The Original SpineChillers™ Books

by Fred E. Katz

SPINECHILLERS™
MYSTERIES

3 BOOKS IN ONE

DR. SHIVERS' CARNIVAL

ATTACK OF THE KILLER HOUSE

BIRTHDAY CAKE AND I SCREAM

FRED E. KATZ

Tommy NELSON

A Division of Thomas Nelson Publishers

NASHVILLE   DALLAS   MEXICO CITY   RIO DE JANEIRO

SpineChillers™ Mysteries 3-in-1
© 1996, 1997, 2010 by Thomas Nelson, Inc.

Previously published in three separate volumes:
Dr. Shivers' Carnival ©1996, 1997
Attack of the Killer House ©1996, 1997
Birthday Cake and I Scream ©1996, 1997

Storylines for *Dr. Shivers' Carnival* and *Attack of the Killer House* by
Tim Myers.

Published in Nashville, Tennessee, by Tommy Nelson. Tommy Nelson is a
registered trademark of Thomas Nelson, Inc.

Scripture is quoted from *The Holy Bible, International Children's Bible*®, ©
1986, 1988, 1999 by Thomas Nelson, Inc. All rights reserved.

Library of Congress Cataloging-in-Publication Data

An application for Cataloging-in-Publication Data has been been filed.

ISBN 978-1-4003-1642-7

Mfr.: HH / Shenzhen, China / July 2010 / PPO#106912

DR. SHIVERS' CARNIVAL

Kyle Conlon discovers that a bizarre
carnival has mysteriously appeared
overnight—right next door to his uncle's
house. He and his three friends, Sara,
Sammy, and Brent, set out to investigate.
The carnival's owner, Dr. Shivers, invites
the four of them to try all the amusements
for free—if they're brave enough.

A blood-chilling scream woke me up. I jumped from the bed in my uncle's guest room and slid across the hardwood floor to the window.

I couldn't believe what I saw. In the field next to my uncle's Hollywood house was a carnival! It wasn't there when I arrived yesterday from the airport. It wasn't there last night when I went to bed. Where had it and the scream come from?

I grabbed my sweatshirt and ran out of the room and down the long hallway to the stairs. As I raced down the stairs and into the family room, I heard my uncle talking in the kitchen. He was hanging up the telephone when I walked through the kitchen doorway.

"Uncle Rex, where did the carnival come from?" I asked.

"That's exactly why I was on the phone. The local police said that the carnival owners rented the field to put up their carnival. It looks like it'll be there for a few days," he told me.

"So, what do we do now, Uncle Rex?" I was hoping he'd say that I could go over and see the carnival.

Uncle Rex pretended like he was thinking really hard. "Now, let me see here, Kyle. Maybe you should wake up your traveling companions and go check it out. How does that sound?"

I didn't even wait to answer him. I ran out of the kitchen and up the stairs to wake up my three friends.

* * *

I guess I should tell you a little about myself and how I got to Hollywood from my little hometown of Carverville. My name is Kyle Conlon. Uncle Rex called my dad and asked if I could visit over Christmas vacation. My uncle is a big-time TV producer. He produced a lot of the hits from last season. Every time he calls my dad, he tells him about the latest big movie star he's worked with. Uncle Rex knows a lot of Hollywood's famous people. But the great thing about my uncle is that it doesn't go to his head. He always says God has really blessed him and he has a lot to be thankful for.

Uncle Rex was working on a new TV show and needed a few teens to screen some of the early film clips. Uncle Rex wanted "regular" kids from the Midwest. Carverville is about as Midwest as a town can get. We've got corn everywhere. And next to the corn there are cows. Yes, Carverville is the Midwest.

I asked my three best friends, Brent, Sammy, and Sara, to come along. My uncle's film studio paid for our plane tickets and sent a big black limo to pick us up at the airport. The limo had a small refrigerator, filled with health food and carrot juice. Dad warned me that California was different from Carverville. I began to understand what he meant after I saw the foods in the limo.

During the ride from the airport to my uncle's house, Sammy was preoccupied with the buttons and gadgets in the limo. Brent looked around for movie stars. Sara and I looked at the trees and neat buildings. California didn't look anything like Carverville. The palm trees and flowering bushes made everything around us seem so fresh and beautiful. And the temperature outside was warm even though it was December. I was going to like California.

When we arrived at Uncle Rex's house, Sara's mouth dropped open. The house was bigger than any we had seen back home. The entrance hallway of the house was bigger than my parents' living room. Sammy got into trouble before our suitcases were even on the shiny marble floor.

The staircase was very long, and it had a winding railing along it. The railing was perfect for sliding down. The temptation got to Sammy before I could.

Suddenly, I heard him cry out as if he'd been shot.

"You got me!" Sammy wailed dramatically to make sure we all noticed him.

"Sammy, don't do that! This isn't your house. My aunt will kill us if she catches you," I scolded.

It was too late. Aunt Janet had already walked into the entryway. The sound of her shoes on the marble made me spin around quickly.

"That's all right, Kyle. It's been so long since kids played on that railing that I am glad to see someone using it the proper way," she said.

Sara leaned over and whispered in my ear, "This is going to be fun. Your aunt is really cool."

Aunt Janet continued. "Kyle, Uncle Rex won't be home from the TV studio till later. I'll make us some dinner and then we can go swimming in the pool."

Aunt Janet made us something to eat, showed us around the house, and led us to our bedrooms. My room was on the side of the house that overlooked an empty field next to some large warehouses.

When my aunt finally led us to the pool, we were awestruck. It was the biggest pool we had ever seen! Half of the pool was inside the house, and the other half was outside. A wall of glass separated the inside from the outside. We jumped into the pool inside the house, swam under the glass wall, and came up outside the house. It was nothing like the public pool we had in Carverville.

Uncle Rex came home while we were swimming. My uncle was very tall, and his black hair was starting to turn gray. Dad sometimes kidded him about that. Uncle Rex usually retorted that at least he still had hair.

It was really great to see Uncle Rex. He had brought home a scary movie for us to watch that was going to hit the theaters in a few weeks. We changed into dry clothes and Uncle Rex led us to a home theater room complete with reclining seats, surround sound, and a wall-to-wall movie screen. There was even a popcorn cart and a refrigerator stocked with sodas and bottled water. "Whoa!" we all said in unison as we took in the room. We all got popcorn and sodas while Uncle Rex started the DVD player. Then we all settled into our seats.

When the movie ended it was late, and we all went sleepily off to bed. The movie must have affected my dreams. In the middle of the night I had a terrible nightmare. In it, the four of us from Carverville were trapped inside a gigantic cuckoo clock with a time bomb. The seconds ticked away, bringing us closer to the explosion. The scream woke me up before the bomb could explode.

I couldn't believe that my friends had slept through that scream, but they had. My room was the only one on the side of the house next to the carnival. I guess that's why I heard it and they didn't.

***

I banged on Sammy's door. "Sammy, wake up! You won't believe this!"

Brent and Sara heard me pound on Sammy's door, and all three came into the hallway. "Come on," I said with a grin. "You guys have to see this."

We raced into my room and hurried over to look out the window. "Uncle Rex said that this carnival rented the field next door to his house and maybe we should go check it out. What do you think?" I asked.

Sammy, Sara, and I had already turned away from the window when we heard Brent scream. When I turned back around, I saw a gigantic, monstrous face just outside the bedroom window.

Sara was on the floor. I thought she was having a panic attack until I listened to the noises she was making. She was laughing. I looked at the face in the window. It was a balloon that had floated up from the carnival. I had never seen one that had a monster's face painted on it.

Sammy said, "Hey, if the balloons can scare us that bad, maybe the rides can give us some good scares too." He loved being scared. To Sammy, being scared was a way to know that you were a living, breathing human being. That wasn't my favorite thing, but I had to admit that the carnival looked like a great time. Both Aunt Janet and Uncle Rex had to work. Going to the carnival would definitely be more exciting than hanging around the house all day with the house-keeper, even if the house did have a pool, a home theater, and an endless library of movies to watch.

It only took us a half hour to shower, get dressed, and make it to the breakfast table. My aunt knew we wanted to get to the carnival quickly. She already had sweet rolls, juice, and cereal on the table. Brent and Sammy started to eat before Sara and I even sat down. I had just poured cereal into my bowl when Aunt Janet walked into the room.

"Aunt Janet, thanks for breakfast. We can't wait to get to the carnival."

A big smile spread across her face. "Have a great time. If I wasn't scheduled to be in L.A. for a meeting, I would join you. It looks like a lot of fun. If you need anything, the housekeeper will be here all day."

We gulped down our food and headed for the door. Aunt Janet caught me by the arm as I was walking out. "You might need some of this. Rex left it for you before going to the studio." She handed me some money. I couldn't believe that I almost forgot money! I gave Aunt Janet a hug and then ran to catch up with the others.

I ran so fast that I didn't notice that the others had stopped dead in their tracks. I slid to a halt in the gravel in front of the carnival gate. My three friends were staring up at it.

"What's up?" I asked.

Sammy pointed to the banner across the top of the gate. DR. SHIVERS' CARNIVAL OF TERROR, it read. Sammy looked at me. "Yes!" he said.

"That's kind of creepy, huh?" Brent's voice cracked as he spoke.

Sammy started to walk toward the gate as he answered Brent. "This looks like a great place to spend the day. California is way cool. You'd never see anything like this back in our little town."

"We have got some great stuff there too," Sara retorted.

"Like what?" Sammy laughed. "The last big thing that happened in Carverville was when the baptistry flooded at the church and Pastor Christensen had to wear wading boots when he gave the sermon." Just a reminder of that day made us all laugh.

"So why are we just standing here?" Brent asked. "Let's go check it out!"

Everyone walked through the gate except for me. I was a little uneasy about this place. After all, the carnival had appeared so quickly and mysteriously. And there was that scream that woke me up. But what really got to me was the banner on the gate. I called the other three back to me so we could talk.

"Maybe we better think this through. You know, it doesn't really look like they're ready for customers. I'm thinking that it might be better if we went back to the house," I said nervously.

Sammy gave me his you've-got-to-be-kidding look, and then he said, "Time out. What are you talking about? You were the first one to want to come over here. I'm all excited and ready to go."

"I'm just thinking about your safety. Remember, I

invited all of you out here to California with me. If something happens to any of you, your parents will kill me. I'm not sure that an amusement park called Dr. Shivers' Carnival of Terror is safe," I argued.

Sara chimed in next. "Am I hanging out with a bunch of scaredy-cats? Let's just go in. If for some reason we get afraid of anything, we can leave. I mean, what can they do, lock us in there?"

"Have a mummy chase us through a tomb?" Brent added, pointing out the silliness of my fear.

"All right. I guess I'm being a little too careful. What can it hurt?" I told them, hoping we weren't being foolish. I said a silent prayer asking the Lord to protect us. He'd been doing a lot of that lately. It seems the four of us have a way of getting ourselves into tough spots. And I had a feeling that this was going to be one of them.

The four of us went through the gate one at a time. Since I was the least eager one in the bunch, I was the last one through. My shoes had shuffled only a few steps from the gate when I was stopped by an eerie realization. Nobody else was here. No families. No kids. No workers. No one. Maybe *we* shouldn't be here either. At that moment, a wicked laugh came from behind me and a bony hand gripped my shoulder. I let out a scream.

We all spun around. I stared up into the long, sharp-featured face of a man. A thin mustache connected to a goatee gave the man's face a sinister look. On the top of his head sat a top hat like the one Abraham Lincoln wore. My jaw dropped open as I scanned the rest of the guy's clothing. He wore a tuxedo jacket, the kind with tails on it. It seemed very weird to me but, then again, this was California. The man's dark eyes stared down at me, and my mouth went dry.

"Can I help you, my young friends?" he asked slowly. His voice sounded like he was deep inside a barrel. It sent a tingle up my spine. Even his eyes were spooky. He opened them wide at first and then squinted at me. When his eyes popped open, his eyebrows raised and then they dropped as he squinted.

Sammy jumped right in. "We're staying with Kyle's uncle. He's a TV producer and he lives next door. When we woke up and saw the carnival, we wanted to be your first customers." He talked so fast that his words almost ran together.

"And that you are. But I'm afraid we're not open yet. There is still much work to be done." The man smiled at us as he spoke. "Oh, I'm sorry. I forgot to introduce myself. I am Dr. Shivers, the owner of this little traveling carnival. It is my distinct pleasure to welcome you."

I finally found my voice. "Nice to meet you, sir. When will you be open?"

"Not until tomorrow. I do hope you can come back then. I'm sure you're dying to try the carnival's amusements, games, and rides," he said. I didn't like how he said the word *dying*. I was kind of relieved that we couldn't stay.

We started to head for the gate when he called to us. "On second thought, kids, wait a moment. I've got some new rides and games. I would truly love it if you would test out my slight amusements, as we here at the carnival call our little rides and *harmless* games."

"Wow, yeah. That would be great! Like I was saying to my friends, nothing like this happens back in our little town." Sammy was nearly jumping up and down with excitement.

"Would you be so kind as to follow me back to my office? I'll give you special free admission passes that will allow you unpaid access to all of my amusements except for one, Dracula's Castle. It isn't quite finished yet. Dracula's coffin hasn't arrived from Transylvania. In case you didn't know, it has to sit on dirt from that country. When the Transylvanians sent the dirt, I told them, 'Fangs very much.'" He laughed with eerie glee at his own joke and then continued. "There's just so much to do in a carnival like this. So please, go ahead and enjoy yourselves as my guests, my very special guests. But I do have one request of you," he said.

Brent spoke first. "Sure. What can we do?"

"When you're done, that is, when you feel like you're just about *dead* from exhaustion, return to my office and tell me what you think of my little carnival of terror," Dr. Shivers answered. I nodded my head that we would. I was not sure I ever wanted to see him again, but a promise was a promise.

Dr. Shivers motioned for us to follow him. We slipped between some tents and amusements. I looked at the names on the games and rides. There were some very strange things at this carnival.

His office was in a dented trailer. His picture was painted on the side, along with the words DR. SHIVERS' CARNIVAL OF TERROR. The painting was faded as if it had been in the sun for a lot of years.

Dr. Shivers opened the door and I walked inside. The room was filled with odd items. It looked like the set of a science-fiction movie. A big stuffed raven

stood on a perch in the corner of the office. At least,
I think it was stuffed. For a moment I was sure the
bird winked at me.

Dr. Shivers gave each of us a small skeleton on a
necklace. But it wasn't an ordinary skeleton. It had
the face of our bizarre Dr. Shivers on the skull. He
told us to show them at any ride or refreshment
stand and we could have what we wanted for free.
Sammy was right. Nothing like this would ever happen back in our hometown.

Dr. Shivers gave us one last twisted smile before
we left. As we walked away from his office, I heard
him laugh, and something told me that this carnival
wasn't going to be all fun and games. I started to feel
like it might indeed be filled with terror. There was
definitely something sinister about his laugh. I
closed my eyes for another quick prayer. *Lord, I
know I can't go anywhere without You. Watch over us
here and protect us from anything evil.*

Brent walked toward the right side of the midway, and Sammy and Sara headed down the left. I decided to join Brent. I was amazed. These were the
strangest rides and games I had ever seen. I was sure
the others felt the same way. Friends can sense
things like that.

Brent, Sammy, and Sara were my best friends.
Brent and I had met a few months ago at the new
church my family started going to. I liked hanging

out with him. He is a little smaller than most of the kids our age. I supposed some of the others at middle school might have picked on him except that he's a great guy. Everyone likes him. He really cares about people.

Sara's dad is the pastor of our church. She loves baseball and has an impressive pitching arm. Her dark brown hair is straight and hangs to her shoulders, but most of the time she pulls it back in a ponytail. The most interesting thing about her is how she lives out her Christianity. It's not like she's trying to live up to the reputation of being a preacher's kid. It's more like she lives what she believes.

Sammy makes life interesting and fun. Everything is an adventure to him. Sammy was born in Mexico, and his family later moved to Texas. His dad's a Roadway engineer, and his company transferred him to a city near Carverville a couple of years ago. Sammy's the kind of guy who jumps right into whatever comes along. Unfortunately, he has one drawback: he plays too many practical jokes on us. A place like Dr. Shivers' Carnival of Terror was ripe for Sammy's sense of humor.

Brent and I walked by two rides that sat on top of mobile trailers. As we were looking around, Brent said, "You know, Dr. Shivers looks familiar. There was something about his eyes. He reminded me of a guy I saw on TV."

I scoffed, "Come on, Brent, a guy like Dr. Shivers would never be on TV. He's probably traveled all over the world with this carnival. Besides, if you saw him before, it was probably a picture on a 'Wanted' poster in the post office. He looked like a pretty rough character to me."

"No, he seemed okay. I know I've seen him, and if I keep thinking about it, it will come to me," he insisted.

While we were talking, someone called to us. "Hey, kids. Come on, try your luck in the Gremlins' Shooting Gallery. Three bull's-eyes and you can win a teddy bear. What do you say, kids? Give it a try. Impress your friends with your skill." The words came from a man standing in front of a shooting gallery.

I laughed and looked at Brent. "I thought this was a carnival of terror. This is like something you'd see at a carnival back home. Let's try to find something a little more exciting."

The guy yelled to us again. "Try the Gremlins' Gallery. Don't be afraid!"

"Who's afraid?" said a voice from behind us. I spun around and Sammy and Sara were standing there. "We're not afraid. What's there to be afraid of in a shooting gallery?" Sara responded.

"I'm sorry, kids. I thought I was talking to a gang of middle schoolers. This might be too frightening for you," the man by the gallery taunted Sara.

"I'm going in. Anybody joining me?" Sara called as she walked forward. Normally, Sara felt pretty sure of herself and didn't have to prove anything. But we weren't quite ourselves in this place and were ready to take a dare. We fell in line behind her.

"Just follow the stairs up to the gallery and walk down the hall, folks," the guy instructed as we entered.

The stairway got darker as we neared the top. When we reached the hall, the others started goofing around, and I moved to the front of the line. I bumped into a wall at the end of the hallway, then Sammy bumped into me, and Brent and Sara bumped into Sammy.

Sammy yelled, "Hey, this hallway ended. Where do we go now?"

"If it doesn't go anywhere, then maybe we need to turn around and go back," Sara suggested. She had barely gotten the words out of her mouth when a panel slid across the hallway behind us, sealing us inside.

"Hey, what is this? What's happening? I can't see a thing," I yelled.

"Attention please. Welcome to the Gremlins' Shooting Gallery. In a moment the wall before you will open, and you will have three seconds to seek cover before the gremlins begin shooting. And re- member, if they hit three of you, you win a teddy bear . . . that is, if you're still around to collect your prize." The voice came from a speaker above us.

"I'm scared," Brent whispered.

"It's a joke. It's got to be a joke. Don't you think, Sammy?" I asked.

"Of course it is," Sammy said fearlessly.

Then the wall slid open. This was no joke after all. Before us was a group of large wooden ducks, and on the other side of the shooting gallery counter stood a bunch of gremlins. Their beady eyes peered through the scopes on their water rifles as they stood there cackling.

The voice from the speaker screamed with urgency, "Your three seconds are up. Take cover!"

I heard pumping and then streams of water shot toward us. We were the targets in a wet shooting gallery.

I dived behind one of the ducks. Sammy and Sara were right behind me. In the dim light I could see them crouching to take cover. Then Brent screamed in mock terror: "I've been hit."

I dived from behind the large wooden duck and slid across the wet floor to Brent's feet. I regained my footing and grabbed him by the waist, pulling him down. He fell next to me.

"How do we get out of here?" he whispered, giggling.

"I don't know. I think the doors have sealed us in. Sammy, Sara, are you all right?" I called to them.

"What's going on? This is crazy," Sara laughed back over the sound of water streams splashing.

"Sara, crawl back toward the wall and see if you can get the doors open. But stay down so you don't get soaked," I told her.

Sammy asked, "Brent, are you okay?"

"Yeah, the water just surprised me," he answered.

"Sara, did you find anything yet?" I called.

"Nothing. This door is sealed off tight. Try the wall by you, and I'll try the one by me."

As long as we stayed low or behind the wooden

ducks, we were safe. The gremlins were just tall enough to reach the water rifles. They couldn't aim their rifles downward unless they were on the counter separating us. I crawled low to the ground all the way to the side wall. I pushed and kicked the wall. I felt for an opening. Nothing. There wasn't even a seam dividing the pieces of wood. We were sealed inside.

I kicked the wall again and then felt a stream of water hit just above my head. I spun around. The gremlins had figured it out. They were crawling onto the counter.

"Kyle, get back behind the ducks. The gremlins are on the counter. They could nail you. Sara, do the same thing," Sammy yelled to us.

"Heading back now," Sara responded as she took a headlong dive toward the ducks. She landed next to Sammy. I saw what she did and imitated it. Sara and Sammy were behind one duck and Brent and I were behind another. We were stuck. There didn't appear to be a way out.

The water started hitting the ducks harder. The force of the spray was soaking us even behind the ducks. The gremlins had changed weapons. Now they each had something that looked and felt more like a fire hose. The force of the water would knock us down if we didn't stay behind the ducks.

"Ouch! This isn't fun anymore," Sara shouted after nearly being knocked across the room.

I was getting angry too, and worried. "What now? Any ideas?" I asked.

"Anybody up for an old-fashioned prayer meeting?" Sammy joked to relieve our frustration at being trapped. I figured even he had to be scared now.

But I didn't have time to feel any relief because other gremlins were climbing onto the counter. The situation was getting worse. Water was several inches deep everywhere.

"Sammy, how many gremlins are on the counter now?" Sara asked.

Sammy carefully peeked around the corner of the duck. The moment his eyes moved to the edge of the duck, water exploded against the wall behind him. "I didn't have time to count, but it must be all of them, and I think they've sent out for more friends."

"I wish they'd send out for pizza and leave us alone." Brent crossed his arms over his chest and sank deeper behind the duck as he spoke.

"We'll get out, Brent," Sammy encouraged. "And we'll certainly have an earful of feedback for Dr. Shivers."

"Shooting at us isn't good for customer loyalty," Brent chirped in.

We all laughed.

Just then I heard the sound of padded, clawed feet hitting the floor. The gremlins were jumping off the counter. Not even the ducks could protect us now.

As the gremlins moved toward us, I held my breath. More than anything, I wished we could get out of this place. I also wished I'd listened to my instincts and not come in the first place.

"Do you hear that?" Brent whispered to me.

"The gremlins," I answered.

"No, that humming noise. I can feel a vibration underneath the floor. What's going on?"

The floor moved. It started to tilt. I tried to hold on to a duck, but the floor's tilt increased by the second. Soon, Sammy and Sara banged into Brent and me, and the four of us slid toward the wall. We were going to smack right into it.

The gremlins were screaming behind us. Their section of the floor hadn't tilted. I saw them jumping up and down in frustration. We slid closer to the wall. In a few seconds we would crash into it.

We hit the wall and went through it. The tilted floor had exposed a section of black plastic wall that wasn't attached at the bottom. We slid out into the daylight and fell on air mattresses next to the amusement's side wall.

"That was great!" Sammy yelled. "This place is fantastic. What do we do next?"

"Next? I think we ought to get out of here," I said. "We could have really been hurt in there."

"Come on, it was just a game. I mean, we got out of there, right? Besides, we just got here. This place could be a lot of fun. Let's try another one, just to see."

"Sammy's right. Let's try something else. What else do we have to do? And don't forget that Dr. Shivers is counting on us to give him some feedback," Brent said.

"Hey, what's this?" Sara asked as she reached down and picked up what looked like a marble. As she rolled it around in her hand, I realized what she had.

"It's an eye!" I gasped.

"Let me see that," Brent said as he snatched it from her hand. "Yep, it's an eye all right," he stated matter-of-factly. He suddenly realized what he'd said. He yelled and tossed the eyeball into the air. Sammy caught it as it fell.

"It is only a marble that looks like an eye," he observed.

"What's it doing here?" I asked.

"I guess someone is keeping an eye out for us," Sammy responded.

Sara interrupted our snickers. "I think it's a clue."

"A clue to what?" Sammy asked with a doubtful look.

"I think she's right," I told them. "Maybe it will make sense later. Let's go check out more of this carnival."

Sammy agreed and headed for the Shoot the Chute. It was a very tall structure with a series of inflated plastic tubes that branched off the center. The whole thing looked like a really tall spider with a dozen legs. The tubes ran all over the place. Some to the front, some to the back, and a few even stretched to other parts of the carnival. I had to admit it looked like fun.

A long stairway led to the top. We ran up the first twenty steps. Brent and I took the rest of the stairs a little slower. I was panting by the time I reached the top. I collapsed next to Brent, who had already sat down to catch his breath.

Sammy and Sara stood on the platform. They scanned the tube openings, trying to decide which ones they would choose.

"Sara, this is great," Sammy said. "Hey guys, each tube has a name on it. This one is the Devil's Doorway, and this one is the Twister."

"Do they have one called Tube to Oblivion? That's where I'm going if I can ever stand up again. My legs feel like rubber," I joked.

Sara said seriously, "That's why I'm choosing the longest tube I can find. I want to sit for a few minutes." Sara chose a tube, climbed inside, and started to slide. We could hear her yelling, "This is fantastic," the whole way down.

Sammy picked the Twister and hopped in. "Woohoo!" he screamed as he slid down.

"I'm taking the Lizard's Leap," Brent said. He dropped out of sight.

I was glad that the others had already gone down. I didn't want anyone to see me when I plopped my legs inside the tube marked Soft and Smooshy. It sounded like something for little kids. That was okay with me. All I wanted was a rest and no weird twists and turns.

I slid down, then shot upward, and then downward again. A few times I bounced off the rubbery plastic sides and spun around in the tube. This was fun! I wished now that I had taken one of the other tubes so the ride would have lasted longer. I was really enjoying myself. At least, that's what I thought until my tube ride ended.

I expected to land on the ground outside the Shoot the Chute. Instead, I dropped a few feet into a spongy, slippery, gooey mess. It was definitely soft and smooshy. The more I struggled to get out, the deeper I sank. I was inside something, but I didn't know what that something was. It was pitch black. What now? I yelled for help.

At the exact moment I yelled, something crashed into the goo next to me. I heard it thud, then thrash around. Whatever it was, it fell too close for my comfort.

I screamed. It screamed back.

"Sara, is that you?" I asked with relief.

"Yeah, it's me. But where are we?" I could tell from her voice that she was shaken up by the goo.

"I don't know, but if you keep moving around in this stuff, you'll sink both of us. Stand still for a second," I told her. Each time she moved I could feel her sinking deeper. When she grabbed on to me, I started to sink as well. We had to get out.

"Kyle, have you tried calling for help?" Sara asked.

"A few seconds before you got here," I said, desperately looking for a way out. "Sara, we need to do this slowly. Let's each walk in a different direction until we reach the wall. We must be inside the Shoot the Chute. There has got to be a wall at the edge. Maybe we can punch through it or go under it."

We moved in opposite directions. It was hard pushing my body through the goo. It didn't seem wet, but my feet and legs worked very hard with each step. I made a mental note to not tell our gym teacher, Ms. Muscles Moreno, about this stuff. She'd install one of these pits at the middle school.

"Kyle, I reached the wall," Sara said.

"Good, I think I'm almost there too," I called back.

"I'm touching the wall now. I feel a rope," she said.

"Don't pu—"

I was too late. She had already pulled it. At Dr. Shivers' Carnival of Terror, you didn't want to do anything that could make things worse. A gremlin could drop through one of those tubes next.

"What's that sound, Kyle?"

We heard a hissing. It sounded like air escaping from a tire—a huge tire, like they use on those monster pickup trucks.

I screamed to Sara, "Quick, go back to the middle. This place is starting to deflate. We'll be crushed by the walls."

I heard Sara huffing and groaning as she sloshed through the goo. I moved toward her sounds and she moved toward mine. The hissing grew louder. I could almost feel the heavy plastic sagging around us.

Then the walls collapsed. I closed my eyes and waited.

I heard laughing.

I opened my eyes and saw that the Shoot the Chute had collapsed all around us and we were standing in the warm California sun again. Sammy and Brent were laughing at us.

"What are you guys laughing at?" Sara asked.

"You two," Sammy said. "How did you get in there and why were your eyes closed? You look like you expected the world to come to an end."

"Close enough. Help us out of here," I responded.

Sara stopped me. She was still holding the rope she'd pulled. At the end of it was a tea bag. "Kyle, why is there a tea bag on this rope?"

"It must be clue number two," I said.

"Clue to what?" Brent asked.

"I don't know. I just know that we have an eye and a tea bag," I answered.

"An eye and a tea—wait a second! That could be it! Maybe the two represent the letters *I* and *T*," Sammy said.

"This is really strange," Sara added. "I think I'm ready for a more normal ride."

"How about the merry-go-round? Maybe a kiddy ride will be just the ticket," Sammy mocked as he helped pull Sara and me out of the goo.

In truth, I disagreed with Sammy. I'd thought soft and smooshy would be a safe and easy ride. We had asked the Lord to protect us and He had. Now we were running headlong into who knew what else. *Were we going from trusting God to testing God?*

Sara and I headed to the restrooms to wash off the

goo. Then we followed the others to the merry-go-round. Brent was the first one on. He seemed really happy to find a ride that couldn't hurt us, splash us, or dump us in goo. Sammy bounded onto the biggest horse he could find. Sara and I climbed onto the two smaller horses between Sammy's and Brent's. The merry-go-round started slowly. I didn't see an operator, but that didn't surprise me. Everything at Dr. Shivers' carnival was a little strange.

"Hey look, a brass ring," Sammy called to us.

He was trying to reach it. It was too far away from me, so I didn't try. On the third time around, I read the sign over it. It said, DON'T PULL THE BRASS RING.

I yelled to Sammy, "The sign says 'Don't pull the—'" But it was too late. His finger slipped inside the ring and grabbed it. Out it came.

"I got it!" he said triumphantly.

I was about to tell him what the sign said and that he was crazy when the merry-go-round started to speed up. Sammy thought it was great fun, but I saw fear on Brent's face. Each second it spun faster and faster.

I started to climb off my horse and reach for Brent when the wooden pony bucked me. I grabbed for the neck of the horse and held on. Soon all the horses were bucking.

"Hold on. It looks like we're in for a wild ride," Sara said.

Our horses bucked up and down as the carousel spun faster and faster. I was getting dizzy and could barely hold on.

I gripped the horse's neck tighter, but each time it bucked it loosened my grip. I went a few inches into the air. I noticed some letters were branded into the leather reins of my horse. The bucking made it hard to read them.

PULL— I read, but the horse bucked me into the air before I could finish reading.

PULL BACK— I read when I landed on the horse. Then another buck sent me a few inches higher. The merry-go-round was spinning faster. I didn't have much time.

PULL BACK ON THE— I noticed Sara was slipping off her horse. The force of the spinning carousel would soon throw her into the midway.

PULL BACK ON THE REINS— The wooden animal tossed me a few inches higher that time.

PULL BACK ON THE REINS HARD— I needed to stay seated long enough to read all the words, but the up-and-down motion and the spinning made it very difficult. Sammy looked like he was having a great time.

PULL BACK ON THE REINS HARD TO— To what? What happens when I pull back hard on the reins? I had to find out. The next buck of the horse dropped me hard. I slipped sideways on the horse. I struggled back into the saddle just before the next toss hit me. This time I had to hold on and read the letters.

PULL BACK ON THE REINS HARD TO STOP, it read.

"Everybody, pull back hard on your reins. It will stop the merry-go-round," I yelled. They did as I said. The carousel started to slow. The bucking stopped, and soon the merry-go-round came to a halt.

I let out a long sigh. Brent and Sara did the same, but Sammy had jumped down from his horse and was running into the midway. He looked at us and motioned for us to follow him. "What do we go on next?" he asked. The three of us staggered off the carousel with our heads spinning from the wild ride.

"Next, we go home," Brent shot back.

"Not yet," Sara called. "I want to look for more clues."

I was curious too. I turned back toward the carousel. Looking up at the horses, I stopped. I couldn't believe it. The clue was all over the place.

"Sara, look at the brand on the horses," I called.

"*S!*" she answered. "We have an *I*, a *T*, and an *S*. That spells *its*, but what does that mean?"

"I don't know. All I know is that there's nothing like this back in our little town. I want to keep going." Sammy was pleading. I thought if he put down "our little town" one more time, I was going to scream.

"Look," he said, "there's a Ferris wheel. We can get high enough to look down on the whole carnival. Then we'll pick out a couple of safe-looking rides that Dr. Shivers can't turn into something that will give you a heart attack. How about it?"

"Okay, but if we don't see anything, then that is it. We go back to Kyle's uncle's house." Brent was insistent.

We staggered to the Ferris wheel and jammed ourselves in a bucket. After I sat down I looked up. I shouldn't have because every time I saw a sign around this place it scared me. This one read, THE FEAR-US WHEEL.

"This isn't a Ferris wheel," I said. My three friends stared back at me like I had lost some of my brains on the merry-go-round. "Look, Dr. Shivers calls this a *Fear-Us Wheel.* I think we should get out before something crazy happens on this thing."

I spoke too late. The safety bar snapped down on us, making it impossible to get out. A glass cage covered the front and sides of the bucket. We started to move.

At first it was just the slow, usual circular movements of a Ferris wheel. The others laughed off my concern. We looked out of the glass for other rides we wanted to go on.

I still didn't trust this place. I wished my aunt or uncle would come get us for some reason. Any reason would be good. I didn't want my friends to think I was afraid, but this place was creepy.

The Fear-Us Wheel bucket was rounding the top when it stopped. "I warned you guys, but nobody ever listens to me," I mumbled, using my best I-told-you-so voice.

"It'll start again. Someone else must be getting on," Sara said hopefully.

"Like who?" I scoffed.

The Fear-Us Wheel swayed from side to side. My stomach was getting upset. I think I discovered what seasickness felt like.

"What do we do now?" Brent asked.

"Wait. All we can do is wait and see what Dr. Shivers has up his sleeve," Sara answered.

"Spiders," Sammy said.

"Dr. Shivers has spiders up his sleeve?" Sara was puzzled.

"No, there are spiders on our Fear-Us Wheel bucket." He said it like he was answering a teacher's question. He was very calm. Brent wasn't.

"Don't say that. I really hate spiders. I mean, *really*." Brent covered his eyes with his hands as he spoke.

"Brent, he's not kidding. There are spiders on the outside of the glass. But in here we should be safe. Besides, the four of us should be able to handle a handful of spiders." As I said that, more and more began to crawl onto the outside of the glass. In a couple of minutes the glass was covered with spiders— hundreds of them.

Brent opened his eyes and saw them. I thought he was going to climb out of the bucket and jump. Sara and I held him down.

"Don't look," Sara warned him.

"What do you mean, don't look! I'm in a nest of spiders and you tell me not to look! I want to see what is going to wrap me in its web and come back to devour me! I'm going to be spider stew! Who is going to explain to my mother that I was a snack for a bunch of spiders? Someone get us out of here!" he yelled.

We all started to scream for help. The bucket rocked back and forth. We swayed from side to side. I hoped the movement would shake off the spiders. It didn't affect them at all. They continued to crawl all over the glass. I was surprised that none got inside.

The swaying stopped. The Fear-Us Wheel began to move again. It slowly descended to the bottom. We stopped with a jolt, the safety bar flew up, the glass slid back, and we bolted from the ride.

"Keep the spiders away from me," Brent said.

I looked back. There wasn't a spider anywhere. Not on the ground, not on the bucket, and not on the glass. That was weird—very weird.

"What now?" Sammy was still optimistic that this place was great.

"I'm up for leaving, except there should be another clue," Sara said. Something hit her from behind. She spun around and watched an inner tube flop to the ground.

"Oh, there's my clue."

"If that's a clue, then what does it mean?" Brent asked.

"It means that a big wave is going to crash into the carnival and we'll all need inner tubes," Sammy joked.

"No, I think we've found another letter. It's the letter *O*," I told him.

"What is this, *Sesame Street*? Can we at least win a stuffed animal before we go?" Sammy asked.

It seemed like a reasonable request. Maybe it would help us forget the spiders. And besides, searching for clues was fun. Everything had turned out okay so far.

Sammy was the first one to the game booth. "All we've got to do is hit one of those two black dots with a ball. It looks easy enough."

"You three go ahead," Brent said. "I want to sit down. Spiders make me a little weak in the knees."

Sammy grabbed the first ball, wound up, and let the ball fly. It missed by a foot. He shrugged his shoulders and moved out of the way.

I took the next try. Baseball wasn't really my sport, and pitching was what I was the worst at. I probably would have done better if I had closed my eyes. At least I wouldn't have seen the ball miss the target by three feet. I did hit one of the stuffed animals on the shelf behind the targets.

"Do I get to keep what I hit?" I joked. I thought it was pretty funny, but the others just rolled their eyes.

"My turn," Sara said as she grabbed the ball. Sara was our last chance at winning. She was also our best chance. She pitched for our Little League team. Last year she even threw a no-hitter. She rubbed the ball and eyed one of the targets. Sara wound up, and the pitch was good. It struck right in the center of one of the black spots.

"You did it!" Brent yelled. "I knew you could, Sara."

"All those tips I gave you really worked," Sammy kidded.

"They're moving," I said nervously.

"What's moving, Kyle?" Sara asked.

"The black spots are moving. Look—they're starting to get higher." I pointed at the targets, and we saw two long antennae rise over the shelf. They were attached to a greenish, fish-scaled head. Long, jagged teeth appeared when the beast roared at us.

"Those weren't targets. They were eyes. And it is really mad!" Sammy yelled.

"Run for it!" Brent yelled.

We turned around as the doors to the carnival game began to slide shut. *Not again*, I thought. Sammy dived out and Sara was only inches behind him. I pushed Brent as the sliding doors got closer and closer.

Sara saw a pole leaning against the outside wall of the ball-toss game. She grabbed it and wedged the pole between the sliding doors. It stopped them, and she and Sammy pulled Brent through.

I dived for the opening. I had just cleared it when a slimy hand grabbed my leg. I felt the scales and the claws wrap tight around my calf.

"It's got me! It's going to pull me back in!" I yelled. I figured that I was going to be this green sea monster's mid-morning snack. I tried kicking its hand away, but this refugee from the sea was too strong.

Sammy jumped up to see what he could do. His

head bumped the pole holding the doors open and knocked it loose. The doors continued to slide together until they closed on the monster's arm. I heard it moan, and then it let go of me.

This place was weirder than I imagined. I lay on the ground breathing a sigh of relief when something moved between me and the sun. It was a shadow. I turned my head to see what it was.

A clown stood over us. He honked his horn. I think he was saying hello. Everybody turned when they heard the horn.

"Hey, it's a clown," exclaimed Sara.

"Brilliant deduction, Sherlock," Sammy mocked.

"Maybe he can tell us about this place. Mr. Clown, sir, we've run into some very weird stuff around here. What's behind all this?" Brent asked.

The clown didn't answer. He reached deep into his pants pocket and pulled out a coin. He held it in one hand and then grabbed it with the other. The clown waved the empty open hand over the one with the coin in it, beeped his horn, and then opened his hand. The coin was gone.

He walked over to me, reached behind my ear, and took out the coin. He never said a word.

Sara looked puzzled. She turned to us and said, "I think he was trying to tell us something. The trick means something."

"Oh, good, we're all going to disappear and then

reappear in Kyle's ear. That's comforting." Sammy laughed as he spoke.

"Let me ask him another question." Sara turned again to the clown. "Are you an important person at the carnival?"

"Why ask him something stupid like that? He's just a clown," Sammy tossed in.

The clown ignored Sammy's comment and reached into his pocket again. He pulled out a large, red cloth with his left hand and draped it over his right. He held his right hand in front of him with his palm up. He passed his left hand over the cloth three times, beeped his horn, and grabbed the cloth. When he lifted it, he had a flower in his hand.

We applauded.

Sammy turned to Sara and asked, "Okay, so what does a flower have to do with his being important?"

"I get it," Brent said. "The flower is a forget-me-not. I guess we shouldn't forget him."

"I think it will be hard to forget anything around this place," I said. "I've got another question. Are we in danger here? What will happen if we stay?"

The clown smiled and pulled the coin from his pocket again. He tossed it to me and walked away. I stared at him and then at the coin. Scratched on one side was the letter N. It was our clue, but on the other side of the coin there was a more important message: "In God We Trust."

"I'm getting hungry," Sammy said. "Anyone else want something to eat?"

We walked to a food stand. Inside the stand, an older woman gave us a big smile and said, "I see you're wearing the special necklaces. Can I get you kids something, compliments of Dr. Shivers?"

Sammy answered, "Sure, I want a hot dog."

She grabbed one from the shelf behind her. It was wrapped in foil.

"And what can I get you?" the vendor asked the rest of us with a big smile.

"Cotton candy, please," Brent responded. Maybe fear gave Brent a sweet tooth. Neither Sara nor I wanted anything. I was just ready to go home.

The woman was very kind. Her smile gave me hope that Dr. Shivers' Carnival of Terror was not all bad. As we turned to walk away, the woman closed the refreshment stand.

Sammy bit into his hot dog and it barked. We all turned and looked at him.

"It wasn't me," he said. "My hot dog barked."

"Sure it did," Sara scoffed.

"It did. Listen." He bit into the hot dog again. It barked. Sara started laughing. Sammy then caught the giggles, and when he laughs it doesn't take long until he's on the ground. I was walking over to look at the hot dog when I heard Brent scream.

"Sick! My cotton candy is filled with worms!" He dropped it.

Brent hopped up and down, shaking his hands in the air. The worms really grossed him out. Sara and I nearly bumped heads reaching down to pick up the cotton candy. Sammy was still laughing. His barking hot dog had struck him so funny that he couldn't stop. Sara grabbed the cotton candy first, scooped it up, and checked it out. The worms freaked her out too.

"Come on, I want to see too," I said in frustration. This carnival kept getting weirder by the minute.

Sara gagged and turned her head away from the pink spun sugar. "You don't really."

"I do," I snapped. I grabbed the paper cone of cotton candy by its point. I didn't want to get worms on me. When I tipped it up and looked inside, I saw worms creeping and crawling up the paper. It was gross.

I looked at Brent. "Did you eat any of it?"

"Yes," he said, gagging.

Sammy was still laughing. "At least you got some protein with every bite."

"That's not funny, Sammy," Brent shot back.

"Hold it, now. We can't get mad at each other. We're supposed to be having fun here," I said as I moved between the two.

"If you think eating worms is fun, then I'm having a ball," Brent said, and then he broke out in giggles. He realized how ridiculous we sounded. My laughter followed. At first I only snickered, then it grew into full-fledged belly laughs.

Sammy stopped laughing long enough to stand up to see the cotton candy. But when he looked at it, he burst into laughter again, falling to the ground and holding his stomach. "Somebody stop me. It hurts."

Sara alternated between gagging and giggling. When Sara laughed she threw her head back in the air and let out the funniest and loudest laughs I ever heard.

"My hot dog barked," Sammy howled from the ground.

"And I had the cotton candy that ate Hollywood," Brent snorted out.

The laughter helped us relax. We sat up and then slowly got to our feet. Sammy was still on the ground and Sara reached her hand down to help him up. Sara looked at him and asked, "Don't you think there's a lot of weird stuff around here?"

"This could all be a dream," Sammy said.

"If this is a dream," I answered, "then someone pinch me."

No one pinched me.

Sara turned to us and said, "I forgot to look for another clue. So far we have *I*, *T*, *S*, *O*, and *N*."

"If you add an apostrophe between the *T* and *S*, it spells *it's on*," Brent added.

"I don't see anything," I said. "But I'd like to know what *it* is and what *it* is *on*. Let's keep looking."

I think my confidence in God's protection was growing with each event. Sometimes I need to be reminded that the Lord is always faithful. Dr. Shivers' carnival was reminding me over and over again.

We started to walk down the midway, looking at all the amusements and wondering what the next clue would be. None of us could explain what was going on, but Dr. Shivers' Carnival of Terror seemed to be living up to its name.

"It all seems a little fishy to me," Sara said. "I mean, think about it. Gremlins? Sea monsters? Barking hot dogs? These things can't be real, right?"

Sammy butted in. "And why did the spiders disappear when we got off the Fear-Us Wheel? I agree, there's something fishy going on."

"Then what do we do next?" I was ready for some answers.

Sara looked at me and said, "I say that we stay

here and figure out where this alphabet mystery is heading."

"Great," Sammy added. "Then let's hit another ride." He looked around. We had reached the end of the midway. "Nothing's here. Let's head back the other way."

Brent stood in front of the last tent on the midway. "The sign says the next show is in two minutes. I could use a few minutes to sit down."

Sara and I shrugged our shoulders as if to say, "That's okay by us." I thought, *It isn't a ride, a shooting gallery, or even food. It must be okay.* Sammy didn't want to see the show. He wanted to go on another ride. Brent, Sara, and I went into the tent without him and sat in the front.

The sign above the stage read, GREAT CHARACTERS OF ITERATURE. The *L* in *literature* was missing. Sara and I looked at each other. We had just discovered the next clue. It must be the *L*. This made me feel better about being there. I jabbed Sara in the ribs and whispered, "Who do you think they'll have from the world of literature? Or is that *iterature*?" I had no more than finished my question when a man in a white lab coat pushed clumsily through the curtains.

"You are about to witness some of the great experiments in our history. Behind this curtain is one of the marvels of the world," he said.

"First you will meet my associate, Dr. Jekyll. He has

created a new soft drink that is better than anything on the market today. It is the kind of drink that can change your life. It is so good that you won't be able to control yourself. You will want more and more. And now, here is Dr. Jekyll," the scientist told us.

The curtain opened to reveal Dr. Jekyll standing behind a lab table. Tubes ran everywhere, and different colored liquids pulsed through them. A bottle of bubbly, bluish liquid stood in the middle of the table.

"Most of us want to change something about ourselves. We either want to be taller or stronger, prettier or more outgoing. I have created a drink that makes you into what you want to be," the doctor lectured.

Sara leaned over and whispered, "So that's why Dr. Jekyll made his famous potion. And look what it did to him. I'm glad Jesus is my friend and is going to make me into what I want to be without stupid drinks and pills and hocus-pocus."

I knew she was right, but I leaned over to Brent and snickered. "Hey, Brent, I wish I'd had that last week at the football game. I wanted to be a tank to break through the other team's line. Do you think that I could be a tank if I drank that stuff?"

Brent laughed, and Dr. Jekyll glared at us.

"Hey, you two, I think you're making him mad," Sara said. "Just cool it! I don't want him to come out here after us."

I sat up straight in my seat and so did Brent. The doctor continued talking about his drink. I was getting a little bored and stopped watching just as the old guy raised the bottle to his lips. Then I heard Sara gasp.

I glanced at her, then looked back at the stage. Dr. Jekyll's body shook, and he jumped around the stage, screaming at the top of his voice. He raced from side to side, then off the side of the stage, then back on again. His appearance began to change.

Dropping to the floor, the doctor kicked his feet like he was having a temper tantrum. I leaned over to Brent and said, "Where are we? Baby-sitting your little brother?"

Brent laughed again. Bad move. Dr. Jekyll stood up. He had gone through a total transformation. A beastly set of eyes glared out of his twisted and distorted face. His crooked body stepped around the lab table and started our way. He dragged his limp left leg behind him.

I started to panic. He was almost to the edge of the stage when the curtains closed and stopped him.

"That was close," Brent sighed. Sara sighed too.

The man in the lab coat walked out from the stage wings and smiled at us. "I'm so sorry. My friend Dr. Jekyll can't always control his emotions when he is being heckled." He smirked at us and continued. "I am so sorry I forgot to introduce myself. I am Dr.

Frankenstein, and behind this curtain stands my creation."

The three of us looked at one another. This place had taken a wrong turn again. The curtains began to move a little, then a nonhuman voice cried out, "Argh!" The red velvet curtains drew open, and before us stood Frankenstein's monster.

Sara stood up immediately. "Quick, get out, get out!"

The monster was only a few rows away from us. He looked at us, then at Dr. Frankenstein.

The doctor tried to hold him back, but the monster swung his large arm at the doctor, knocking him to the stage. The monster headed toward us.

I turned to Brent and grabbed him by the arm. Frozen with fear, he was glued to his seat. Sara tried to get him to stand.

"Come on, Brent, let's get out of here," I yelled as I pulled him to his feet and out into the aisle. Sara pushed him and I pulled at him all the way to the exit doors.

As I reached the doors, all I could think about were the times that the doors to an amusement had slid shut on us. I prayed that this time the doors would be open.

I turned my head and saw that the monster was only a few feet behind us. *The doors have to open*, I thought.

My hand reached for the crash bar on the door. "Please, Lord, make them open," I prayed aloud. I pressed with all my weight against the metal door. Brent and Sara crashed against me.

I heard the monster's big feet thud on the ground right behind us. "Let's get out of—"

"He's got me!" Sara screamed.

I turned my head quickly. For a moment I forgot the door. Something happened in my head. The only thing I could think to do was to karate chop the monster's arm. I leaped in the air, gave my best kung fu scream, and came down hard on the arm.

"Ow!" I yelled. The monster felt like he was made of steel. I looked the monster in the eyes. He was shocked and let go of Sara's arm.

By then, Brent had pushed the door open and we went flying into the sunlight, stumbling and falling into the dirt of the midway. On the other side of the door, the monster yelled, "Why?" over and over again.

Sammy stood over us. "You guys didn't stay very long. Was the show that bad?"

I was breathing hard as I tried to explain. "A monster—Frankenstein—grabbed Sara—the door—" Sammy's face beamed. "Wow! I can't believe I missed all that fun. I'm not sitting out one more thing around this place. Everything is better than what it seems. Let's go back inside."

"Everything is *weirder* than it seems, you mean," Sara said. "I'm not going back inside for anything."

Brent caught his breath and stepped between us. "Listen, I'm not sure I know what's going on, but I want to solve the mystery."

"We've already got the next two clues," Sara told him.

"I know about the *L*, but what's the next clue?" I asked with my puzzled, crunched-eyebrow look.

"What did Frankenstein's monster yell?" Sara asked me.

"Why?" Sammy asked.

"That's it!" she exclaimed.

"That's what? Why do you care what that monster yelled?" Sammy asked, confused.

That's when I jumped in. "I get it. The monster yelled, 'Why?' but it wasn't a question."

"It was the letter *Y*," Brent said as he realized what we were talking about.

"That means we have *I*, *T*, *S*, *O*, *N*, *L*, and *Y*. What does that spell?" Sara asked.

"What are we doing here, cheering for a basketball team or trying to solve a mystery?" Sammy joked.

"*It's only*," I said. "It spells *It's only*. I wonder where the next clue will come from."

Sammy poked Brent and pointed. Brent's face lit up. "Look! There's a Tilt-a-Whirl over there. That's my favorite ride in the world. I'm going to go on it. I bet I've ridden Tilt-a-Whirls a hundred times. Nothing weird can happen there."

Brent marched toward the ride before I could stop him. Dr. Shivers had been able to make everything else twice as frightening as it should be. I was sure that the Tilt-a-Whirl wouldn't be any different.

"Wait up, Brent. If you're going on that ride, we all are. From now on, we stick together," I called after him.

The Tilt-a-Whirl is a basic spinning ride that rises and falls on small hills. Sometimes it goes really fast. I've always liked it too.

But everything at Dr. Shivers' Carnival of Terror was unpredictable. I thought about the merry-go-round. I had little hope that the Tilt-a-Whirl would be normal.

Brent was the first one on. Then Sammy and Sara climbed on. I looked around for spiders, Frankenstein's monster, barking hot dogs, or strange clowns. I didn't see anything or anybody, not even a person to run the ride. I cautiously got on.

When I sat down, the safety bar dropped and secured us in. The ride began to move slowly, then faster and faster.

"You would think that Dr. Shivers would come up with something different. We've already gone fast. We've already been trapped on rides," Sammy said with disappointment in his voice.

Then he startled us all by yelling, "Dr. Shivers, this ride isn't very frightening!"

"It will be!" came a voice from a loudspeaker.

"Thanks, Sammy. Thanks a lot," I said. "Now he's going to make this one more frightening than all the others."

The entire ride began to sink into the ground. It was lowered a foot every couple of seconds until we were in some kind of pit. Ghostly faces appeared along the walls of the pit. "I've got to get off this ride!" I screamed.

"Not now! The force of the spin will toss you like a rag doll. Stay in the car. I'll figure something out," Sara screamed back to me.

While Sara thought, I prayed: *Lord, thank You for keeping us safe. I know You're still with us.*

We dropped another three feet. The carnival had disappeared from sight. It looked like gremlins and skeletons were racing next to our car. This ride was too weird, way too weird.

Then it suddenly slowed down and started to rise toward the surface again. Once we were back at the top, the car stopped and the safety bar opened. I breathed a sigh of relief.

The Tilt-a-Whirl had barely stopped before we hit the ground. I had only taken two steps when I heard something crack. I looked up to see the *A* from the sign come loose. It fell with a thud into the car we had been riding in. I ran after the others.

Sammy had turned down an alley of the midway. "I think the gate out is this way," he said.

As we followed him, I told the others about the *A* that had fallen from the sign. Brent put it together. He said, "*It's only a*—but what is it only?"

Sammy planted his shoes into the dirt so quickly that we almost ran into him.

I saw why he stopped so suddenly.

There before us was a stage. On the stage was a ventriloquist with his dummy. The dummy was dressed in a plaid shirt and bib overalls. The ventriloquist wore a dark suit and a red bow tie.

We stared at them.

"Hello, kids," the dummy said. "It's time for another terrible show—not. Get it? *Knot*." He chuckled and pointed to the ventriloquist's bow tie.

"Hey, kids. I went to the doctor the other day because I thought I caught the flu bug. He said, 'Here's something for the bug,' and he gave me a woodpecker. Get it? Woodpecker. Ha, ha, ha. I've got a million of them."

Sammy laughed right along with him. I shifted from foot to foot. This whole place made me feel tense. Nothing here was what it was supposed to be.

Nothing turned out the way it should.

Nothing made sense.

I knew I wasn't looking at it from the right perspective, but I wasn't sure what the right perspective was. If this were a dream or something in a book, all this stuff would be understandable, even funny.

But this wasn't a book. It wasn't TV. It wasn't a dream. I, Kyle Conlon, was living through a real, live, crazy adventure. And why? What was I supposed to be learning? That "God's spirit, who is in you, is greater than the evil that is in the world"? That God can be trusted in every situation? That the Lord watches over us at all times?

Sara snapped me from my thoughts when she asked the dummy a question. "Would you tell us some more jokes?"

"Would I? Get it? *Wood eye*," the dummy answered, pointing to his eyeball. "Ha, ha, ha. I got a million of them."

The ventriloquist looked at us and smiled. His teeth were white and perfectly straight. His blue eyes had a blank look, as if there was little behind them.

"I've got a better idea. Instead of more jokes, how about a nice trick or two? I will need a volunteer from the audience."

Sara leaped to the stage. "I'm ready. What do I need to do?"

"Come closer, my friend," said the dummy.

What was Sara trying to prove? I had a bad feeling about this, and it was confirmed when the dummy leaped off the ventriloquist's lap and onto Sara. The force of the dummy hitting her knocked Sara to the stage floor.

It didn't look like the ventriloquist threw him. I was almost sure the dummy had jumped on his own.

But dummies don't do anything on their own. The ventriloquist does all the moving.

The dummy's wooden hands and fingers grabbed at Sara, frightening her. She screamed for help.

I cupped my hands around my mouth and yelled to the ventriloquist. He just sat there.

I leaped onto the stage and raced up to him. I pushed his arm to get his attention, but the ventriloquist slumped into the chair.

Then he slid off, making a heavy wooden thud on the stage. He was lifeless, and I saw the joints in his jawbone. They were hinged together by bolts.

He was the dummy.

Whatever had grabbed Sara was not a dummy. It was alive, and Sara needed help.

Sammy saw what happened with the ventriloquist and jumped onto the stage. He was thinking like I was. We both dived for the mysterious fiend at the same time and smacked our heads hard against each other.

I tumbled off the back of the stage. Sammy rolled off the front. Sara screamed again.

Brent moved so quickly that by the time I was able to pull my aching head and body onto the stage again, he was reaching for the impostor dummy. The moment his hands grabbed the menace, it went limp. We stared at the body, now lying lifeless on the stage. It, too, was made of wood.

"Thanks, Brent. I was beginning to think that you three were drawing straws to see who had to help me," Sara said as she took in some deep breaths to calm herself.

"I don't get it," Brent said. "This was a dummy too. How could it have acted so lifelike?"

"I don't know," I said. "But I don't think I want to hang around here and find out."

Sammy seemed unfazed by the experience, as though he had just witnessed nothing more than a magic trick. "So what's next?" he asked.

"Nothing!" Brent and I said simultaneously. We had had enough of this mania and wanted to leave.

Sammy stomped his feet in a mock temper tantrum. "I don't want to go. I don't want to go."

Sara sided with Brent and me. "I don't think we should stay any longer. Let's just get out of here. I think the gate is this way." She started walking, and we all followed along.

"Okay," Sammy said, "but if we leave now we'll never solve the mystery of Dr. Shivers' Carnival of Terror."

Brent added his two cents' worth. "I don't care. I'm out of here."

"There is something really strange going on around here," Sara said. "I wish we could figure it out. But frankly, I'm too spooked to stay."

"The sign said THE MAGIC DUMMY. Do you think it's magic?" I asked. I don't believe in such things, but this place was so weird.

"Magic is just a bunch of tricks that magicians learn. It's not real. But I wonder what's really going on here," Sara answered with a puzzled look on her face.

Sammy wanted to make sure we knew where he stood. "I love this place. I'm thinking of coming back tomorrow when it opens up. I feel like I've missed some of the best stuff. Besides, I've got to get one of those barking hot dogs to take back home with us. I've got to scare my little brother with it."

"Well, I don't ever want to see this place again," Brent said. "Tomorrow is too soon. Next week is too soon. Next month is too soon. Next—"

I stopped Brent in the middle of his sentence. I heard something.

We were only thirty feet from the gate when I heard footsteps, lots of footsteps heading our way. We spun around and saw a large crowd of people stampeding toward us. I saw several clowns in the crowd.

They must have known we were getting ready to leave. Dr. Shivers' gang was going to make sure we didn't.

As they got closer, the four of us jumped out of the way. They didn't even slow down. They ran right by us.

Why would they race toward us as fast as they could and then not grab us? It didn't make sense.

Then I saw the reason. A large, roaring lion bounded around the corner. His hungry eyes looked directly at us.

I looked around. Our only escape was to enter the closest amusement. It was only three feet away. The lion was about twenty feet away.

I had no choice. I grabbed Brent and Sammy by the arms and yelled to Sara. In two seconds we were falling backward through the door of a place called THE MUMMY'S TOMB. It had an unusual sign. Most of the letters were big, squared shapes. But one of the *M*s was exactly like the cursive *M* in the magic dummy sign. Could that be our next clue?

Inside, the scene looked like the set of an Egyptian movie. Fake sandstone blocks were stacked along the walls. Flat human forms with their arms bent funny were painted on the blocks. It didn't look very scary.

Sara looked around at the paintings. "Hey, this could be really educational. I've been doing research on ancient Egypt for a report, so I can say that I did research on my Christmas vacation."

"Yeah, research on how to get scared to death," Brent piped in.

"What I'm scared of right now is that lion outside. At least we're safe from it in here. Besides, maybe I can learn something," Sara said.

"About all you're going to learn is how to make a cheesy movie set. Let's just leave," I said.

"If you want to be eaten by a lion, go ahead. I'm staying in here for a while," she answered.

Sara had a point. Our options were to stay inside the Mummy's Tomb or leave and risk becoming lunch for a hungry lion.

"You're right," I said. "We're safer in here than we are out there. I don't see anything in here that looks threatening."

We descended a staircase. Behind large panes of glass we saw wax mummies authentically positioned in their tombs. Interesting historical facts were printed on metal plaques next to each window.

Sammy was bored. "Hey, let's hurry it along here."

We descended more stairs and passed more and more windows. After about forty steps, I stopped everyone. "Have any of you noticed the same thing I noticed?"

Brent was the first to answer. "Yeah, why are we going downstairs? How could we go any deeper? This carnival was put up just last night while we slept. Nobody would have had time to dig out a hole this deep. Now I've got the shivers."

"This whole place gives me the shivers," I added.

Sammy chimed in. "Yeah, Dr. Shivers."

"Let's turn around and get out of here," Brent said. "I don't think there's anything else worth seeing. That lion's got to be gone by now."

"I'm with Brent," I said. With that, I turned to walk back up the stairs.

I froze.

My voice caught in my throat and my mouth went dry.

Only three steps away from me was a figure wrapped in cloth strips. It was a mummy.

My friends twisted their heads quickly and saw the mummy standing behind me.

My mouth was wide open. After everything we had seen, I should have been ready for another fright. I wasn't. No one else was either.

We had been looking at all the glass-encased wax mummies and didn't expect that a real one would suddenly appear behind us.

I was still trying to form words when Brent screamed, "Run, everybody, run!"

Holding on to the rail for balance, we took three steps at a time down the staircase. How many more steps we took I don't know. I was too frightened to count, and the mummy was bounding down behind us. Its wrappings kept it from moving too fast, and that may have saved us.

The mummy yelled, "You have violated my tomb. I am coming for you."

His eerie, deep, rough voice was enough to keep us running.

Sammy stumbled when he hit bottom. He fell against the wall and slipped to the floor.

Sara leaped over him to keep from tripping, but Brent wasn't so lucky. He went sprawling along the ground as well. I was able to stop myself in front of them.

"Quick, get up. We don't have time for a rest," I yelled.

"Who's resting?" Brent answered. "Sammy fell, and I tripped over him. Help us up."

"You have violated my tomb." The voice was closer as it called to us.

"This way!" Sara yelled. "I've found another room."

Sammy scrambled to his feet as I pulled Brent to his. "We've got to find a way out of here. I don't think this guy likes houseguests," I said to the others.

Even Sammy seemed nervous now. He shot back, "Another brilliant deduction, Sherlock. I really don't need you to give me a running commentary of what is going on. I just want to get out of here."

We raced behind Sara into the big room. All around us we saw gold jewelry and statues with human bodies and animal heads. It was really strange.

"Great," Sammy snapped at Sara. "Now we're trapped in some room with no way out. We've got an angry mummy that doesn't plan on just grounding us but putting us into the ground, and there isn't a way out. Can this get any worse?"

"You have violated my tomb. I am coming for you."
The mummy sounded very close.

"I think it just got worse. He's right outside," Sara
said.

I yelled instructions to everyone. "Quick, grab
some of those statues and push them in front of the
door. It will keep him out for a few minutes. Brent,
start looking for a way out of here."

Brent panicked. "Like what, Kyle?"

"A button, a switch. Anything that might move a
wall. All of Dr. Shivers' amusements have had a trick
to get out. Look for the one here."

Brent felt along the walls while the rest of us
pushed statues across the door. After the third one,
I felt we might keep the mummy out long enough
to find an escape.

"You cannot stop me. I am coming for you. You
have violated my tomb," he called to us in his low,
raspy voice.

I didn't want to stick around to find out whether
he meant it or not. I began pushing on the walls. I
thought there might be a fake wall or a hidden door.

Brent pulled everything in sight to see if he could
open up a sliding door to another passageway.

Sammy and Sara piled more Egyptian artifacts in
front of the door to keep the mummy out.

The mummy continued to call to us, "You have
violated my tomb. I am coming for you."

Sammy ran toward me. As he neared me, he slipped on an Egyptian necklace and slid across the room. He landed, half sprawled on top of a casket. As he fell back away from it, the door to the casket popped open. A dim light shone from somewhere deep within the casket.

Brent turned and yelled, "Sammy, what did you do?"

I didn't have time to see the damage caused by his fall. Our mummy friend pushed through the statues in front of the doorway and was stepping over them.

Soon he would have us in his grasp.

"No!" I yelled.

Sara jumped out of the mummy's way and headed right toward us, then she made a quick cut and ran for the open casket. "Follow me and don't ask questions," she called as she raced by.

Sammy and Brent bumped into each other as they dived through the casket door. I turned to see where the mummy was. My delay cost me big time. His large, wrapped hands grabbed me by the shoulders. I was only inches from the casket.

Four hands reached from inside the casket and grabbed me. *Oh, no*, I thought. *I'm part of a mummy tug-of-war.* I could see the newspaper headline now: BOY TORN APART BY MUMMIES. I was scared.

The four hands inside the casket won the battle, pulling me hard into another room. I was moving so fast that I fell and landed facedown onto the dirty floor. Rolling over, I opened my eyes.

It couldn't be.

I was lying between Sammy and Sara on the dusty

floor of another room in the tomb. "Thanks. That one was really close. I wasn't sure if I was ever going to get out of the mummy's hands. Do you have any idea where we are?"

"I haven't had time to look around, but this looks like the room where they prepared the mummies for burial. If I'm right, there will be a secret door here that leads to the outside. The people who prepared the mummies had to confuse grave robbers so the treasure would be safe," Sara explained.

"Let's get going. I want out of here as quickly as possible," Brent added.

Each of us searched the room for the secret door. Sammy climbed the rocks that jutted out from the wall to search the ceiling, while Sara searched the floor. Brent felt along the stone wall.

"Nothing. There is nothing here," Sara said with frustration in her voice.

"Keep looking, Sara. We have to find a way out. Besides, that mummy knows all the ways into this place. I wouldn't be surprised if he mysteriously showed up out of the shadows. So keep looking," Brent insisted.

She went back to feeling and tugging on each rock. Brent pushed every painted symbol on the wall. There wasn't much light inside our mummy preparation room.

A torch on the wall gave us enough light to see,

but that most likely would not last as long as we needed it.

Sara stood up and straightened her spine. "I'm getting sore bending over. I wish we were back at your uncle's house watching movies and relaxing, Kyle."

"I want to swim in the pool and get some of this dirt off me," Sammy called down from his search of the high points of the wall.

"Now you're making sense, Sammy. I hope this means you don't want to go on any more rides," I said.

"Yeah," Brent said. "There may not be anything like this back in our little town, but I, for one, am mighty glad."

The torchlight was getting dimmer. I needed to do something to stretch our lighting. While the others looked for the passage, I went through the bottles of fluids and stone boxes.

If I could find a liquid that burned, I would dip some old cloth strips in it and wrap them around a torch. I saw that in a movie once.

It worked for the hero on the big screen. I hoped it would work for me as well.

There was one large vial on the top shelf over a stone table. I grabbed it, but I couldn't lift it off the shelf. Instead, it fell forward as if it were hinged.

I stood on tiptoe to get a better look, when all of a sudden a horrible grinding noise made me spin around.

"What's that noise? What's happening?" I hurriedly asked the others.

"That large stone over there is moving," Brent answered fearfully.

We all watched as a square piece of stone about the size of a refrigerator began to slide forward. As it inched toward us, I felt the hairs rise on the back of my neck and chills run up and down my spine. What could this be? What would come out of there?

A hand curled around the stone. It was wrapped heavily in cloth strips. I was sure the mummy was coming again.

Sara jumped back and bumped into Brent, who was already retreating. When her body struck Brent's, he stumbled over some stones on the floor and lost his balance. Brent hit the ground hard. I heard the thud and raced toward him.

Sammy leaped away from the wall and grabbed a wooden beam. From there he swung like a monkey to a torch holder. When he grabbed the torch holder, it gave way and flipped downward.

By accident, Sammy had found the hidden lever that opened the secret passage to the outside.

Unfortunately, the mummy was already slipping in the other passageway and three of us were lying on the floor.

I yanked hard on Brent's arm and pulled him to his feet. Sara was already scrambling up, and Sammy's tumble to the ground lasted only a second.

We had to get out of there before the mummy reached us. I didn't know what this mummy wanted to do to us, but I was certain he didn't intend to befriend us.

Brent was still groggy from his fall. I guided him toward the passageway and pushed his body through. He stumbled again and fell. Inside the opening was another staircase.

Sara and I hoisted Brent up. Sara supported Brent under one of his arms and I took the other. We began to drag him up the steps.

Sammy was left with the unfortunate job of holding the mummy back until we climbed the stairs. I don't know what he did, but whatever it was, it worked.

The three of us had reached the top when I heard Sammy's shoes slapping the stone stairway. He was only a few inches behind us as we turned the corner and discovered ourselves at a fork in the staircase.

The mummy was halfway up the steps. We heard him shouting his favorite and only phrase, "You have violated my tomb. I am coming for you."

"Which way do we go?" I asked the others.

Sara thought a moment and said, "Left."

Sammy said, "Right."

"We only have a few more seconds to make the decision here. Which way?" I pressed for one unified answer.

Brent stood on his own now and studied the stairways. "Definitely left," he said.

"That's good enough for me." I reached to help Brent up the steps, but it was obvious he no longer needed help. The four of us ran up the stairs.

I was near the top of the staircase when I looked behind me to see where my friends were. I should have been looking ahead, because as I reached the top landing my body crunched into another one.

I looked up. It was the mummy. His big hands locked me in a tight hold. He said over and over again, "You have violated my tomb. I am coming for you." Only he didn't have to come for me. He already had me.

"Don't come the rest of the way up the stairs!" I yelled, panic straining my voice. My friends stopped below me.

"What do we do?" Sammy asked.

Sara didn't wait to find out what the others were going to say. She ran as fast as she could back down the steps.

The mummy dragged me along the hallway. I twisted from side to side, trying to break free, but the mummy was too strong. He picked me up and slung me over his shoulder.

I could hear Brent panicking. "It's my fault! I chose this staircase. Kyle's caught and it's my fault!"

The mummy turned a bend in the corridor, then halted. I didn't know if that was a good or bad sign. I twisted around to see what made him stop.

Sara stood in front of us with a flaming torch. "All

right, mummy. There is nothing that this blazing, fiery torch would like more than to set fire to a bunch of old rags wrapped around some two-thousand-year-old withered body. So, drop my friend and you go free."

The move was extremely bold. And it worked. The mummy hurried away to some other part of his Egyptian tomb. Sara had saved me. "Hurry!" she said, not waiting for me to thank her. "Let's get back to the staircase."

"Thanks," I said as I started running. "That was a brave thing you did. What made you think of it?"

"I didn't know what else to do but pray," Sara said with a twinkle in her eye. "And God gave me the courage to stand up to that mummy!"

Sara and I ran back down the hall and found Brent and Sammy seemingly frozen on the steps, their eyes opened wide in fear. When Brent saw me he let out a wail. "Kyle, I thought you were—"

"Come on," I interrupted. "No time for that now. Let's get moving."

We raced to the bottom of the steps and got to the other staircase. We climbed it to the top. We walked another few steps and came to a dead end in the stone-lined hallway. There was no way out.

"I can't figure this out," I said. "One of these stair-ways should have led us out of here." I turned to tell the others that we needed to go back.

There was no one behind me. My friends had vanished.

19

"Sara! Sammy! Brent!" I called their names, but no answer came back to me. They'd been right behind me only a moment before.

I imagined that the mummy had grabbed them. I needed to save them, but how? Feeling helpless and hopeless, I slumped down in the corner.

For the first time that day, I felt like crying. I wanted out of this mummy's tomb and out of the carnival.

I heaved a breath. *Lord*, I prayed, *if I were all by myself, I'd be no match for a mummy. But I've got You with me. I know I'll be all right.*

I stood up and started back down the dark passageway. I moved slowly and quietly until I heard voices. I stopped.

My heart beat so loudly that I couldn't hear what was being said. I knew I needed to go closer, but I was too scared. For several moments I stood silently, leaning against the stone wall.

Then I pulled together all the courage I had and made a step toward the voices. They were barely audible, but I recognized them—Sammy, Sara, and Brent.

"Hey guys! I'm here! It's me!" I shouted, but they didn't hear me.

I could hear Sammy say, "The mummy must have grabbed Kyle. He was up ahead of us and then he was gone. I think we need to go back and look for him."

"How are we going to look for him? We don't have a torch since Sara's burned out. We don't have a flashlight. We don't have any idea where he might be," Brent said.

"That doesn't make any difference to me. Kyle is lost and we need to find him," Sara objected. "Besides, we've hit a dead end. This passage leads nowhere."

They were in the same predicament that I was in. I went down another corridor that led to nowhere and so did they. If the ones we chose did not lead to safety, then there must not be a way out. Or there must be another passage we missed as we traveled along the stone hallway.

"Let's go find him," Sara said. I could hear her footsteps coming toward me. The others were right behind her. Their steps sounded so close to me. "Hey, you guys! I'm here! This way!"

I waited, but their steps never got any closer. In fact, they now headed away from me. They must have found the passageway out. I had to catch up to them.

I started down the corridor, feeling my way along the rocks. I moved slowly, touching from side to side. I knew that if I could feel the opening I would find my friends. It was my only hope.

After a few minutes, I thought that I should have found the passage opening. I started to get frightened.

I felt from one side to the other as I prayed.

My right hand touched stone. My left hand touched stone.

My right hand touched stone. My left hand touched rags.

I pulled it away quickly. What was that? I heard deep, heavy breathing, then a growling whisper that moved closer and closer to my ear.

"You have violated my tomb. I am coming for you."

"Aah!" I shrieked. I backed away from the mummy. When I did that I felt no stone behind me. The passageway was right there.

The monster's hand reached out and grabbed me, but it didn't get a good hold on me. I broke free and went hurtling down the open corridor behind me.

The mummy's cloth-wrapped feet thudded along the stones. It was too close for me to feel safe.

"Help! Sammy, Sara, Brent, where are you? The mummy is right behind me. We need to get out of here and we need to do it right now."

"Kyle, run toward my voice," Sara yelled.

She was close, but I suddenly realized how stupid I was. I had just led the mummy right to my friends. We had not found the way out yet. The mummy was inches away from me.

In the dark, I couldn't tell how close I was to them. I found out soon enough; I slammed into them and we all went flying into the stones at the end of the hallway.

When we hit the wall, I felt it move slightly and then pop open. The sunlight bathed us as we tumbled to the dirt midway of Dr. Shivers' Carnival of Terror. We had to shut our eyes to protect them from the brightness.

Brent let out a long breath. Sara gasped. I was confused. Sammy had a very different response from the rest of us and a very typical one for him. He was giggling.

"That was great," Sammy said. "I like this place more and more."

"Maybe you like it so much because you weren't grabbed by a mummy," I snapped back at him as I stood dusting myself off.

"Or because you didn't eat any worm-filled cotton candy," Brent added.

"And you didn't get attacked by a living dummy," Sara threw in for good measure. "I vote that we get out of here. I don't even care about the mystery anymore." Sara moved into the center of our group and looked each of us in the eyes. I was with her all the way until I took a step back onto something slippery. I lost my balance and went crashing to the ground once again.

"What's the matter? Are you so worn out that you need a nap before we leave?" Sammy kidded.

"No, I slipped on something," I snapped back.

"You slipped on our clue," Sara said, suddenly interested in the mystery again as she pointed downward. "There's an *O* painted on the ground. The plot thickens, my friends. If we add that to the *M* from the mummy's tomb sign, we know that *It's only a mo* . . . But what is a mo?"

We all tried to finish the phrase.

"It's only a mouse."

"It's only a mockingbird."

"Mocha candy."

"Monkey."

"Mongoose."

"Monster."

When Brent said *monster*, we all mouthed the phrase together. "It's only a monster." Shivers ran up and down my spine.

Then Sammy piped up again. "So it's only a monster. I still want a prize before we go. There's a ball toss over there. Let me do that and then we can get out of here quickly." Sammy ran toward the game booth before any of us had time to respond.

A barker appeared as we approached the game. He had a big, beaming smile. Glancing at our necklaces, he said, "Ah, you are friends of Dr. Shivers. What can I do for you? Do you want to win a prize?"

"That's what we're here for. What do we have to do, sir?" Sammy asked.

"Simple, my friends. Just knock over the bottles in three tries," the barker answered.

Sammy picked up the balls, but then paused. He looked at Sara. "You're the best pitcher here. Why don't you try? If you win me a prize, I'll gladly leave."

"All right," Sara agreed. "Anything to get out of here quickly."

Sara tossed the first ball. It hit the bottles and the top one fell off. The next time, she hit the center one and they all fell but one. On her third attempt, the last bottle fell.

"You won!" Brent shouted. "But where did the guy go?"

"Right here. I just had to get the prize."

His back was to us. When he turned around, his beaming smile had turned into bloodstained fangs. His face was covered with dripping green skin, and his eyes glowed bright red.

"Aah!" we yelled in unison.

The barker laughed and gripped his face with his hands. He pulled off a mask. He was now howling with laughter. "That gets them every time. I love doing that to kids."

Sammy grabbed the mask right away, but Brent took it from his hands.

Brent put it on and tried to scare us all with it. After what we had been through, a little mask didn't seem to have much effect.

I looked at the barker while Brent tried to scare Sara. He raised his hand and gave me a victory sign.

Then Brent handed the mask to Sammy, and he slipped it over his head. He goofed off a little with it then tried to remove it.

"Hey, I can't get it off," Sammy cried out.

"Quit messing around, Samuel," Brent said very seriously.

"I agree," I said with emphasis.

"Help me. It feels like it's sticking to my skin. It's starting to feel *like* my skin. Quick, help me," Sammy whimpered.

His body started to twist away from us. I thought he was in pain. Suddenly he stood straight up with his back to us.

I felt relieved that he seemed to be back to himself. Sammy turned very slowly. His arms were raised in the air. His eyes were red and horrible looking. He spoke to us, "Dr. Shivers has sent me to eliminate all of you. I must do as the good doctor says."

The mask had been loose when Sammy first put it on. Now it was drawn tightly over his face and neck.

He took a step toward us. We huddled together. I don't know what the others were thinking, but I was torn. *Do I help my friend or do I run for my life?*

I turned to the other two. "Sara, you and I will hold Sammy down while Brent pulls off the mask." They nodded in agreement.

We lunged at Sammy. Sara and I held Sammy on the ground while Brent pounced on Sammy's chest. Brent grabbed for the mask and I heard Sammy laugh.

"Got you, didn't I?" he said.

It was the first time I ever saw Brent look as if he wanted to hit somebody. He formed a fist with his right hand and grimaced, but he held back.

"I guess I shouldn't have done that. I'm sorry, everyone. I thought it would be funny. I guess I'm ready to leave if you are. Which way is out?"

"I kind of remember that the front gate was over by that balloon stand. We can all get one of those really scary balloons and head back to Kyle's uncle's," Brent said.

"To the balloons!" Sara yelled, and I raced toward the booth. I stopped dead in my tracks in front of it. The balloons were there, but the vendor wasn't.

A moment before, a woman dressed in a bright red jacket had been standing next to the balloons smiling at us. Now she was gone.

Sara ran up behind me. She laughed and said, "I'm second."

Then she gasped. "Where is the woman who was here a minute ago?"

"That's what I was just wondering. I saw her, and I don't remember taking my eyes off the balloons. How could she have slipped away so quickly? Let's just skip the balloons and get out of this place," I told her.

Brent was with us next. "I really want to get a balloon," he said.

"All right. But after this I'm going home," I told him firmly.

"We all keep saying that and then something else happens. This is not an easy place to get out of," Sara added.

The three of us started pulling at the balloon strings. Sara chose one that had Dracula painted on it. Hers came out easily.

Brent's was a little tougher. He tugged and tugged on the string of a balloon with a face that looked more like a monster than most monster masks in stores. It finally came loose, and he stood waiting for me.

My choice was a little less frightening. It was a cute little animal face. The problem was that my string wouldn't come loose at all. The three of us grabbed the string and yanked it. It wouldn't budge.

"I surrender. I'll take something else."

The moment I said that, the balloon popped loose and started floating in the air. We all jumped for it, but the helium was lighter than we were and the balloon continued to rise.

"This just isn't my day. I can't even pick a balloon without something strange happening. I'll choose another one."

I walked back toward the balloons, but my eyes were still focused on the one I lost.

Bang!

"Somebody is shooting at us!" Brent said. "Hit the dirt!"

We were on the ground in a second.

"Who is shooting at us?" Sara asked. She was quiet for a minute and then cried out, "Where's Sammy? Where did he go? Have either one of you two seen him?"

I sat up and stared around, but I didn't see Sammy. I yelled for him, "Sammy, where are you? Quit goofing around, Sammy. Come on, don't joke around like this."

No answer. I climbed to my feet just as another shot rang out.

Bang!

Before I could hit the ground again, balloon fragments fell on my head. I shook them off and looked up.

I saw a piece of paper floating to the ground. It must have been inside the balloon. The shot must have been to break the balloon.

"What is it?" Brent asked.

I picked up the paper. "It's a message to us. I think it has something to do with Sammy."

Sara grabbed the paper out of my hand.

"What does it say, Sara?" Brent asked.

"'We have something that you may want back. Come to the Tunnel of the Weird.'"

"What do you think it means?" I asked.

"I think you were right. I think someone has kidnapped Sammy and we have to get him back. He's probably at this Tunnel of the Weird," Sara said.

"Where is it?" I asked. "Everything in this place is weird. I think we need to have that old-fashioned prayer meeting. Let's pray for Sammy's protection." We formed a circle, held hands, and prayed for a few minutes. There was real power in our prayer, and we all could feel it.

"Now, let's find that tunnel," Sara said with a new strength in her voice.

"I haven't seen anything like that anywhere in the carnival," Brent said.

"We better split up and look for it. I don't think we have much time. We need to find him now," Sara said firmly.

"I think we should ask someone where it is," Brent said.

"Where are we going to find someone to ask?" I snapped.

Brent looked around, his eyes growing wider and wider. "Over there," he said.

Sara and I turned around quickly on our heels.

It was the clown.

The clown lifted his arm and waved. He motioned to us to follow him. Then he started to walk down another midway of rides and games, ones that we had not seen before. I couldn't believe how big the carnival was. How could they have built this overnight?

The clown stayed about ten feet ahead of us. I didn't mind that. He was a strange character to say the least.

He passed a lemonade stand and turned right, disappearing from our sight. By the time we got around the corner, he was gone. I wasn't sure where to look for him.

There were several rides and other amusements that he could have slipped into. But it didn't make any difference where he had gone. We were looking for the Tunnel of the Weird.

"I see it over there," Sara said, pointing straight ahead. The sign over the entrance looked old, and it hung by one rusty nail from one side. The wind was making it swing back and forth. We heard it squeak.

"Do you hear that?" I asked.

"What?" Sara said.

"I can hear the sign squeaking."

Sara looked at me like I was crazy.

"The music over the loud speakers has been turned off. I'm beginning to think that this Tunnel of the Weird is not a safe place for any of us," I said fearfully.

Brent put his hand on my shoulder, then stepped toward the tunnel. "We don't have a choice. Sammy has been kidnapped and we need to find him."

"I'm all for it, but I think we should have some sort of game plan," Sara added.

"I've got one. Let's go in and get Sammy and get back out alive," Brent said matter-of-factly. "We don't know what's in there. We need to stay close together and grab Sammy as soon as we can.

"I'll guide us in. Sara, you guide us out. Kyle will take the lead against any monster that we might find in there. Agreed?"

"I'm ready," Sara said.

"Me too," I added.

We walked the few feet toward the tunnel with slow, fearful steps. The entrance was a heavy, dark brown, wooden door. We slowly pushed our way through it.

Inside, it was very dark. I could hear an amusement ride car on a track near me.

"I'll go first," Brent said as he moved by me. "Can you see the cars for the ride?"

"Over here, children."

The voice came out of the dim light. My eyes had adjusted to the low lights by now. A soft glow lit the face of a man on the other side of the tracks.

He continued. "Welcome to the Tunnel of the Weird. Many go in. Few come out. Would you have a seat please?"

The bar to the car popped up and the three of us climbed in. I looked at the man and asked, "What do you mean by 'few come out'?" He didn't answer. In another moment the car lurched forward. I turned back to look at the man, but he was gone. We were entering the tunnel.

Brent relaxed. "I've seen this ride before. They have it at the Big America Theme Park."

"What happens?" Sara quizzed.

"I don't know for sure. I mean, I've never ridden the one at Big America. I've only seen it. I've heard that a bunch of things jump out and try to scare you. None of it is real. Relax and enjoy the ride," he said. I wanted to believe him.

The first thing we saw was a headless woman sitting in a rocking chair. Her head was in her lap and it was talking to us. "Turn back now. Go no farther, or you may never come out of here again."

"I think we should believe her and leave," I said.

"You want to leave Sammy?" Brent asked.

"No. You're right, we have to find him. But I hope we can do it fast," I answered, just as the headless woman receded into the darkness.

The car turned a corner and came alongside a lumberjack dressed in a red plaid shirt, stocking cap, and jeans. He flashed a giant smile and raised his ax.

"I don't like the looks of this," I said.

Brent tried to assure me. "Haven't you ever seen one of those before? It's a robot. He'll lower the ax in a minute."

And he did.

He started to lower it quickly and let go of it. The handle and glistening ax head flew our way. We dived for the floor of the amusement car. I heard the ax smash into the front of the car with a loud bang.

I was afraid to look, but I raised my head just slightly and peeked outside the car.

The lumberjack was gone. I looked at the front of the amusement car, and the ax was gone too. There was no sign of either one anywhere.

"It's all right. The lumberjack is gone and his ax never really hit us," I said, exhaling a sigh of relief.

Sara popped up and looked at me. "What happened?" she asked.

Before I could reply, Brent spoke up. "It was weird, and we are in the Tunnel of the Weird."

Sara's mouth fell open and she spit out the words, "Weirdness ahead!"

Brent and I turned to see our car heading directly for a spinning buzz saw. "Jump out of the car," I screamed.

"That's crazy. There's nothing but wall on both sides of us. We're about to become split personalities!" Sara said, panic rising in her voice.

In another minute we would be doing more than panicking. In another minute we would be going to pieces—literally.

"Move to the sides of the car and let the blade pass down the middle," I yelled to the others.

Sara and Brent moved to the left side of the car and I went for the right.

The car moved closer and closer to the blade. The sound got louder.

We were about a foot from the blade. I could feel the breeze from the fast-turning toothed wheel. I prayed that we would survive the cut.

Then we were about six inches away. Suddenly the car shifted and my body faced the blade.

I gulped.

23

"Help!" I screamed. As I did that the car leaped forward, pulling us out of the way of the whirling blade.

"That was close," Sara cried.

"Too close," I agreed.

Brent sat back and spoke. "We came in here to save Sammy, and it looks like we may not make it out of here."

"Yes, we will," I said, trying to banish Brent's fears, although I wasn't convinced myself that we would make it out of the Tunnel of the Weird. "The Lord will show us where Sammy is and help us get out of this place."

"Then let's get to work and find him, because I want to get out of here as quickly as possible," Sara added.

Her statement was almost drowned out by the sound of rushing water. We looked at each other and then at what was ahead of us.

Our car had gone into a flowing stream of water

that ran through the tunnel. And that stream headed straight for a waterfall. We couldn't tell how far down it was, but the crashing water sounds at the bottom were loud and violent.

"Hang on!" Sara yelled to make sure her voice sounded out above the water.

We all gripped the bar in front of us. I looked over at Brent. His eyes were closed and his lips were moving. I think he was praying. Sara was praying out loud.

We hit the edge and tipped forward.

Down and down the car fell.

The air rushed by us faster and faster.

We anticipated the crash, but it seemed like it was never going to come.

"I don't think we're going to come out of this one. I'm really sorry for inviting you out here to my uncle's house. I wanted us to have fun, but it seems like the fun ends right here," I apologized as we dropped through the rushing water.

Brent opened his mouth to say something when the car blasted into a pool of water and came to a dead stop, tossing us forward against the crash bar. It saved us from flying out and into the water. None of us were hurt.

"Wow! That was fantastic," Sara exclaimed. "I wonder what we're in for next?"

I looked at Brent. His face was greenish. "I'm not

feeling too good," he said. "All this excitement is making my stomach tie in knots."

Sara didn't hear what he said. Her eyes were fixed on something in front of us—a castle. Its turrets were built from large stones.

I wondered again how the carnival workers built all this in one night. I needed to remember to ask Dr. Shivers when we got out of here. *If* we got out of here.

Our little car was moving again, heading straight for a big wooden door. It was a drawbridge, but it had not been let down yet. After the other weird things we had encountered in this tunnel, I fully expected it to lower and take us inside. I was right.

The drawbridge eased down as we got closer. By the time our car got to the moat, the bridge was all the way down. We crossed it. Not one of us said a word. Our silence told me that each of us was frightened about what we would encounter next. We entered the castle. It was so dark inside that we could not see a thing. I heard the drawbridge rise again and close tightly behind us. We were not going to go back that way. We had no choice but to press ahead. Then the amusement car stopped. Sara sucked in a breath. Brent let out his breath, and I felt thankful to still have mine running through my lungs.

"What's next?" Brent asked.

"We have to stay calm."

We heard the sound of several feet stomping toward us in the dark. It sounded like people wearing some type of armor.

The clanking metal grew louder, and we knew our welcoming committee was almost on us.

Sara yelled, "Run for it!" I felt the car shift as Sara leaped out of it and then I heard a crash against metal. "Let me go!" Sara yelled.

"Sara, are you all right?" Brent called out into the darkness. I felt hands brush by me, and Brent yelped and began to struggle. Then two strong hands grabbed me under my arms and another pair took hold of my legs.

We had been captured, but by what?

"Where are you taking us?" I demanded. No answer. Only the sound of our captors' grunts.

Sara's and Brent's voices were not too far from me. The captors carried us off in the dark. I had no idea where we were going, and I was afraid of where it could be.

Even though it was too dark to see, I could sense that we were placed inside a room. Brent breathed heavily and Sara whispered a prayer. But I was sure there was another person in the room with us.

"Who's there?" I asked.

"Me," a voice replied.

"Sammy!" we yelled in unison.

"Man, am I glad to see you," I said. "That is, if we could really see you. How did you get in here?"

"I'm not sure. When the three of you went to get balloons, I saw one of those hot dog stands and I wanted to get a barking hot dog for my little brother. When I got closer to the hot dog stand, one of the carnival workers invited me to try a new ride called the Well of Doom.

"I guess I'm a real sucker. I sat down in a bucket, and suddenly a dozen crazy things happened to me. To make a really weird story short, I ended up here," he told us.

"That's pretty close to how we got here. Now we need to find a way out of here. Any ideas?" Sara asked.

"Have you found the walls or a door yet?" I asked.

"No, I just got here a few seconds before you did. It's too dark to see anything," he answered.

"I have an idea," Brent said with excitement.

"Spit it out," Sara said. "Anything would be helpful right now."

"We need to find a wall, but we don't know where the closest one is. I have a way to find it," he said. "I have some of that glow-in-the-dark putty that comes in an egg in my pocket.

"We can roll it into a ball that we can throw against the walls. When it hits, it will bounce back. Then we head to the closest wall," he told us with pride.

"That is the best idea I've heard in the last five minutes. I say we go for it," I encouraged.

The next thing I knew, Brent was throwing the putty ball in the four directions around us. The first one took awhile to come back. The second and third throws returned faster. The fourth one told us that we were only about three feet from a wall.

Sara got to the wall first and pushed on it. Brent felt around for an opening. Sammy got frustrated and kicked the wall.

I was about to tell him to not lose his temper when the wall gave a cracking sound. He kicked again. Something popped open.

"It's the door!" Brent yelled happily.

"Pure luck," Sara told Sammy.

"What do you mean? I knew exactly what I was doing," he joked.

"I think we should get out of here before something else happens," I warned them.

We passed through the doorway and stopped. We had stepped into what looked like a beautiful field. Bright lights shone above us, and what looked like green plastic grass covered the ground.

I looked behind us. The door we came through was in the side of a wall. The number sixteen was painted on it.

"Where are we?" Brent asked with bewilderment.

"It looks like a big, green field," I told him as I

walked forward and looked around for a clue. "It doesn't look familiar, but we must be outside the carnival. Let's find our way back to my uncle's."

I raised my foot to take another step, but something grabbed me by the belt and hurled me to the ground.

"Why did you do that, Sammy?" I lay on my back on the ground and stared up at him.

"Hey, bozo, you better watch where you're walking. You almost stepped into a big hole," Sammy said with a big laugh.

"A big hole in the middle of a green plastic field. It sounds like a miniature golf course to me. But that's silly. Everything on a miniature golf course is miniature," I said.

"Unless it is a giant miniature golf course," Sara interrupted.

I pulled myself up from the artificial grass and responded to Sara. "Why would you say that?"

"I didn't say that," she said. "The sign over there said it. I can't believe that we didn't see it before. It could have run us over, we were so close to it."

"The sign may not run us over, but there is a good chance that the big orange ball rolling toward us might," Brent said quickly.

"Golf course!" Sammy yelled.

"Big ball!" Sara screamed.

"Jump in the hole, everyone," I commanded.

The other three went in before me. Once inside, we found ourselves sliding through a bent tube that led to a lower platform where there was a second hole.

We had to get to the bottom of the tube before the ball followed us. But that wasn't what happened.

Only seconds after I jumped into the hole, the ball fell in. Just our luck. The giant got a hole in one. We all slid down the tube with the ball behind us. It gained inches at a time. If it hit us, we would be crushed inside the tube.

I wondered how giants could exist and why they would play miniature golf.

Up ahead the tube split into two. To avoid getting crushed, we needed to go down one and the ball needed to go down another.

I yelled to the others, "Go down the left tube!"

Sara shifted her body and angled down the left side. Sammy and Brent followed. The ball was only a foot from my head. I had to take a gamble and go to the left. If the ball came after me, that would be the end of the game. I slid feet first into the left tube and pushed off the side to give myself more speed so my head would clear the split before the ball got there.

The golf ball nailed the divider and bounced to the side. I prayed that it would go down the right side. I prayed hard. If ever I needed the Lord to answer my prayers, this was the time.

I looked back over my head. Was it going to follow me? I closed my eyes and kept sliding downward.

After a few seconds, I opened my eyes again and looked back. The ball was gone. It had gone down the right tube. In another moment I popped out of the bottom and fell onto the artificial grass.

"How did you know that we needed to take the left one?" Brent asked me excitedly.

"I'll tell you as soon as we are off of this green," I answered. "As long as we are here, the ball can get us any time. I don't feel like repeating that last experience. Jump the wall."

We scrambled over the side and landed on another green.

"It looks like this is taking another bad turn," Sara whispered.

I nodded in agreement, then said, "Sara, if we get out of this one, then I'm heading straight for the front gate and back to my uncle's pool. I've decided that I don't need any more excitement in my life."

"Actually, things are looking up," Sammy assured us.

"How?" asked Sara.

"There's a number seventeen painted on this wall. That means we only have to get through two more holes," he informed us.

"Great, but I still want to know how Kyle knew that we should take the left tube," Brent insisted.

"It was easy. My dad and I play miniature golf all the time. Any time there is a split tube, the builders put in a slight bump to send the ball down the side farthest from the hole.

"I could see that the hole was near the opening on the left side. I assumed the ball would bounce down the right side."

"It saved us, Kyle. Thanks," Sammy added.

"Does anyone know where we should go now?" Brent quizzed.

"To get to the next hole, we have to go through there."

Sara pointed to several large objects that were swinging back and forth. In their enlarged size, I couldn't tell what they were. I guessed the swinging objects were golf clubs.

"What do we have to do, Kyle?" Sara said, placing her hand on my shoulder.

"Avoid the next ball," Sammy called to us as he bolted from our spot toward the center of the fairway.

We turned our heads and saw another huge golf ball rolling toward us.

We leaped in step behind Sammy, running toward the clubs. We had little choice if we wanted to avoid the ball rolling toward us.

But the clubs were swinging back and forth in such a motion that we had to time it perfectly. And we didn't even have time to think, let alone plan our run.

Sara reached the clubs first. She was the most athletic one of us. She dodged and weaved. The first club missed her by only an inch. She let out a muffled scream.

She knew it was too close, but she couldn't turn back now.

The second one nipped her back heel. For a second she lost her balance. The delay worked in her favor. The third one went by easily. But I noticed that the fourth one moved at a faster speed.

"Dive for it, Sara!" Sammy yelled. He must have noticed the speed increase as well.

Without hesitating, Sara did as she was told and

leaped forward like she was sliding into second base. It was a perfect base-stealing move.

Sammy faced the run next. I prayed that he'd be as attentive to his own run as he had been to Sara's. He ran past the first club and stopped dead in his tracks as he waited for the second to pass him.

It worked.

Brent watched Sammy to plan his moves and made it through safely.

I was glad that they made it, but I had forgotten to watch out for my own run. The first club narrowly missed me. The second one tossed me into the air. I was flying.

The air rushed through my hair and I felt gravity pulling at the skin of my face.

I looked down and saw the other three watching me with their mouths open. I felt more like a bird than a boy.

The club threw me up and over the wall. I started my fall back to earth and then realized that the artificial grass on the other side of the wall was very near. That saved me from broken bones and maybe even worse when I hit the grass. I had not fallen far enough to pick up much momentum. "Kyle, are you all right?" Brent yelled up to me.

"I'm fine. You have got to get up here before the ball makes it through the clubs," I called down.

There was only one way and we all knew it. They

would have to let the clubs throw them over the wall. The giant's ball was already slicing through the barriers and would soon be rolling where they were standing.

The giant's ball bounced and hit the back wall. The ball rolled within a few feet of my friends.

"You've got to hitch a ride on one of the clubs and get up here before the next bounce nails you," I bellowed down to them.

My friends ran toward the clubs. The ball rolled even closer to them. The next time would get them for sure.

Sara leaped first. It was the perfect jump. She grabbed on with her hands and swung off the club as it reached the high point. She dropped down next to me.

Brent was caught by the club and flew much like I did to the top of the wall. He fell with more impact, and I heard his breath rush out of him. The only one left was Sammy.

He followed Sara's lead and grabbed on. His body flew off the club with great momentum, and the sound of him hitting the ground was loud.

He didn't move at first. He opened his eyes slowly. "I don't feel so good. Can we just go home now?" Sammy asked in a pained whisper.

"More than gladly, but first we have to get out of here," Sara said.

"What do we do now?" Brent asked.

I stood up and pointed to the next green. "If I am right, that should be the eighteenth hole and we are out of here."

I ran toward the hole and skidded to a stop. I had seen one of these before at Cascade Park Miniature Golf. It was the most difficult hole ever. The ball had to roll into a special cup at the exact time that a powerful blast of air shot out of the cup. The ball would fly into the air and fall into the hole.

I explained to the others what we had to do. Everyone understood except Sammy.

"So we get in the hole, then what?"

"The last hole is actually a tube that leads somewhere," I explained.

"Leads where?" Sammy asked.

"Out. I hope," I told him. "I hope—and pray."

We only had two choices. We could stay and risk getting crushed by a giant golf ball or we could risk getting into the last hole. The second choice provided the best chance to escape.

"Brent, you go first. Sammy, you go second, and Sara, since you're the fastest, you'll need to go third. There won't be any time for mistakes. Since I know the hole the best, I'll go last. Keep moving once you're on the green in case a ball heads our way," I instructed them.

We had all just jumped to the eighteenth green when Sammy yelled, "Look out!"

Another ball was rolling toward us as Brent headed for the cup and the blast of air. He leaped in the cup and the air blasted him upward. He dropped into the hole and was out of sight.

Sammy was in the cup before Brent reached the hole. Sammy flew upward, but he twisted wrong and came back down into the cup. I turned around and saw the ball rolling closer to Sara and me.

"I don't think we're going to make it before the ball arrives. Watch yourself as you run for the cup. Keep looking back because that ball is going to head for the hole as well."

I turned to look at Sammy. He was just dropping into the hole. That was two of us safe. Sara raced across the green. The ball was right behind her. She dived for the cup, and the blast of air shot her straight upward.

The ball was so close to her that the rushing air pushed it backward. I was glad she beat the golf ball, but it was heading back toward me.

Sara dropped inside the hole. I was the only one left. The ball was rolling my way.

As the orange ball rolled back toward me, I felt a

rumble and saw a white one moving up behind me. I was about to be sandwiched between two golf balls.

I looked in front of me and then behind me. The two were about equal distance from me. I could not run fast enough to get away from the rolling menaces.

As the balls approached, I dived from between them. They hit each other and flew off in different directions. I lay on the artificial turf, watching them.

The orange one bounced off the wall and came directly toward me. I rolled out of its way.

This was a good short-term solution, but I needed a long-term one that would send me sliding down the eighteenth hole. I jumped to my feet and started jamming my shoes into the turf. I picked up speed, but so did the white ball. I hit the cup and was propelled into the air. I saw the hole that I needed to drop into below me. I twisted my body and down I went into the escape route.

I dropped out of the chute into the middle of my friends. I looked up to see who pulled me up. Sammy and Brent smiled back at me.

"We did it. We got out of there," I told them with relief showing across my face. "Where are we now?"

Sammy pointed to a door. "Sara went over to that door to see what was on the other side. She'll be back in a minute. Just take a break and rest."

"I don't think we should do that. A golf ball will be heading out of that hole in a second," I said.

We scrambled to our feet and ran for the door. Sara was waiting for us.

Sara smiled when she saw us. "I think this is all over," she yelled. "On the other side of this door is the nicest sight I've seen all day."

We opened the door and before us was a sign that said, TRANSYLVANIA TRAM TO DR. SHIVERS' CARNIVAL OF TERROR. We were finally out of the Tunnel of the Weird and on our way home, or at least to the place that led to home.

"All aboard," said a voice from the speaker system above our heads. We slipped through the doors into a brand-new tram car. It looked more like a small subway car, but that didn't make any difference to us.

Our feet hurt and we were tired.

Brent stared at the walls around us. "Doesn't it seem strange that there isn't another person on this tram?" he asked.

"No, what's strange to me is that in one night Dr. Shivers could have set up a carnival and a tram system. I'm beginning to think that there is more to this place than we can see," I told them.

The tram slowed down and came to a stop. I looked out the window. It wasn't our stop. The sign read WEREVILLE. I thought that was a strange name for a town. "We have stopped at Wereville."

"What an odd name for a town. I wonder what it

means. I wonder how you're supposed to pronounce it," Sammy added. "*Where-* or *were-* or *we're*-ville?"

"Quiet. The door is opening and someone's getting on," Brent whispered to us.

A boy about our age slid through the open door. He smiled at us and said hello. We all returned his greeting. He sat down at the other end of the tram car.

When he did, the Wereville sign shook. The *I* shifted and then spun around.

"There's our next clue," Sara said. "*It's only a m-o-i.*"

"It's only a moist cookie," Sammy guessed.

"What? Why would the mysterious clues lead us to *It's only a moist cookie*?" Brent scoffed.

"They don't. There was another letter after the *O*," I told them. "When we were at the game booth with the mask, the man there gave me the victory sign. You know, *V.*"

"Then it's *M-O-V-I*," Sara said thoughtfully.

Sammy looked at the sign distractedly and asked, "What do they say in Wereville? Do they say *where* in *Wereville*? Or do they say *we're* in Wereville?"

"Or is it the werewolf of Wereville?" Sara joked, giving up on the mystery clues for a moment.

"The werewolf of Wereville," I said slowly. Then I said it again. "The werewolf of Wereville. That has a nice ring to it."

"Next you will be saying that the guy sitting down there is a werewolf," Brent said, chuckling.

28

We all laughed at Brent's joke and sat back in our seats. We were exhausted and needed to rest. The only sound was that of the tram moving over the tracks. The clickety-clack soothed me and I closed my eyes.

I was just about asleep when the tram slowed down again. I groggily asked, "Where are we?"

Brent put his face to the glass and looked outside. He turned around and told us that this stop was called Full Moon Junction.

"Werewolf of Wereville traveling through Full Moon Junction. Can this get any stranger?" I asked.

As I joked, the boy at the other end of the tram started to twitch and jerk. He held a hand up in the air. It was covered with hair. Then he leaped to his feet and growled. The boy twisted in the other direction and ran into the next car.

"What was that?" Sammy asked.

"It was really weird," Brent added.

"It was also a werewolf. The boy got on at Wereville, and then when we passed through Full Moon Junction, he started to transform into a werewolf. Any minute now, he will walk through that door with only one thing on his mind," I explained.

"What?" Sara asked.

"Dinner. We are going to be his dinner," I expressed with unnatural calmness.

"Do you have any suggestions?" Sammy quizzed.

The doors to the other tram car opened and the werewolf leaped through them.

"I have one suggestion—run!" I yelled loudly.

We all ran from our tram car to the next one. The werewolf didn't waste any time. He smashed into the door and then through it.

We only had a few seconds to open the next door and leap through it. The werewolf jumped from seat to seat. He was tearing them up with his claws.

Sammy used his belt to tie the door handle to one of the metal bars people use to steady themselves. The belt held for a few minutes.

The werewolf got madder and madder as he hit and pulled at the door.

"How many more tram cars do we have till we reach the end?" I asked.

Sammy pulled open the door and looked inside. When he turned around, his eyes were filled with real fright. "The next car is the last one, and it's filled with all kinds of boxes and junk. There's no place to run after that one."

"Great!" Sara said.

"What do you mean, 'great'? We could be dinner for a werewolf and you say that's great?"

Sammy was getting more animated as he spoke. His arms were flying in the air and his eyes were bugging out.

"I don't want to get eaten. I just want out of here."

The belt holding out the werewolf was stretching. The leather showed signs of splitting. I didn't think that we had more than another minute to move to the next car.

"Let's get into that other car. Once we're there we can block the door with boxes," I called to my friends.

We yanked open the last door just as the werewolf ripped the leather belt. The werewolf's yellow eyes glared at us as he let out a tremendous howl.

Sammy, Sara, and I passed into the last tram car. After Brent joined us, Sara slammed the door shut behind him, picked up a broom that was lying on the floor, and jammed it into the door to hold it shut. The werewolf smashed his face against the glass of the door. His hot breath steamed the window.

We backed against the stuff in the last car and started looking and scrambling through the boxes.

"I found something that might work," Brent yelled out as he pulled a chain from under a stack of rags.

He and Sammy ran to the door and wrapped the chain through the handle and around the bottom of a spare seat stored in the car.

"What do we lock it with, Brent?" Sammy asked.

"I don't know. What can we lock it with, Kyle?"

I found a small rope. I looked at it and then looked back at the chain. It could work, but then the chain could still break. We didn't have a lot of choices. I tossed it to Brent. "Try this. It won't hold for long, but it will keep him out while we try to figure out something else."

Brent and Sammy tied the chain together with the rope and wrapped it as tightly as they could.

The werewolf continued to smash his body against the door. His howls were getting louder.

I glanced around at my friends. Fear strained their faces as they wildly tore through the boxes of junk, looking for something to use for protection. We were reacting out of panic. I needed to say something to calm everyone down. In a flash I knew everything would be all right.

"Hey, we've been in some pretty tight spots in Dr. Shivers' carnival, but the Lord got us out of each one, right? What are we so worried about? The werewolf could change back any minute or turn around and run off the tram."

Sara stared at me. The tension was getting to us all. I had to do something to get rid of this werewolf and save my friends. I climbed down off the stack of boxes and spotted a shovel. I picked it up and walked toward the door.

Sammy stepped between the door and me. "What are you doing?" he asked.

"I'm going to get us out of this. When I open the door and smash the werewolf with the shovel, you guys jump out the back door. Run as fast as you can, and I'll hold him off as long as I can."

My voice quivered with fear as I spoke.

One of us had to stop him, and it was going to be me. I pushed Sammy out of the way and took a few more steps toward the door. Suddenly the tram lurched forward, then backward. I didn't have to walk the last few steps to the door. The tram tossed me toward the door, and I hit it with a heavy thud.

The werewolf was just inches away.

The werewolf was pressed against the other side of the window. His fierce eyes glowered at me.

The tram had come to a complete stop. The werewolf backed up. I thought he was getting ready to run right through the door.

I bent down and picked up my shovel. He was not going to get through me.

When I stood up again, he was gone. I thought he might be hiding. I waited. The werewolf could attack again, and I wanted to be ready for him.

"Look!" Brent screamed with excitement. "The werewolf got off at this stop. We are safe."

"Where are we?" Sara asked.

Sammy looked at the nearest sign. "This is the stop for Monster Middle School. Why would he be out of school at this time of the day?"

"He went out for lunch. We were going to be his fast food. 'I'll take four kids, please, and hold the mustard,'" Sammy blurted out.

I started laughing. Then Sara picked it up, then Brent. We kept laughing until the tram began moving again. As we pulled away from the Monster Middle School, a voice came over the speaker above us.

"Last stop coming up, Dr. Shivers' Carnival of Terror. We hope you enjoyed your ride. Please ride the Transylvania Tram again soon."

"Finally, we're back at the carnival. I never thought that I'd be glad to be back at the Carnival of Terror," Sara said. We all agreed as we sat motionless, waiting to see the carnival up ahead. The tram came to a slow and easy stop. The door opened and we entered an enclosed area. Up ahead was a large Exit sign, but only the *E* was lit up. It was in that second that Sara and I turned to each other and said in unison, *"It's only a movie!"*

We stumbled into the sunlight and out onto the midway. There we saw the clown and several others walking toward us.

Something was different about the clown. He had taken off his makeup. I recognized him. I couldn't believe who it was.

It was Uncle Rex. Behind him were several men and women with clipboards and communication headsets. We ran up to him.

"Uncle Rex, you've got to have this place closed down. It's too frightening. Kids will be scared to death here. Dr. Shivers has monsters that tried to eat us and rides that tried to knock us off. He even has giants that play miniature golf."

The words tumbled out of my mouth.

Finally, it hit me—Uncle Rex was wearing the clown suit. I was puzzled.

"Uncle Rex, why are you dressed like a clown?"

Then I heard a gruesome laugh come from behind me. I spun around and saw Dr. Shivers. He looked different as well. Brent gasped.

Uncle Rex looked at me. "Great! You kids were great."

We must have given him the most puzzled looks he ever saw. He started to laugh. "Kids, I wanted you all to come to this carnival."

"Why? Did my dad do something to you when you were a kid that you needed to get revenge for?" I asked.

"No, this is the set for a made-for-TV movie. If it goes well, it will be a new series called, of course, *Dr. Shivers' Carnival of Terror.* I wanted to test the rides on kids who didn't know anything about them. We wanted four kids from the Midwest. So I called your dad and told him what I had planned. You four were fantastic."

Sara's face broke into a big smile. "Then everything we saw was made by illusions and special effects?"

"Exactly," Uncle Rex answered.

"Then I never ate any worms?" Brent said with relief.

"Nope, it was real cotton candy with a hologram inside it. Pretty neat, huh?" my uncle responded. "Now, I want you to meet Dr. Shivers. I'm sure you recognize him. This is Johnny Tate."

Brent looked at him with a smug smile. "I knew you looked familiar," he said, giving the famous teen television star an I-knew-it-all-along look.

"Then we were right about the clues spelling out *It's only a movie*," I said.

"Yep. I've been concerned by all the horror books middle school kids are reading. Even worse is that some of them believe that stuff. I want kids to have fun, but they need to separate what's of God and what's of the imagination," Uncle Rex explained.

"How did you get us to follow the correct order for the letters?" Brent wondered out loud.

Uncle Rex smiled and put his arm around Sammy. "Last night I filled Sammy in on the whole plan. He guided you to the clues.

"And we filmed everything you kids did. Mostly we wanted to see how you'd react. We'll use those scenes for the opening credits of the TV movie. And better yet, you'll all get paid for it," my uncle rattled on.

Sammy jumped in front of me. "Do you mean we'll be on TV? I'll be a star?"

"Kind of, Sammy. In fact, you gave us some of our best footage. After we take it back to the studio and make the edits and cuts, I'll bring it home for you all to see.

"Now, I need to get my crew together to close things down. Why don't you kids head back to the house and we'll have dinner together," Uncle Rex said.

"Will Johnny Tate be coming?" Sara asked.

"I wouldn't have it any other way," Uncle Rex responded.

All the danger, all the excitement, had only been gimmicks and tricks. I felt a little sheepish, but mostly I felt relieved. *Thank You, Lord*, I prayed. *I should've known You were in charge all along.*

We had started back to the gate when my uncle called, "Hey, Sammy, catch."

Through the air came the barking hot dog. Sammy caught it and we all laughed. He got his souvenir of Dr. Shivers' Carnival of Terror after all.

As we walked back to the house, Sammy nudged me and said, "There's nothing like this back in our little town."

ATTACK OF THE KILLER HOUSE

Anna and Jonny Greger are looking
forward to a quiet day at home. When
Jonny's science project—a robot—attacks
Anna, she thinks it's just Jonny playing a
joke. But she knows something is terribly
wrong when her hair dryer flies, their
video game shoots back at them, and the
lawn mower takes off on its own. But a
house can't attack people. Or can it?

I live in a strange house. Everybody says so. But some days are weirder than others. I suppose it has a lot to do with my parents. It might even have something to do with us kids. My brother Jonny and I are two years apart in age. He's ten and definitely the little brother type. Sometimes it's hard to believe we're from the same family because we're nothing alike. He takes after Dad, Dr. Randall Greger, the original computer genius. Dad's even designed entire homes that are run by computer.

Thanks to Dad, I'm the only kid in my middle school who takes notes electronically. I write on a screen that translates everything I scribble into typed letters. Dad set it up so the screen even sends the notes back to the computer in my room automatically. When I get home from school, all I have to do is print out my notes.

That wasn't enough for Dad. He also attached a voice module to the computer. It turns the typed words into spoken words. Along with my typed-out notes I get an MP3 sent to my e-mail inbox of the day's work so I can listen to my notes as I study them. Now if he could just figure out how to plant a computer chip in my brain so I could remember all this stuff. I get pretty good grades, but I'm much better at sports.

On the other hand, my brother Jonny spends hours building electronic gadgets in his bedroom. Our basement looks like a mad scientist's laboratory. It's filled with dials and switches that do all sorts of amazing things.

Jonny's school science project was a robot teacher, which he remote-controlled from the principal's office. He almost won first place. Then Ashley Cross unveiled her kitchen of the future. It cooked, baked, did dishes, and mopped the floor on its own. Even our dad voted for it. I guess that's partly because, as the Science Fair judges walked around the gym looking at all the entries, Jonny's robot teacher went berserk. The robot didn't do anything really bad. It just asked people a bunch of math problems. But if they answered incorrectly, the robot chased them with a ruler.

After a while the gym was filled with people being chased by the robot. A few people chased Jonny to get him to stop the thing. Jonny never did figure out what went wrong with his project, and, if I can help it, he never will.

My mom teaches at our Christian school. Actually, as the reading specialist, she spends a lot of her time teaching kids accelerated reading skills. Mom always brings home great books from her classes. She often reads from them as we eat dinner together.

That's enough about my family. I better get to the really weird day at our house. Mom had to go to school even though we kids didn't have to. It was a teachers' workday. I guess they have to work at least one day a year. (Just kidding.)

For all Mom's good qualities, she has one drawback: she is always late. That morning she scurried around upstairs getting dressed. Dad had been in his office tapping away at his computer keyboard. He came into the kitchen for coffee at the same time Mom flew in. I thought we were going to see a head-on collision, but Dad slammed on his brakes. He burst out laughing. Mom didn't.

"Anna," she said distractedly as she put on an earring.

"Yes, Mom. How can I help you make it on time?" I answered. I couldn't wait till Mom and Dad left. But not because I was going to do anything devious. I wanted to work on my painting of the two of them. I figured I could finish it after I cleaned the kitchen. I wish we had the kitchen Ashley Cross invented.

"Anna, I want you two to stay in today," she said.

Jonny started to groan over in the corner.

"The weather report said we're going to have severe thunder and lightning. I'd feel better if I knew you two were inside," she continued.

"We'll come in when it starts to rain." Jonny wanted to negotiate a better deal.

Dad started to laugh. "Look outside. It's already starting to rain," he said.

"Oh, my! I've got to make it to the car before it pours." Mom scooped up her briefcase filled with books. At the door, she turned to Jonny and me and said, "Please try to leave the house in one piece. Several teachers and librarians are coming over for pie and coffee tonight."

Dad headed out right behind her. He had to speak at a big technology convention downtown. Their cars hadn't even hit the end of the driveway before Jonny raced out of the kitchen, leaving me with all the dishes. There wasn't too much to do, so I didn't make a big deal out of it.

I was just scrubbing the last dish when something poked me from behind. I turned around and saw two bright red eyes staring at me. Then the thing spoke, "Earthling, come with me to my spaceship."

"Jonny, get your stupid robot out of here," I yelled. "Why do you keep trying to scare me like that?" I knew he was nearby and could hear every word I said. I heard his laugh. At only ten years old, he already had the laugh of a mad scientist. Sometimes I feel like I'm living in one of those old late-night horror movies. He peeked his blond head around the corner.

"I just wanted to show you the changes Dad and I made to the robot. Look what he can do now," he said with excitement.

Jonny pushed a few buttons on the remote, and the robot pushed me out of the way.

"I see, you've taught him to beat up on me," I said with a smirk.

"No, just wait. Watch this." His eyes were gleaming. I almost like him when he's this excited about a project. The robot moved over to the sink. He reached into the soapy water and pulled up the last lonely dish in one of his hooked claws. With the other one he took the dishcloth and thoroughly scrubbed the plate. "Ashley Cross, look out. Here I come," Jonny said.

"Jon, I think he has to do more than just wash dishes. Ashley's kitchen also cooked and baked and cleaned. All this metallic hunk of junk can do is wash dishes and chase people with rulers," I told him.

"Hey, that ruler thing wasn't my fault. Somebody else was controlling him with a more powerful remote," he snapped back. "Somebody who knew the codes and hacked into my computer."

"Are you accusing me, your loving sister, your own flesh and blood? How dare you?" I was laughing on the inside. After a few months he had finally figured out who sabotaged his little science project. I had owed him one, though.

Last year at a swim meet, he'd rigged the clock so it went faster when I swam. I always ended up with the worst time. But I knew I wasn't the slowest swimmer. I figured my little brother, sitting up in the stands, had something to do with my times.

A giggle escaped me, giving Jonny his "proof" that I had meddled with his science project. I decided to quickly change the subject.

"Have Rusty the Robot finish up the kitchen. I've got things to do in my room," I said as I left the kitchen. When I got to my bedroom, I pulled a canvas from under my bed and set it on the windowsill. I used the windowsill as my easel. I knew Dad would have made me one if I'd asked, but I didn't want him to know what I was doing. Their anniversary was coming soon. I wanted to make them something different this year.

I got a photo of Mom and Dad enlarged. Then I glued it to the canvas and painted over it, using the photo as a guide. That way the finished painting would look just like them. If I could get in a good day's work, I might finish it today. It had to be framed and ready by the anniversary dinner that Jonny and I planned to cook for them. It was going to be our way of saying thanks for being our parents.

I started to fill in the lines on Dad's face when I heard a tremendous bang downstairs. It wasn't that unusual for Jonny to have broken, dropped, or smashed something in the house. I went down to check on him. As I reached the middle of the stairway, I could see Jonny flat on his back on the floor.

I leaped over the railing. "Jonny, are you okay?"

He was moaning, "Kill me."

"Kill you? Jonny, as much as I'd like to sometimes, I'm not going to kill you. You're my little brother—"

He cut me off mid-sentence. "I didn't say I wanted you to kill me. I said that Mom is going to kill me."

"What did you do?" I asked him. I was worried that it was something that could get us both in trouble.

"I didn't do anything. The robot moved too quickly and knocked that glass dish off the counter," he told me. He grimaced.

"Don't worry. Mom won't kill you for that," I re-assured him with a big smile.

"She won't?" He was so happy to hear me say that. I almost hated to finish my statement.

"No, she won't kill you, but I'm pretty sure she'll ground you for close to eternity." I laughed. "Come on, get up and show me the damage."

The glass dish was one of Mom's favorites. She would not be happy that it was broken. I thought a little glue might be able to put the busted section back on.

"Pick up the pieces and put them on the counter. I'll see if I can fix it later. Right now, I want to finish my painting. And you ought to get that walking house wrecker back to your room. Take his batteries out before we both get into big trouble," I told him. Then I headed back toward the stairs.

The storm had been getting worse each minute. Lightning and thunder got closer than I liked. The sky was getting darker too. It almost looked like nighttime out there. Jonny was scared of the dark. I noticed he had most of the lights on downstairs.

Moments later, lightning hit our house. The lights went off in every room. It was as dark as night. The next lightning bolt snaked its way through the sky. It gave off an eerie glow as it cracked near the house. I swallowed hard. The storm scared me, but not nearly as much as the cold, sweaty hands that grabbed my arm.

"Anna, what's happening?" Jonny had grabbed me. The sudden darkness gave him a fright. As I turned to him, lightning flashed again. His eyes told me that he wanted me to do something about it.

"Don't worry, Jon," I reassured him. "Let's grab some candles and shed some light on our problem. Mom keeps them in the top drawer in the dining room. And the matches are in the kitchen."

I wished somebody could reassure me too. I've never liked the dark. When I was little, I was sure that some monster would leap out from behind a door or be standing in the shadows at the top of the stairs. The top-of-the-stairs monster was the worst. I dreamed about it almost every night until I got into first grade. After that, my dreams took a strange turn. I dreamed that I went to school in my pajamas. Both dreams were silly, but when I was a kid, they were real to me.

Jonny went to the kitchen while I looked for a flashlight. I knew the fuse box was in the basement.

I wasn't sure what to do once I got there, but I knew I should look inside it. Mom always did. I wish I had paid more attention to what she did next.

The lightning flashed again. The thunder sounded like it was in the living room. The walls actually vibrated. I could hear the glasses in the china closet shake. I hoped nothing would break. Jonny and I were probably in enough trouble over the glass dish he broke.

I got close to the basement door and reached out for the knob. Another crack of thunder boomed and bright lightning lit up our house again. Jonny raced around the corner.

"Anna, I can't find the candles. Why don't the lights come back on?" he yelled.

"Jon, I'm going down to the basement to check the fuses. Maybe one blew, and that's all I've got to fix. Wait up here and tell me when the lights go on," I said.

"Do you have to?"

"Do you have another idea?" I asked.

Jonny grabbed me. "Can I go with you? You know, just in case you need help or something."

"Sure." I smiled as I answered.

As we took our first steps down the pitch-black stairway, another bolt of lightning struck nearby. I felt things rattle and shake. The thunder was like a sonic boom. Suddenly the lights came on. But everything seemed brighter than bright. Then the lights went back to normal.

"See, Jonny, I told you everything would be okay. I don't think we'll have any more problems. Let's get back to what we were doing," I said. Then I ran up the stairs to my room. Jonny headed toward his room. I'm sure he was dreaming up some new electronic device to bug me with.

When we got upstairs, I could hear a strange buzzing noise coming from the bathroom. It sounded like bees were loose behind the shower curtain.

I slowly pushed open the door. I knew there shouldn't be bees in the house, but with my parents, you never knew what you might find. I looked to the left. No bees in sight. I looked to the right. Still no bees anywhere. The buzzing continued. I walked to the tub and pulled back the shower curtain.

Dad's electric razor was trimming a terry cloth towel hanging over the edge of the tub. It was shaving it clean. How could a razor shave a towel on its own?

I figured Dad had forgotten to turn it off, and its vibration made it jump around. All I needed to do was pick it up and turn it off. But when I reached for it, the razor stopped.

I guess I did my job. But when I pulled my hand away, it turned on again. I thought, *All right, somebody is playing games with me. Is this one of Jonny's practical jokes or one of Dad's?* Dad was a practical joker. Mom was just practical. I think I generally took more after Mom.

I reached for the razor again. It turned off again.

I pulled my hand away, and it turned on again. I was starting to get a little tired of the joke. I decided the joker could shut it off.

I turned to walk out of the bathroom. The buzzing suddenly got louder and closer. I looked down, and the electric razor was inches from my feet. It was shaving the rug.

I jumped up, and the thing cut a pathway through the rug. As I jumped, I grabbed the pole that held the shower curtain. I swung myself into the tub. *That radical razor can't get me inside the tub,* I thought. But I was wrong.

The razor reversed itself and headed for me. When it bumped against the tub, it got ahold of the bath mat hanging over its side. As it made its way up the mat, I jumped again. I swung my body out of the tub and landed on the clothes hamper. My next step would be to the floor and out the door.

I turned to see where the razor was. It wasn't in the tub. It wasn't on the floor. I couldn't see it, and worst of all, I couldn't hear it. It was time to make my escape.

I hopped off the clothes hamper. Just one jump and another second and I'd be out the door. As my feet hit the floor, the bathroom door swung shut. Then I heard the razor. It had been hiding behind the door.

Buzzzzzzzz! It was heading at me again.

The razor inched toward me while cutting a jagged pathway through the rug.

Thinking quickly, I grabbed the wastebasket next to me and dropped it over the electric razor. The razor pushed against the sides of the basket but was trapped. I could finally make my escape. I jumped over the basket, quickly yanked the door open, and tumbled through the doorway. Safe!

I grabbed the bathroom door and pulled it shut. Leaning against it, I said quietly to myself, "That was a close shave." Then I started to giggle.

When I turned my head, I saw something staring into my eyes.

"Jonny, where do you think you're going?" I asked, startled.

"I don't think I've got to report to you each and every time I go into the bathroom, do I?" he shot back at me.

"I don't think you want to go in there right now," I told him with caution in my voice.

"Don't try to boss me around. Mom and Dad didn't make you dictator of the house," he said.

I was ready to argue with him some more, but I decided that maybe going into the bathroom was exactly what he needed to do.

So I said to him, "Go ahead. Be my guest." I turned around and bounced back to my room whistling. I waited to hear him come screaming out of the bathroom. Nothing happened. Then the sound of his thumping feet came down the hallway.

"Anna, it's bad enough you used Dad's razor to trim the rugs and towels. You should at least put it away when you're done," Jonny told me. He tossed the razor onto my bed.

"Aaaahhhh! Why did you do that? Get that thing out of here," I yelled at him.

"It's just a harmless electric razor. Why are you so upset about it?" he asked.

It didn't turn on again. I looked at it and then at Jonny. "I was a little bossy a few minutes ago. I'm sorry," I told him. "I'm right in the middle of something important. If you put it back for me, then I'll do something for you later. Deal?"

"Anything I want?" he asked.

I had to think a minute. Whatever he would ask couldn't be as bad as having a razor chase me around. "Sure, anything," I answered.

"Great. How about moving out of the house so I can live in peace?" He laughed.

I felt relieved when he picked up the razor and left. I could finally get to my project. The thunder sounded farther away. The lightning had stopped. The storm was easing up.

I settled in to paint. After a while, I noticed the TV downstairs was on pretty loud. I walked into the hallway to yell down to Jonny.

"Jon, could you turn that down?"

Jonny came out of his room. "What? How come the TV's on so loud?"

"I thought you did it," I said to him.

"Not me. I've been in my room since I put the razor away," he said.

"Then who turned the TV on?" I wanted to know, but I wasn't sure that I wanted to walk downstairs by myself. "Why don't you go down and turn it off?"

"No way. You still owe me one from the razor."

"How about if you turn off the TV while I check Dad's office? We should have thought of it earlier. I hope his computers are all right. Who knows what the lightning could have ruined in there," I said.

"Fair enough," Jonny responded. Then he looked at me like he had a serious question to ask. "Anna, I was wondering. What time did you go to bed last night?"

"What does that have to do with anything?" I asked him as we headed down the stairs.

He looked at me and smiled. "When I was downstairs with my robot, I noticed something in the microwave."

"I made popcorn last night. Did I leave some kernels behind?"

"No, you didn't leave any *kernels*, but you did put the whole box away—in the microwave!" He shouted it at me partly for effect and partly to be heard over the TV. It was really loud.

"I was pretty tired," I yelled back. "I stayed up late to watch a spooky movie. It was about aliens that came to earth and took over the computers. They eventually took over the planet. Mom and Dad probably wouldn't have liked it. When it was over, I was kind of in a hurry to get upstairs."

"Before the aliens got you?" Jonny joked.

I made a face at Jonny and walked into Dad's office. It looked like a computer store with flat-screen monitors, hard drives, flash drives, and keyboards everywhere. There were five different computer stations on his oversized, u-shaped desk. I can't say that Dad was neat, but he would tell you that there was perfect order in this room. The rest of the family couldn't see it.

I glanced at each monitor. Two of the monitors showed messages that said SYSTEM ERROR. The lightning could have caused that. The monitor by the window was *blinking* SYSTEM TERROR. I thought that was odd. I knew enough about computers to know my father would have a real problem getting everything back in working condition. But Dad would probably love the challenge of making things run smoothly again.

One of the smaller monitors had a different message: "The angel said to her, 'Don't be afraid.'" I recognized the verse from the gospel of Luke.

Then I noticed something on the main monitor that Dad used most often. As I got closer, I could make out the face of a man. He was moving his mouth, but the volume was turned down. The guy's face was really weird. His eyes seemed too big for the rest of his face. The long crooked nose led my eyes to a dark pointed beard. He was pretty creepy. Why in the world would Dad have him on his computer? I would have to ask him that.

I wanted to find out what the man was saying. Using the computer mouse, I chose the volume control to make the sound louder.

At first his words sounded like a foreign language. I couldn't understand anything. The voice was high-pitched and spooky sounding. Then he seemed to turn his eyes to look right at me. He said, "I'm coming to visit."

Just then the doorbell rang.

"I'll get it," my brother yelled. I could hear him running toward the front door. His feet smacked the floor hard. Each step struck fear in me. The guy on the computer monitor had said he was coming to visit. The bizarre-looking face from the computer didn't look like someone I wanted in the house. *Lord,* I prayed, *give me the speed and strength to stop Jonny.*

"Jonny, stop! Don't open the door!" I yelled as loud as I could. He didn't answer. I screamed again as loud as I could, "Jonny, don't open the door!"

"What? Let me see who's at the door, then I'll be right there," Jon called back to me.

I knew I had to stop him. Could I get there in enough time? I started to run from the room, but I hadn't looked at the floor in front of me. Dad had left a stack of thick computer coding manuals in the middle of the room. Like I said, Dad thought he was orderly, but the rest of us didn't believe it.

My shin slammed into the books, sending them

sliding across the floor. I followed behind them, crashing to the carpet. "Ow!" I cried out. My cry stopped Jonny.

"What happened, sis? Are you all right?" he called to me.

"I'm okay, but don't open the—"

The doorbell rang again.

"Let me get the door, and then I'll be right back."

I scrambled to my feet. I had to stop him from opening the door. I bolted out of Dad's office. When I reached the hallway, I cut to my left quickly on the hardwood floor. I could see that Jonny was only a few feet from inviting evil into the house. I had to stop him.

"Jonny, no!"

He turned. That extra second was all I needed. I took three more steps and dived through the air. In another second, my body slammed into Jonny's, driving us both down to the floor.

"What did you do that for?" he cried out in shock.

"There was this creepy guy on Dad's computer. He said that he was coming to visit. Then the doorbell rang, and I think it's him. So don't open it," I was rattling on.

Jonny shook his head, a little dazed. He started to stand but lost his balance. "Huh? Wow. Have you ever thought of trying out for the football team?" He slowly got to his feet.

The doorbell rang again. He took a step toward the door. My arm snapped out and went for his ankle. My fingers snaked around it. I yanked on it and down he went again.

"Anna, what is your problem? Someone's waiting for us to answer the door. It could be that contest guy who gives away a million dollars. Please stop goofing off." He spit the words out.

"I'm not goofing off. I don't want you to open the door," I said.

The doorbell rang again. "I'm tired of you bossing me around," Jonny said angrily.

He reached for the knob. I didn't know what to do next. Then an idea struck me. If I couldn't stop Jonny from opening the door, then I needed to stop the door from opening. I leaped up and smashed my now-bruised body against the door. I lay in front of it, making sure Jonny couldn't open the wooden barrier against evil.

"What's wrong with you?" Jonny asked even more angrily.

"Don't open the door. We're not supposed to open the door when Mom and Dad are gone." I hoped he would listen to me this time. I slid up the door until I was standing. Jonny was looking at me as if I had a few screws loose in my head. I was ready to agree with him. I had to convince him that I hadn't gone nuts.

"What happened to you in Dad's office? Did your brain get zapped?" he asked as he pushed me away from the door. He grabbed the doorknob and twisted it.

A gust of wind caught the door and pushed it wide open. The strength of the wind almost knocked Jonny down. From around the corner of the house, a black ghostly form appeared. It raced toward the open door. I tried to slam the door, but I wasn't fast enough.

I pushed the form away from me and dived for the floor. The figure floated over my head and smacked against the wall. I could feel liquid dripping from it as it passed over. I was afraid to look.

Whatever it was had rattled the pictures hanging on the wall. Mom had her favorite family photos on display in the entryway. I hated that my friends could see what I looked like as a kid. When I was little, I had ears that made me look like a cab with open doors.

The black form attacked the pictures, knocking several to the floor with a loud crash. I didn't want to look, but I had to. What if its next move was to get me or my brother? I peeked with one eye. The thing had slid down the wall. It fell forward onto me. I started kicking and punching at it. I felt like it was suffocating me.

"Help me. It's attacking me!" I yelled to Jonny.

I heard him howl. *Oh, no!* I thought. *There must be*

another one attacking him. I had to get free so I could help him. I struggled harder, and Jonny howled louder. But it sounded different. He wasn't yelling. He wasn't in pain. He wasn't crying. He was laughing as loud as he could.

I stopped struggling for a moment and yelled, "What are you laughing at?"

"You. You look really funny, Anna. Let me help you," he said between his chuckles.

I felt him grab the thing on top of me and yank it off. Jonny was standing over me with a black plastic tarp. Dad had used it to cover the flowers in the front yard. It must have been picked up by the wind and blown in when Jonny opened the door. I sat up and looked at it. I could not believe how embarrassed I felt.

"Throw that back outside and then help me pick up the photo frames. The glass broke on a few of them. What a great day. You broke one of Mom's favorite dishes and a black tarp broke some of her favorite photos. I guess that should be enough damage for one day," I told him.

He tossed the tarp outside and turned around to give me a puzzled look. He asked, "Hey, Anna, why were you trying to stop me from opening the door? What were you yelling about?"

"When I was in Dad's office, I saw this face on the computer. It looked really scary. It said, 'I'm coming to visit.' Then I heard the doorbell ring. I was sure the man from the computer was at the door. I was sure that he was here to get us. I didn't think we were safe. Why didn't you listen to me?"

He looked at me strangely again. "Anna, if there wasn't anyone at the door, then why did the doorbell ring?"

"I don't know. Maybe rain got in the button. Or the wind could have blown a stick against it," I answered.

"Four times?" he said.

"I guess. I don't know."

"Maybe Dad can explain it when he gets home," Jonny said. He started back up the stairs to go to his room.

I headed off to the kitchen to see whether I could fix the broken glass dish. When I passed Dad's office, something caught my eye. There was another verse on the computer screen. I recognized the psalm: "The Lord is my light and the one who saves me. I fear no one."

What a great verse for a day like this, I thought. *But I wonder how it got on Dad's screen. It wasn't there a few minutes ago.*

After a moment, I shrugged my shoulders and went into the kitchen. The freezer door was wide open, and the ice maker was working overtime. It kept popping out ice cubes and sending them smashing against the wall. My foot slipped on a melting ice cube on the floor.

My feet went up in the air, and my bottom came down. I thudded against the tile floor. I knew that I would be sore later on from the fall. Before I could call Jonny to help, an ice cube whistled past my head. Another one smashed on the floor next to me. I rolled from side to side trying to keep out of the way of flying chunks of frozen water. They barely missed me.

The freezer had a pretty good aim. We could use it on our baseball team. I could see the newspaper headline: REFRIGERATOR PITCHES NO-HITTER. I was almost back on my feet when the ice maker quit shooting ice cubes at me. It started on the frozen foods.

A pepperoni pizza flew past me like a Frisbee. It smacked against a kitchen chair and knocked it over. Then a bag of frozen peas was lobbed my way. When it hit the tile floor, the bag came open, spilling frozen green peas everywhere.

I knew I needed to get over to the fridge and push the freezer door shut. I couldn't walk across the frozen peas without falling, but I realized I could slide. I sat down, put my feet against the wall, and pushed away from it. My body went sailing across the little green peas like they were marbles.

The only thing I didn't calculate was how hard to push with my legs. I flew toward the refrigerator pretty fast. Luckily my aim was perfect. I ran into the refrigerator section, reached my arm out to the left, and slammed the freezer side shut.

I was not having a good day. In fact, I was having a really strange day. What a chilling experience. I couldn't figure out how or why it happened. One more thing to ask Dad about. Or should I be talking to my evil-scientist brother, the practical joker from the weird zone?

While I sat there imagining ways to get even with Jonny for the flying peas and the robot scare, his bucket of bolts rolled into the kitchen again. I pulled myself to my feet and yelled to Jonny, "Stop it! This joke is getting old." He didn't answer. Where was he? And why was the robot reaching for me?

"Jonny! Jonny! Come get your robot," I screamed. "Jonny, I know you're out there. Stop your robot now." There was no response from Jonny. I began to doubt that he was in the hallway. But if he wasn't around the corner, why was the robot here? The robot's eyes were blinking. Its arms were moving closer.

"Jonny, stop your robot!" I yelled again.

Still no response. The robot whirred and moved an inch closer. It was getting too close, so I slid along the sink another foot away from it. The robot turned. Its tank track wheels were grinding along the kitchen floor right behind me. The eyes spun in its head. I thought they were looking right at me. I moved. The robot's eyes moved.

The kitchen TV turned on and words appeared. It was another verse from Psalms: "The Lord is my strength and shield. I trust him, and he helps me." I liked that verse, especially the part about Him helping me.

I realized the robot had inched closer while I was distracted by the verse.

"Jonny!" I yelled at the top of my lungs.

"What is it? I'm trying to build something up here," he said.

"Your robot is trying to kill me," I hollered with a little extra drama and exaggeration.

"He can't be. I've got the remote control up here," he said.

"Well, it's sending signals to him, and somebody is pushing the buttons. I won't mention his name, but his initials are Jonny Greger."

"Anna, it's impossible!" he called.

"Try telling him that. Every step I take, he takes with me. Please stop it!" I was starting to get angry.

"It's impossible. I took the batteries out of the remote control," he shouted down the stairs.

That really scared me. I began to wonder who, or what, was controlling the robot.

Jonny's feet slapped the stairs hard as he ran down them and into the hallway. He skidded to a stop at the doorway to the kitchen.

"Sis, I can't believe it," he gasped.

"Just believe it, little brother. And stop this thing from attacking me," I said as calmly as possible. I took two steps toward the refrigerator, and the robot moved closer again. Its little pinching metal fingers started opening and closing as its arms moved toward me.

"Jonny, you better do something now," I said, beginning to lose my temper.

"I'm going to run back upstairs and grab the remote. That ought to help," Jonny said. He disappeared from the doorway.

I hoped it would work. But if it wasn't controlling the robot to begin with, could it stop its attack?

The robot's eyes blinked quickly. I heard sounds coming from the voice box that Jonny had added. He seemed to be trying to say something. I didn't want to listen.

The sounds started to clear up. Words became more distinct. "I'm coming" was all I could make out at first.

Then the robot finally spit out: "I'm coming for a visit."

I yelled for Jonny again. He had been gone only a few minutes. In that time, I tried moving closer to the door, but the robot blocked me. It seemed to be reading my mind.

An idea struck me. What if I jumped up on the kitchen counter and crawled across to the door? I turned to make my move. The robot's arm extended and grabbed me by the belt loop on my jeans. I dropped to the floor.

I couldn't move. If I started to crawl away, the robot blocked my path. If I tried to stand, the arm knocked me back down again. All I could do was wait for Jonny to return with the remote.

"Anna, what are you doing on the floor? Get up," my brother called to me.

"That thing grabbed me and threw me down here. Turn on that remote control, and make it go away," I said sternly.

Jonny was standing behind the robot and pushing buttons on the remote. Nothing worked. Something else was guiding the monstrous bag of bolts.

The robot moved closer and closer to me.

"Anna, I can't stop him. What else can I do? Think of something." Jonny sounded panicked.

"I've got an idea," I said. I really didn't have one yet, but I was praying that God would give me one by the time I opened my mouth again.

"Tell me. I'll do anything you want," Jonny said urgently.

"Would it be possible for you to get a screwdriver and take this thing apart?" I wondered aloud.

"That would take hours. What else can you think of?" he responded.

"I'm out of ideas." I was ready to cry. I just wanted the thing to leave me alone. It had been only a few minutes since the robot appeared, but it seemed like an hour.

I looked up. The robot's eyes grew brighter and blinked at me. Its metal arms moved toward me. The mechanical monster was only inches away. This was it. I felt cold steel touch my skin.

"Help!" I screamed.

I looked at Jonny and pleaded, "Do something—"

The robot stopped. The eyes quit blinking, the wheels ceased whirring, and the reject from the science fair stood frozen with its hands poised around my arm. "Jonny, what did you do?"

He stuck his head around the robot's body and smiled. Then he brought his big toothy grin and skinny body around to help me up. "You know, Anna, he almost had you there. If it weren't for me, you would have been crushed like a walnut."

"What did you do, you little punk? And why didn't you do it earlier?" I was ready to choke him when he thrust his hand out so I could see what he held.

"Why didn't we think of that before?" I asked in surprise.

"That's exactly what I was wondering after I thought of it. It was so easy to reach inside and pull out his batteries. No juice. No kill. Although, with the way you were treating me, I began to wonder if I should stop him or not. Then I decided that I would get really lonely around here without someone to annoy. That's when I yanked out the batteries," he said.

"Thanks," I said with a smile. There were times when he wasn't so bad as a little brother. "What do you think caused that metal maniac to come after me?"

"I'm trying to figure that out. If the remote control wasn't controlling him, then something else was. I bet I know what was doing it. It's happened before. This remote works on the same frequency as a garage door opener. I'll bet somebody's garage door opener was hit by the lightning, and the signals are getting crossed," he explained. I think Jonny thought I would buy that idea. I didn't. I began to think there was more going on than we could see. My first instinct was to get out of the house, but Mom had told us to stay inside. Besides, I wanted to figure out what was going on. I've always loved a good mystery.

"I can't believe how scared I was. I'm beginning to wonder about us. If we tried to tell someone about all this, they'd think that we're a few sandwiches short of a picnic."

"A few bricks short of a load," Jonny added.

"Our elevators don't go all the way to the top," I finished. Mom had started doing that to us whenever we used a cliché. She would match it with another just like it. It's become one of our favorite games.

"I'm going to clean up the kitchen. There are peas and puddles everywhere. What are you going to do?" I asked him.

"Not much. I may watch TV awhile," he said. He turned and walked from the room.

The kitchen wasn't too bad. Cleaning up after yourself is part of being in a busy household. Mom comes home from school and has to prepare for the next day and grade papers. Dad always has a project to finish. I have after-school sports activities. Jon spends a lot of time studying and hanging out with his friends.

It took me close to a half hour to clean up all the peas and ice on the floor. I was glad the house didn't do anything else crazy. When I finished, I walked toward the front of the house.

Tap, tap.

What's that noise? I thought. Then I heard it again.

Tap, tap.

It seemed to be coming from somewhere near the front door. I decided to investigate.

As I passed Dad's office on the way to the door, I noticed a new message on his computer screen: "Say to people who are afraid and confused, 'Be strong. Don't be afraid.'" Was that another Bible verse? It seemed like the computer was trying to comfort me. I began to wonder what the computer knew about the strange things going on here.

I tiptoed over to the window by the door. I wanted to peek out, but I wasn't sure that I really wanted to know what was making the tapping sound. I knew I would never be able to relax unless I looked. I pulled the white lace curtain back a little and peered through the glass.

I started to giggle. I couldn't believe how on edge I was getting. It was only a broken branch that had blown onto the porch.

I opened the door to grab the limb and move it. The tapping would drive me crazy if I didn't push it back into the yard. As I pulled the door open, the branch fell into the house. I wondered how it got knocked off the tree. I supposed the lightning could have done it. I examined the end where it broke off. It didn't look as if it had broken off. It looked as if it had been cut off very recently.

I started to scratch my head, puzzled. Then a sound broke my thoughts. It was an electric chain saw.

A chain saw! Why was an electric chain saw flying through the air toward me?

I tossed the branch toward the chain saw and slammed the door.

Frightened, I waited for the sound of the saw edge cutting into our front door. Nothing happened. I carefully went to the window next to the door and peeked out. The chain saw was lying quietly in our front yard. I don't know what I did, but I'm glad I did it.

I jumped up the stairway two steps at a time. I turned the corner at the top and headed toward my room.

As I got to the door, I stopped. I could hear something inside the room. I put my ear on the wooden door. It sounded like a small motorbike was racing around my room. I figured it was Jonny with one of his motorized cars, trucks, or airplanes. He and Dad built those a lot. I threw open the door to catch that pain-in-the-neck little brother of mine making a mess out of my room. Something shot by my face.

I couldn't believe what I saw. My hair dryer flew

past me again. The other day it wouldn't work at all, and now it was zooming around like a jet engine. I wasn't sure I should step into the room. But then the dryer smashed into my mirror and shattered it. I thought that today would be the first day of that dryer's seven years of bad luck. I took three steps toward the plug.

The dryer raced within inches of my face. I dived for the ground, and it dived right behind me. I jumped up, thinking I could race it to the plug. It hovered in midair behind me. Then it began to turn slowly until it was aimed at my head.

The engine raced. The hotheaded dryer shot toward my reddish-blond hair. I wanted to yell for help, but what could I say? I couldn't scream that my dryer was flying like a jet plane around my room. I couldn't yell out, "There's a mad blow dryer in my room." Jonny would have just ignored that.

My hair dryer increased speed as it came at me. I needed to do something, but my feet felt like they were glued down. I screamed, "No, stay away!" But the plastic hot-wind machine just got closer and closer.

I ducked and dropped to the floor next to the bed. The dryer buzzed over me twice. It appeared to be searching for me. The handle turned left, right, up, and then down at me. I could have sworn that I saw it smile. It came right at me. I rolled under the bed and breathed a sigh of relief. I was sure the hopped-up hair dryer couldn't get to me under the bed.

I inched to the center of my mattress. I wasn't sure what to do next. If I crawled out, the hair dryer would buzz me again. If I yelled for Jonny, I'd have to live with him teasing me for the rest of our mortal lives. I'd rather chance it with the dryer.

I moved closer to the other side. I shouldn't have. The dastardly dryer detected my movement and turned toward me. The engine went to a higher pitch as if it was preparing for an attack. Then it bolted beneath the bed, directly at me.

I had never rolled as fast as I did then. I could hear the roaring engine getting closer and closer as I scrambled out from under the bed and hopped on top. The dryer wasn't fooled. It came from beneath the bed and made a quick turn upward. As soon as it came to eye level with me, the thing shifted directions once again. It was heading my way.

Suddenly the most wonderful idea came to me. If I went under the bed again and the dryer followed me, then it would wrap its cord tightly around the mattress and be unable to move. Then I could walk over and unplug my airborne attacker. The battle would be over, and I would have won.

I dropped to the floor again. I was right. The hair dryer followed me. I scooted under the bed. It was right behind me. My plan was working. I shot out the other side of the bed and up and over the top of the mattress. I turned to see the hair dryer struggling to free itself from its prison. I smiled. I'd outsmarted a hair dryer. I better not tell anyone. Outsmarting a hair dryer shouldn't have been as hard as it was. Then again, who would believe that I was attacked by one?

I had taken a few steps toward the plug on the wall. The dryer was making some unusual sounds. I turned to see what was happening. I couldn't believe what I saw. The motorized maniac was unwrapping itself. The chase was ready to start again. I made a mental note to shave my head and never use another hair dryer again.

I tried to think quickly. I knew I couldn't get to the plug before the dryer would get to me. A light went on in my head. I knew how to defeat the flying pest. It would take split-second timing, but I was sure my plan would work.

All I had to do was make it to the opposite corner of the room where my closet was. I remembered that the cord couldn't reach that far. A lot of times when I was drying my hair, I'd try to reach for my shoes or something, but the electrical cord was about a foot short. If I could reach that corner of the room, the dryer would snap its cord tight. The pressure would pull the plug from the wall.

My plan had to work. The dryer took off after me again. I dodged it and zigzagged through the furniture and piles of laundry. Maybe Mom was right; I should put my clothes away. No time for that right now. I had to save my life.

I glanced over my shoulder. The tiny engine roared closer to me. I had just enough time to reach the corner and dive to the floor. I slammed into the wall hard. The impact knocked the wind out of me in a big gush. I didn't even have to think about falling to the floor. I did it quite naturally after smashing up against the side of my room.

The cord snapped straight about a foot short of me. The force and speed of the hair dryer were too much for the plug, and it popped from the wall. The hair dryer bounced on the rug by my feet. *Thank You, Lord!* My slumping body leaned against the wall. I wasn't sure I could go through much more. The morning had been awfully strange. My house was attacking me.

I slid my tired and bruised body up the wall. I looked around the room at everything that had been knocked from the shelves, dresser, and walls. It would take me at least an hour to clean it all up. But I was exhausted. I needed a nap.

As I got to the bed, I turned on my electric blanket. My room's heat vent didn't work. If it had been a computer, Dad could have fixed it. Instead he bought me an electric blanket. I didn't mind because the blanket made the bed toasty warm and comfortable.

I didn't even wait to crawl under the blanket. I plopped down on top of it and closed my eyes. I must have been more tired than I thought. Within seconds I could feel myself falling asleep. For the first time since I had gotten up that morning, I felt comfortable and safe.

I yawned and rolled on my back. That's the last thing I remember before I drifted off to sleep.

Something tapped at my window. I rolled over and looked. I couldn't believe it was dark already. Why didn't my brother wake me up? Why didn't my parents wake me up when they got home? Could I have slept all day after sleeping all night?

I didn't see anything at the window. I tried to sit up, but I couldn't move. I struggled. All I did was work up a sweat. I could feel it dripping down my face and soaking the blanket around me.

The tapping came again. It was in my room. I twisted my head to see what caused it. A shape moved in the dark shadows of my bedroom.

"Who's there?"

No answer.

"Jonny, quit playing games," I warned.

Still no answer.

The shadowy figure moved closer. I could smell him. It was a horrible, stinky smell of rotten vegetables. The figure reached out toward me. Another figure stepped from the shadows next to my bed. He smelled like rotten eggs. The second thing started talking to the first one.

"We have a perfect specimen here."

"Of what species?"

"*Girlus Americanus.*"

"We must make a replacement so no one will know she is gone. Send the mother ship her information. They should be able to make an avatar and have it here before anyone discovers she's missing."

"Yes, Captain. What will happen to her?"

"After the experiments I think she would make a very good midnight snack."

"Stop! You can't eat me. You can't take me away,"

I yelled toward them and leaped from my bed. But I must have jumped too far. I didn't land on the soft rug of my bedroom. I was in the basement. It was dark and damp.

A giant spider chased me through the basement. It caught me with its long, hairy legs and started to weave its web around me. I could feel the web pressing in from all sides.

Suddenly I woke up. It was all a dream. But I was wrapped up in something, and it was holding me tightly. My mind screamed, *Help me, Lord. What is happening to me?*

The dream had seemed too real. I was afraid to open my eyes. A large black spider might be hovering over me with its mouth wide open. But I had to look. I had to know what was going on. I forced an eye open. Then a second one. I couldn't believe it.

The electric blanket was rolled around me like a cocoon. It squeezed me. It was all I could do to scream out to my brother, "Jonny, get in here. This is not funny. Get me out of here right now!"

Jonny didn't respond. I heard him playing a video game in his room. The sound was loud, and he was yelling. I yelled to him three more times. No answer. I had to figure a way out. But how in the world did an ordinary electric blanket wrap itself around me? Before I could figure that out, my electric blanket squeezed me again. I yelled for Jonny. I was beginning to think that this wasn't one of his pranks.

The blanket was getting hotter. The sweat dripped down my face. If I didn't get unrolled soon, I'd be cooked.

I had to unplug the blanket. That had stopped the hair dryer. I had to think of a way to unplug the cotton hot plate.

I started to rock my body back and forth. I moved only an inch or two. I didn't have a lot of confidence that rocking was going to work. I rocked again. Nothing. I rocked harder back and forth, and after ten rocks, I finally rolled over. But I didn't move very far. I stopped to gather my thoughts and prayed aloud, "Heavenly Father, I saw all those verses about not having fear because You are here, but right now I'm a little bit afraid. Help me to be strong and brave."

I realized I had to call for Jonny again. The noises were very loud in his room. I could hear him yelling at his video game. I had never known him to get into a game like that before. I was sure he wouldn't hear me, but I tried screaming one more time. I was right. Jonny didn't answer.

I was trying to come up with another plan when my brother ran into the room.

"Anna, you have to see this," he yelled. Then he stopped at the foot of my bed. "What are you doing? Why are you wrapped up in the blanket like that? Are you cold or something?"

"Listen, you little punk, I know you did this to me while I was asleep. I want you to let me out of this right now. Unwrap me or I'll run your video games through the dishwasher," I cried out to him.

"I didn't do anything. I was in my room playing with this really weird new game I discovered. You've got to see it," he said excitedly.

"I'd like to, but I seem to be all wrapped up at the moment. Maybe I'll stop by after I break free," I joked. I hoped my brother would understand that I was in a serious situation. I needed his help. "Listen, Jonny, I'm sorry. It probably wasn't you, but I can't figure out what is going on around here. A few minutes ago my hair dryer attacked me, and now my electric blanket is trying to do me in. Would you please help me?"

"How?" he asked.

The blanket squeezed tighter. I had to get out of it soon. I said to my brother, "When the hair dryer attacked me, all I had to do was unplug it. I hope that's all we have to do now."

Jonny looked puzzled. "Never mind, it's a long story," I said.

He shrugged and asked, "Where's the blanket plugged in?"

I sighed. "It's under the bed."

"You expect me to crawl under your bed and unplug the blanket? Do you know how dirty it is under there? Forget it!" he said.

"Jonny, I'm going to tie the tails of your remote-control mice together."

"Anna, I'm kidding you. I'll help you out if you'll

come with me and see what is going on in my room. Deal?" Jonny was driving a hard bargain.

"Deal. Now let me out, please," I begged.

Jonny reached under my bed and unplugged the blanket. It unwound and I was free.

"Okay, now you've got to see what's going on in my room," he said. He pulled me off my bed. I followed him down the hallway.

He chattered the whole way there. "I don't know what's causing it, but do you know that video game *Gunslinger*? It's really acting up. I'm supposed to be able to fire the electronic impulse gun at the gunslingers and score points—"

"So what's wrong?" I interrupted.

"Well, they keep firing back at me," he said.

"What do you mean?" I asked as we turned the corner into his room. The moment we stepped inside, something hit Jonny's piggy bank and it exploded, raining pennies, nickels, and dimes all over the place. I looked at the video screen. A gunslinger was aiming at us. I jumped on top of Jonny, and we went tumbling to the floor as another shot struck just above us on the shelf. One of Jonny's books hit the ground. The whole thing gave me goose bumps. *Lord*, I thought, *what is going on?*

I rolled to my left to avoid the next shot coming from the video screen. It bounced off the mirror above us and then smacked Jonny's hairbrush. The brush leaped in the air and fell on top of Jonny's head. I started to laugh.

"Finally that brush got close to your hair," I joked. So many crazy things were happening that I couldn't help laughing.

"Quit joking around, Anna," he cried out. "We're getting shot at by a cowboy in a video game, and you're laughing. Just try to figure out what we should do next."

"Let me see. We could unplug it like I had to do with the hair dryer and the electric blanket," I said as I tried to stifle my giggles.

"That's a great idea. Which one of us is going to crawl out there in the line of fire and unplug that thing?" He rolled over and looked at the game. "Hey! The cowboy is gone, but there's some message on the screen."

I poked my head out and looked. "It's gone," I said. "What did it say?"

"It was something about God defeating our enemies," he told me.

The message made me feel a little better about doing battle with the video game. I was sure we'd be safe.

Jonny interrupted my thoughts. "Anna, before I ran into your room, I was shooting it out with him. Watch this." He picked up one of the electronic pistols. He squeezed the trigger and fired a shot. It missed but struck the animated cactus to the left of the gunslinger. The computer-generated cowboy laughed a deep and scary electronic howl.

"Maybe you need some target practice. Let me try. How does this work?" I asked.

"Aim it and pull the trigger," he instructed. "If your electronic beam hits the circle on his shirt, then you win. If we can stop him, then I can unplug it."

Most sports come easily to me. I've always felt that video games were too easy. I took aim and shot. I missed.

Jonny reached over and grabbed the gun from my hand. "It isn't as easy as it looks. I've been practicing this game for weeks, but never under these circumstances. It might take me a few shots, but I'm sure I can hit the target. The moment I do, you have about five seconds to unplug it before the next gunslinger comes up on the screen. And, Anna, the next one is the toughest of them all."

Another blast from the gun hit a stuffed animal on a shelf. The fuzzy little bear went up in the air until it touched the ceiling. I watched it fall right into my lap. "Okay, Jonny, go for it. I'm ready."

He took another shot. It was closer but still missed. The gunslinger mocked, "Missed me. Now it's my turn, partner." Jonny rolled to avoid the next blast that banged into the floor beside him.

"He is going to tear this place apart. You've got to do something quickly," I pleaded. My sense of humor was almost gone.

Jonny rolled back to his original position, still holding the gun. By instinct he shot again.

"Aw! Ya got me, little buckaroo," the video gunslinger cried out.

"Go now, Anna!" Jonny yelled.

I bolted from my position on the floor. I was a foot away from the plug when I heard the next gunslinger pop into place on the screen. He turned and fired a blast that marked my new shoes.

I dived and slid along the waxed wooden floor until my outstretched hands reached the wall plug. Before I could give it a yank, the gunslinger got off two more shots at Jonny. The first ricocheted off the door behind him and struck something in the hallway. That something was breakable. I didn't want to know what it was.

The second came too close to Jonny. He screamed as I yanked the plug. The noises stopped. The voice stopped.

"I think we're safe, Anna," Jonny said with a long, loud sigh.

"I love it when a plan comes together," I said to him. My smile reached from one side of my face to the other. "We did it!"

We both breathed out a gasp of relief. "What's happening, Anna?" Jonny asked.

"I'm not sure, but our house has taken on a personality of its own. It's like some maniac is controlling it. Don't worry, though. We'll be safe," I told him. Then we became very quiet.

"What's that noise?" Jonny asked.

"Is it coming from outside?"

"I think it is," he answered.

Since I was right under the window, I pulled myself up to the sill and peeked out. I couldn't believe what I saw.

"Jonny, come quick. The lawn mower is cutting the grass and Mom's flowers," I said with surprise. "And no one is pushing it."

The two of us leaped through the doorway and hopped down the staircase to the front door. I hadn't even thought about what could be behind the door. My only thought was how disappointed Mom would be when she saw her flowers cut down. Mom spent every Saturday morning in her flower beds. They were her pride and joy.

Each Sunday she made a bouquet and took it to church. The flowers sat right in front of the podium. The pastor's wife often joked with Mom about how they brightened up an otherwise dull sermon. Then they both laughed. The flowers meant a lot to Mom.

As we ran past the living room, I noticed the TV was blinking a message. It said, "Wait for the Lord. He will make things right."

It was comforting to know Jonny and I would have help as we battled the lawn mower.

I pulled the front door open and heard the buzz

of Dad's electric lawn mower. He had been experimenting with making it run off a remote control.

Jonny ran by me and down the steps of the porch into the front yard. The mower was headed away from us toward the street. As Jonny took his first steps across the grass, the mower turned and raced toward him.

"Jonny, jump up on the steps. The lawn mower is after you," I yelled.

Jon turned and hopped back on the porch with me. He was just in time. The mower smacked into the bottom step as if it wanted to come up and get us.

"What now?" Jonny asked.

"As soon as it heads back the other way, I'll run into the garage and unplug it," I answered. I was sure it would work, considering we'd stopped the video game, electric blanket, and hair dryer that way.

The mower moved away from the front of the house toward the street. It deliberately ran over the flower bed again, cutting down the last of the daisies. That was my chance to make it to the garage. I had only a few seconds because the mower could move fast.

I jumped to the ground and was running as soon as my feet touched the grass. A high-powered motor made the machine faster than I expected. It turned and chased me toward the garage, but I got there just in time.

As I pulled the plug, I sighed in relief and thanked God for giving me quick feet.

"Wow, great job!" Jonny yelled to me from the porch. "You can really move!"

"Thanks," I said as I walked back to join him, and we went inside. "Hey, did you start the washing machine? Laundry was supposed to be my chore. Thanks."

"I didn't start it. I just heard it come on a minute ago. We better see what kind of wacko activity is going on in the laundry room," he told me. "By the way, you're older—you can go first."

The day was taking another weird turn. The washer was old. Mom was glad when it worked. I think Dad had done more repairs on it than Mom had done loads of wash in it.

I pushed open the door to the basement and turned on the light. Jonny was right behind me as we took each step carefully. Too many creepy things had already happened. I kept thinking about the verses that had popped up on screens all over the house. They made me feel better as we descended the stairs.

The washer was spinning and jumping. As it bounced across the floor, wet clothing flew out of the top. The moment my foot hit the basement floor, a wet T-shirt came right at me. I ducked. Jonny wasn't watching, and it hit him in the face.

He started screaming, "Anna, get this octopus off my face. Quick, before it sucks me into its mouth or covers me with black ink."

I reached up and grabbed the shirt. "Relax, little brother, it isn't an octopus."

"I don't care. Just get it off me," he said.

I pulled the shirt from his face. When I turned to put it somewhere safe, a balled-up wet sock came at me. There was no time to duck. It smacked me right in the nose.

"That was terrible," I cried out.

"Are you all right? Did it break your nose?" Jon asked me.

"My nose is all right, but the sock was one of yours. That was the worst-smelling thing I've ever encountered," I joked.

"Quit joking around. We need to stop this maniac machine from destroying the basement. I know just what to do," he told me with authority.

"Yes, sir, general sir," I responded.

"I'm serious. Turn it off." He pointed as he said it.

I laughed. "That's easy for you to say, but how in the world am I going to catch it? It's moving like a bucking bronco."

"Then saddle it and go for a ride, buckaroo." He smiled.

A few other pieces of clothing whistled by me as I approached the washing machine. I got close enough to jump on it. I could hear my little brother yelling, "Ride 'em, cowgirl!"

I turned the washer to the end of the cycle. It stopped. It was an easy victory against our house gone mad.

"Well, Jonny, I think we've conquered the evil basement laundry machine. Let's see if we can conquer the upper regions as well."

But as I spoke, another wet piece of clothing smacked the back of my head.

"Now what?" I asked.

I turned to see my brother's twelve-inch army soldiers walking toward me. I wished they didn't have all those movable parts.

"Jonny, how are those things moving?" I asked in a frightened voice.

"I got bored playing with them. Dad taught me how to motorize them and put in radio controls. They work pretty good, don't they?" he asked. I think he wanted me to praise his work. As I said, our basement is like a mad scientist's lab, and the lab was filled with twelve-inch Frankenstein monsters.

"What can they do to us?" I wanted to know.

He thought for a minute. I thought that was a minute too long. When he took time to answer a question, he usually came up with a long list. Which he started to do. "Well, the one on the far left holding the rocket launcher can shoot that at us."

I broke in. "And what will that do?"

"It only has a small explosive device in it," he said.

"How small is small? Or how large is small? Can it hurt me?"

"It has been known to put holes in plastic houses," he answered.

"What plastic houses?" I asked, then my mouth dropped open in shock. "You were shooting at my old dollhouses! You little monster, I ought to—" I never had time to finish my statement. Around the corner of the furnace came a small marching army of blond-haired fashion dolls. It was hard to recognize them. Each one carried a weapon, and all of them looked more like brides of Frankenstein than like my old doll collection.

"What did you do to them?" I screamed.

"You stopped playing with them years ago. I made them into an army of amazons," he said with a smile. He was hoping that I would think they were vastly improved.

"Jonny, we can talk about your ruining my doll collection later. Right now, we have to find a way to shut off each and every one of them. They are getting very close," I told him in a calm voice.

"I know, the one with the rocket launcher is starting to take aim. I'd duck if I were you," he advised me.

He told me just in time. A rocket went shooting by my head when I dropped down. The rocket hit the wall behind me and exploded. I looked back. There was a small hole in the wood paneling.

"What's controlling these toy-store soldiers, and how can we turn them off?" I quizzed.

"I have a whole remote control board for them. You should see it. Dad and I made it with switches and dials and everything." He sounded excited. I wasn't excited about it at all.

"Okay, punk. Go turn them off," I commanded him.

"I can't. The board's on the other side of my GIs. If I move, they'll get me. They target based on movement. The less we move, the better," he told me.

"Let me get this straight. These tiny androids are controlled by a radio signal sent out from a control board. This control board is on the other side of them. If you move, they will not only chase you, but they could put holes in you as well. So all we have to do is stand here until their batteries run out of juice. Right?" I asked.

"Yes, except for one thing."

"What one thing?"

"Their batteries are the ones Dad made and have an extremely long life. I think we'll be here a long time if we wait for them to run out," he said sadly.

I stood very still and looked at the army heading my way. Little plastic feet in little plastic boots and high heels clicked on the cement basement floor. I needed to get us out of there. There weren't a lot of choices.

Lord, I prayed, *You've gotten us out of a lot of weird stuff today. Please be with us now too.*

Then I turned back to Jonny with an idea. "Listen to me. On the count of ten, I am going to jump up and grab those pipes in the ceiling. I will swing over their heads and drop down beside them. You keep still. They'll follow me, and you can get to the control board," I barked out my orders. The countdown went quick.

"Now!" I yelled as I leaped up for the pipe. Five soldiers spun their rocket launchers, spears, and guns my way. They all let go at once, but I had already vacated the area. They blasted three holes into the wall, and two tiny spears entered the wood.

My plan worked. When I dropped down, I ran toward our old playroom. I was out of the range of the weapons. I heard bombs and missiles explode behind me. They were close but not close enough.

I ran as far into the room as possible. I smashed against the far wall and spun around. The army continued its approach. I had less than a minute before it would make me look like Swiss cheese. "Jonny, are you there yet? Turn off the control board," I yelled.

"Anna, it won't turn off."

"Unplug it. Do it quickly. I don't think I have much time left." I wondered if he could hear the panic in my voice. One soldier and one fashion doll came to the front. They held tiny hand grenades.

Both of them raised their arms and prepared to throw. I was hoping that Jonny could turn them off, but my hopes were running very thin. I needed to protect myself. Our old toy box was next to me. I scanned it and saw the perfect counterattack weapon.

I reached into the pile of toys and pulled out a Ping-Pong paddle. I raised it in time to smack away the first grenade. It went flying back into the midst of the plastic android crowd. The explosion knocked several of them on their backs.

I had to see how many of them I could knock down with each try. My blond doll from the distant past pulled her hand back and let go of the explosive.

It went to my other side. I had to use my backhand spin return. I was glad that I was the youth group Ping-Pong champion. The next grenade flew back at them. Another group of soldiers and fashion models from toyland terror collapsed.

"I did it," I yelled.

"I did it too," Jon screamed. He had unplugged the board. The remaining minimonsters stopped in their tracks. I tested to make sure they weren't trying to trick me. What was I thinking? They were toys; they couldn't think. I was starting to lose my mind.

Jonny met me at the stairs and asked, "What's going on?"

We seemed safe for the moment. I suddenly had a wild thought and decided to tease Jonny.

"Our comfortable little house is attacking us," I said, "and I think I know why."

"Tell me," he begged.

"It's ghosts from the cemetery that this house was built on," I told him. His eyes grew large.

"Ghosts? What do you mean, ghosts?" he asked. We sat down on the basement steps.

"You have to promise me that you will never tell Mom and Dad that I've told you this story. They didn't tell me until I was twelve. It was on the night of my birthday that I got filled in.

"Hundreds of years ago, before people moved here from Europe, this area belonged to a group of Native Americans called the Fulands. They hunted and fished all around here, and this block where we live was considered their holy ground.

"The medicine man did his work in this area, and all the great chiefs were buried here. In fact, they were buried right under our house. The builders discovered the burial site just before they started our house's foundation. The contractor didn't care. He told the men to build right on top of the graves.

"It took a long time to build the house. Each day the carpenters would come to work and find something they had just built ripped down. The contractor had one of the carpenters stay all night to catch the vandals.

"The next morning, the house was again in shambles. The construction crew called for the carpenter who had stayed all night. He didn't answer. They searched everywhere for him. The boss decided he must have quit and gone home. He told his workers to clean up the mess the vandals had made.

"They lifted boards and moved dirt for more than an hour. As the last board was pulled away, they saw it . . . Well, that's enough of that story," I teased Jonny.

"You have to finish the story. You can't stop there," he insisted.

"It gets pretty gruesome and scary from this point on. Are you sure that you want to hear it? I don't want you to blame me when you have nightmares," I said with a victorious smile.

"Please tell me the rest," he pleaded.

I had to finish it after he asked so politely: "Out of the dirt under that last board, a hammer head stuck out. The workers looked at it. One of them said that it looked like the missing man's hammer. They could see his initials engraved on it. They were sure it was his.

"The biggest guy in the bunch reached down and grabbed the hammer. He thought they should keep it for the missing man in case he came back.

"The hammer was stuck in the dirt. The guy with the big muscles couldn't pull it out. Three of them grabbed it and pulled hard. The hammer came flying loose, but something was attached to it.

"We better eat now," I told Jonny.

"No, I'm not hungry. Just finish the story. What happened? What was attached to the hammer?" he whined.

I was using my best storyteller's voice: "The men gasped. One of them screamed and started running. The missing man was no longer missing. He was attached to the hammer. It was firmly in his grip when something buried him. After they pulled the worker from the dirt, he gasped and coughed. His eyes popped open, and he looked around.

"His lips formed words. They couldn't hear them. One of the construction workers leaned over to catch the last words of the dying man. He inched closer and closer. He still couldn't hear. He got closer. He couldn't hear. Finally he placed his ear next to the lips of the dying man.

"A scream rang out. The dying man grabbed the other worker and yelled, 'I am Fuland!'

"The other workers tried to pull his hands away. It was as if he had superhuman strength. Nothing could stop him. He held on tight. His eyes bugged out, and he kept saying, 'I am Fuland.'

"The construction workers never returned. New

workers would come only during the day, and none of them would stay past dinnertime. Each family that lived in this house since that day has lost at least one person to that ghost of the Fuland tribe.

"The ghost takes over the body of one of the family members until the family is frightened away. When Dad bought the house, he knew the story. He knew the ghost never enters anyone until the person turns at least twelve. That's why he waited to tell me."

"So, how do we know when one of us is taken over?" Jonny asked.

I could sense the fear in his voice. "The person will begin twitching. Then the arms will go straight out like a zombie's. The eyes bug out next, and then the person starts saying, 'I am Fuland,'" I told him. "Let's go grab something to eat."

I stood up in front of him. My body began to twitch. He walked past me and then looked me in the eyes. They bugged from their sockets. Jonny moved backward, and my arms snapped out in front of me.

That was all he needed to see. Jonny flew up the steps and into the kitchen, then around the corner toward the staircase upstairs. I went around the other way. It was shorter. I reached the stairs before him. His shoes were skidding against the floor as he ran into me.

I reached out for him and he screamed.

"I am Fuland," I said in a weird monotone voice.

I said it louder the next time: "I am Fuland!"

Jonny screamed and tried to run. He couldn't move because I held him tight. I opened my mouth again, and a very eerie and creepy voice came out. "I am foolin'. I am just a foolin'. I am just a fooling you."

"Anna, why did you do that? That really creeped me out," Jonny said.

"I figured I owed you one for what you did to my dolls," I told him while I laughed.

"Things are scary enough around here without you adding to it," he told me angrily.

I knew I had to get things back to normal after all the excitement. "How about lunch? Riding a wild washing machine always makes me hungry," I told him.

"Being chased by ghosts, even if they turn out to be foolin', usually gives me an appetite too," Jonny added.

I smiled. "You know ghosts aren't real."

We went into the kitchen. "Hasn't this been an awfully strange day?" I asked.

"I keep wondering what kind of crazy thing will happen next. Every time I open a door I expect a face to pop up or an appliance to attack us," Jonny told me. He plopped into a kitchen chair.

"I'm going to make a turkey sandwich. Do you want one?" I asked him.

"Sure," he said.

I started to open the refrigerator door. Jonny let out a bloodcurdling scream. "Don't open the door!"

It was too late to stop. I had already yanked the refrigerator door open. I spun around and dropped to
the floor, throwing my hands over my head. His yell
had scared me. I didn't know what to expect. I lay
on the floor for a few seconds and waited. I slowly un-
covered my head and rolled over to look at the
fridge. It stood with its door wide open. Only a bottle
of olives stared back at me.

"Jonny, nothing happened," I whispered.

He didn't say a thing. Jonny started to giggle and
then broke into full-fledged howling laughter. It
wasn't long before I was doing the same thing. I
had to admit that after a while I just didn't know what
to expect from anything. The two of us just sat and
laughed until we heard a popping sound.

"What's that?" Jon asked.

"Oh, just popcorn popping in the microwave," I
said as if it were perfectly normal.

"Did you turn the microwave on?" he inquired.

"No, did you?"

"Nope, so what is making the corn pop?" he wanted to know.

"I probably turned it on when I opened the fridge," I answered. Then it hit me. Last night, I was so tired when I went to bed that I put the whole box of popcorn in the microwave. Hundreds of kernels were starting to pop. Their pressure against the door pushed it open. Popcorn flew out of the microwave at crazy angles.

Jonny shouted, "Take cover." He jumped up and dived toward the kitchen table. As his body dropped by it, he flipped the table over to protect us.

I looked at him in amazement. "Jonny, that was pretty cool. It was like something in a movie."

"Thanks, it was just a little something I've been working on in my spare time," he said as he laughed. I started laughing again as well.

"Hey, little brother, what do you think is going on here?" I asked.

"It's the attack of the killer house if you ask me."

Mom was going to go nuts when she saw the popcorn all over the kitchen floor. How were we going to explain this day to her? I could hear myself saying, "Mom, the house attacked us. It wasn't our fault." I was sure she wouldn't believe that story.

A dozen late-popping kernels smacked the shelf above us. A book fell from the shelf into my lap. It was Dad's Bible. It had several pages marked. I flipped to one of them and read the verse to Jonny: "'Don't worry, because I am with you.'"

"I guess God's eyes are on us," I said.

The sound of a tiny truck horn surprised me. Two oversized radio-controlled toy trucks sat in the doorway to the kitchen. Their headlights blinked in unison, and the trucks headed for us.

The trucks roared into the kitchen. Jonny and I jumped to our feet and scrambled around the tipped-over table. We wanted to get away from the trucks, but the popcorn made us slip. I fell to my knees, and the trucks began circling me. Jonny's feet were moving fast to get back to me, but his body wasn't going anywhere.

"Jonny, stop your trucks," I yelled at him. They were starting to scare me, and they moved nearer with each circle.

"With what? I don't have their remote, there isn't any plug to pull, and the batteries are underneath them. What can I do?" He was nearly in tears.

"Go get the gun from your video game. Maybe we can stop them with it," I called out.

"I don't know if I can get it fast enough," Jonny said.

"I think I can make it to the doorway before they get me. Let's go as fast as we can," I told him. I leaped over the circling trucks and somersaulted on an inch of popcorn that covered the kitchen floor. I didn't think about hurting myself. All I thought about was how to keep from being a hit-and-run victim in my own kitchen.

I pulled myself to my feet with the stairway railing. The trucks brushed my heels, and I ran faster. "Jonny, hurry up."

Jonny appeared at the top of the stairs with the video pistol in his hand. "Don't worry. Gunslinging Jonny is here," he called down. He raised the pistol and aimed. Nothing happened. The trucks were making a turn right behind me as I ran through the living room.

"Anna, it isn't working. What do I do now?" he called out to me.

I was running and panting. "Here's what we'll do next," I said when I ran by the staircase again. "Remember how we used to dive over the railing on the back porch into the sandbox?"

"Yes, but what does that have to do with saving you from my four-wheel-drive trucks?" he asked, puzzled.

"Just run to the back door and open it. On my next pass through the house, I'll lead them to the porch, and then I'll dive over the railing. They can't get beyond the railing. Slam the door behind them. Then I'll run around front, and you can let me in. The trucks can run around outside until their batteries wear out," I said. I made the next loop around the living room, dining room, and kitchen.

"I'm on my way," he said. He vaulted over the stair railing and into the hall. I could hear his feet crunching on the popcorn.

As I rounded the corner and saw the back door, Jonny was struggling to get the door open. He was yanking hard on it. Nothing happened. I took another run through the house. I was getting tired, and the trucks were gaining on me.

"What's wrong? I'm running out of energy, but your trucks aren't," I yelled to him.

"It won't open. I feel like I'm pulling against a vacuum. The door feels like it's glued shut," he called back. I had to ask him to repeat it a second time so I could hear all the words as I ran from room to room.

"Jonny, that's happened before. All I have to do is open the front door to change the air pressure in the house, and then the back one will open as well," I told him. I slid into the front hallway. The trucks had made the bend and were continuing their circle around the house. I knew that once the trucks returned, they would follow me again.

I yanked the front door. It came open. I was watching behind me for the trucks. I should have been looking at the open front door. That's where the real danger was.

I felt something cold slap against my neck. I wasn't ready for it. The sensation made me jump. I twisted around in midair to see what was behind me. Two legs were swinging freely in the doorway. The rest of the body was above the door. I screamed.

Jonny came running to see what was wrong. That was a mistake on his part. The trucks decided to play follow the leader with him as the leader. Jonny was in good shape. I knew he could outrun his trucks while I dealt with the monster in our doorway.

I turned around. My doorway monster was gone. I took a step onto the front porch. Could I have dreamed it? No, I wasn't asleep. I wished the spooky things were all a dream, but they weren't.

Puzzled, I turned to go in the house. I needed to help Jonny. I didn't get far. The legs I had seen were hanging from the light in the hallway. It wasn't just the legs. A body was attached.

I reached up and pulled the body down from the

light. I turned, opened the door, and drop-kicked the ghoul into the front yard. I swung the door shut and twisted the lock while I wondered how the neighbors' scarecrow got on our porch. The wind must be pretty strong. My brother's cry for help cut into my thoughts.

"Don't just stand there. Get these things off my heels," he panted as he raced by me.

I jumped in between him and the trucks. They stopped and turned toward him and then toward me. They couldn't seem to make up their minds about whether they wanted to leave their big-wheel tracks on Jonny or on me.

They made their choice. It was me.

"Jonny, these little motorized bloodhounds have picked up my scent. They're after me now. We've got to get them outside," I told him.

Jonny sprinted toward the back door. When I rounded the corner of the room, he was smiling and holding the door wide open. I ran past him with the two trucks right behind me. The railing was about six feet from the door. I jumped into the air and flew from the porch, over the rail, and fell into the sandbox on the other side. I always wondered why Mom and Dad kept it, but as I landed, I was glad they had.

I headed around the house to the front porch. The first part of the plan had worked great. Leaping up the front porch steps, I saw that the second part had a snag in it. The front door wasn't open.

"Jonny, open the door!" I yelled at the top of my voice.

"No!" he called back.

I was pounding on the front door. "Why won't you let me in?"

"Remember that guy you saw on Dad's computer? I just saw him on the TV, and he said that he was coming to visit. How do I know that you're not the weird guy from TV pretending to be my sister?" he called back.

"It's me. It's me," I said. I pounded harder on the door.

"Prove it. When's your birthday?" he asked.

"January 14," I answered.

"Lucky guess," he said.

"It wasn't a lucky guess. It's me, and if you don't open that door right now, I'm going to come in there and feed you your worm farm one worm at a time." I was really getting mad.

"Only Anna would say that. I'll open the door," he said. I could hear him twisting the knob. "Anna, it isn't opening. I can't get it open. I'll pull if you push," he called through the door.

Lord, please open the door. My house may not be the safest place, but I have a feeling that things could get worse out here.

As I started to push, I heard a tiny beep from a truck horn. I turned around. Behind me were two monster trucks and the robot.

"Jonny, hurry up and open this door. I've got company out here, and they aren't very friendly," I
screamed. I pounded my fist against the hard
wooden door. I could hear my brother inside trying
to pull the door open.

"Anna, I can't get it unlocked," he called back to me.

The miniature trucks revved their engines. I spun
around to see how close they were. The trucks and
robot were bouncing against the lower step. I was
glad they couldn't get up on the porch easily. My hap-
piness was short-lived, though.

The next time I glanced back, the robot had
moved around behind the trucks and was tipping
them upward. The tiny wheels were rolling up the
front porch steps. They weren't moving fast, but their
progress was steady and aimed right at me.

"Help!" I was screaming as loud as I could.

"What is out there with you?" my brother yelled.

"You don't want to know. Stand back and I'll try

to break the door down," I said. The trucks were blinking their lights and beeping their horns behind me. The robot was following them up the stairs. I didn't want to get too close to the edge of the steps. I backed up and took a fast, hard run at the door. It would hurt when I slammed my body into it, but I had to get inside.

I hurtled forward. I was inches from a whole lot of pain when I heard the yell.

"I got it!" Jonny screamed as he yanked the door wide open. Instead of crushing myself on the hard wood exterior, I went flying through the opening and past my little brother. His eyes were as big as silver dollars when he got a look at me moving toward him. I tried to stop before I hit the wall.

My feet slid along the hardwood floor. I was trying to stop, but I couldn't. The wall and I met. My aching arms and legs toppled to the floor. I still had the presence of mind to tell Jonny, "Close the door, or they'll get in."

"What will get in?" he asked. He spun his head to look through the doorway. The trucks and robot were three inches from the door. Jon pushed the door shut as fast as he could and locked it.

Jonny looked at me with fear in his eyes.

"How did the batteries get back in the robot?" I asked with a touch of anger in my voice. "I thought you took them out."

"I thought I fixed the remote, so I put the batteries back in to see if it worked. That was when you called me to help you. I'm sorry," he said apologetically.

I slowly stood to my feet and said, "That's okay. All we can do now is let them run around outside until the batteries die. Let's try to get some of this mess cleaned up before Mom and Dad get home."

I barely got out the words before the house sounded like a jet went flying through. Every TV, stereo, boom box, and radio turned on at the same time. They were blasting at full volume and shaking the walls, shelves, and pictures.

A small glass horse was vibrating across the top shelf of the bookcase in the living room. It balanced on the edge and then slipped off. It was part of Dad's collection. I had to save it.

I jumped to the footstool and pushed off it, diving along the floor with my hands outstretched. The horse dropped, and I caught it with the tips of my fingers. *Thank You, Lord.* I sat up smiling until I saw the collector's plate slide off the shelf. I was too far away to catch it. I just closed my eyes and waited for the crash.

I didn't hear it. I waited a little longer. I still didn't hear it. I was almost afraid to open my eyes. Jonny was holding the plate and smiling.

"I got that one," he hollered above the noise.

More things were bouncing off the shelves and

leaping to the floor. We both hopped from place to place catching everything we could. A few things broke, but we saved the valuable pieces.

One of Mom's favorite souvenirs from Mexico jumped from the top shelf. I saw it falling and made a dive to capture it. I was just in time. I sat up to show Jonny when three furry things leaped on my back.

I struck out every which way with my arms, knocking the beasts into the air. They flew across the room toward my brother. I could barely hear his screams. The TV, radios, and boom boxes were so loud that Jonny's cries sounded like laughter. I scrambled to my feet to help him. I spun around, facing him. I was ready to take on those monsters one more time to save my brother.

I took a look and realized I couldn't help him. He had crumpled into a corner of the room. The three furry goblins sat on his chest.

He lifted them up in the air and shook them at me. "Hey, Anna, I hope these monsters didn't hurt you," he joked loudly with me. They turned out to be teddy bears from Mom's collection.

I yelled above the noise, "Okay, so I panicked. Big deal. Help me turn these things off. I'll stay here and save anything that falls. You take the batteries out of or unplug anything that's making noise."

Jonny nodded his head and took off for the other

rooms in the house. I only had to catch a few more trinkets before he finished his job. Before Jonny could get back to turn off the TV in the living room, another verse slid across the screen: "Then you will know the truth."

Jonny came back into the living room, and we sat down in the center of the floor.

"What's going on, Anna?" he asked. "I've never seen anything like this before. Our house is going crazy. What's behind it all?"

"I'm really not sure. I've been thinking about it. I don't want to scare you, but I think the house might be haunted," I whispered to him.

"We're Christians. We don't believe in ghosts," he said with his mouth wide open. "And if there aren't any ghosts, then how could the house be haunted?" Jonny asked me quickly.

"You're right, but I don't have any other explanations. I just don't know what to think. I guess we'll have to trust God to show us what's going on."

I was worn out. I wanted to go back upstairs and lie down, but I needed to clean up the chaos.

We both knew that it would take the rest of the day to create order again. Neither of us wanted our parents to walk in and see this mess. I went to the closet to get the vacuum cleaner. I wished we had a normal one. This one had Dad's "computerized advancements."

I pulled it out of the closet and plugged it into the

nearest outlet. I flipped the switch to turn it on. That was a mistake on a day like we were having. The machine revved up and started sucking in the dirt around it. Then it started sucking in the rug beneath it. I tried to unplug the vacuum, but before I could reach it, the thing pulled from my hands and shot down the hallway faster than I could run.

It was gobbling up everything on the floor like a hungry dog. The machine sucked in the edge of a cloth on top of the coffee table in the living room. Jonny tried to reach it before it disappeared. He missed the cloth, but he was able to grab the book and wood statue before they were slurped up.

The cleaner edged toward Jonny. I knew if it latched onto him, I would have a terrible time explaining to my parents how my brother got inside the vacuum cleaner. I had to save him.

The vacuum touched his shoe. The laces started to untie and were being sucked inside. I heard a pop and one lace was gone. Then I heard another pop. The other lace was gone. It had Jonny's shoes and socks off by the time my finger hit the switch.

"Thanks, Anna. I thought I was going to be sucked into that thing. What a terrible place to live if you have an allergy to dust," he joked.

I agreed, but I wasn't really listening. We had to get the house cleaned up, and even the vacuum cleaner was working against us. "I'm going to try an old-fashioned broom this time, Jon. Would you turn on some lights in the living room so we can see better?"

That was another mistake. The moment he flipped on the switch, the wall lights came on but so did the vacuum. Jonny heard it and was out of the living room in a second. The cleaner hadn't gotten enough of him before, and it started after him.

"Help!" he yelled. "It's chasing me again."

I followed him out of the living room in time to see him racing toward the staircase. He was not nearly as fast as the cleaner. The vacuum left the floor and flew directly at him.

"Jonny, jump up in the air!" I yelled.

He jumped. The vacuum sailed into the wall and missed him. The impact seemed to stun the machine. Jonny sighed, relaxed, and sat on the steps.

But the vacuum started rolling up the wall and then turned toward Jon. He saw it and leaped over the railing. He hit the ground running.

"Unplug it, Anna," he called out.

He was right. That was exactly what I had to do. It was how we'd stopped the other crazy machines. Jonny ran for the kitchen, and I darted toward the plug. The vacuum smashed against the front door and pulled it open.

I heard the sound of little beeps. The trucks were still out there.

"Jonny, the trucks are trying to come in again," I yelled to him.

"You unplug the vacuum, and I'll close the door," he called back.

I bolted toward the plug in the other room. I yanked it out. The vacuum quit humming and sucking in our stuff. It was beaten, but we had to face the trucks again.

I watched as Jonny forced the door shut while a truck tried to squeeze in. It didn't make it. Jon tossed his body against the wood again. The truck was forced out, but an arm inserted itself in the door opening.

"It's the robot!" he said with terror in his voice.

At the same time, the TV flashed and the bizarre face appeared. "I'm coming to visit," he said.

"And that creepy face is back too," I answered Jonny. I ran to the door to help him.

"What in the world are you doing?" I questioned.

"I'm twisting his arm out of the socket. That's how they're attached," he told me as he dismembered his robot. He made one last twist, and the arm popped out in his hands. I pressed the door shut, and Jonny locked it. We slid down the door to the floor. Neither of us said anything. I could hear only the sound of our heavy breathing.

I drew in a long, deep breath. Jonny jumped up and said, "Did you hear that?"

"What? Hear what?" I asked.

"Be quiet and listen. Do you hear that music?"

I sat quietly. I strained to hear the music he was talking about. Then I heard it. The tune was very simple. I remembered it from many years ago. I looked at Jonny, and he looked back at me. "Where is it coming from?" I asked him.

"Upstairs," he answered.

We started up the stairway. I was getting scared. *Father, it's pretty crazy around here, but there has to be a reason why our house is attacking us. Show it to me and please continue to protect us,* I prayed silently. As we climbed upward, the music got a little louder. At the top of the stairs, I walked down the hallway, but I couldn't figure out where the tune was coming from.

Something grabbed me by the shoulder, and I screamed.

"It's only me, Anna," Jonny said, laughing.

My nerves were starting to get the best of me. "Don't do that!" I told him as I turned around.

"I figured out where the music is coming from," Jonny told me. He pulled on my arm, directing me down the hallway. "I followed the sound to the door up to the attic. I opened the door a little, and the music got louder. It has to be up there."

Our attic was used only for storing extra stuff. I never liked going up there because it was spooky. When we opened the door to the attic, the music drifted down the steps.

"Are you going up or not?" Jonny asked.

"Only if you come with me. I'm not doing this alone," I told him.

"I planned on it. There's nothing up there except for old toys and old furniture. I have to know what's making that music," he told me.

"Remember that curiosity killed the cat," I joked.

"I'm glad I'm not a cat then."

We went up the staircase into the dark attic. The only light worked with a pull chain at the top of the steps. A bit of daylight was coming through the one dirty window. It didn't cast much light, but it would be enough for me to find the pull chain and get some real light on things.

I got to the top and reached my hand up to grab the pull chain. As I did, a black shape flew through the air at me. I screamed and crashed into Jon. We fell backward down the stairs.

Jonny and I gathered up our crumpled bodies from the bottom of the stairs. We climbed to the top of the steps more slowly and cautiously than before. When I got to the top, I looked around me. The black shape swooped down at me again. I ducked, but it came very close to me.

"Jonny, it's still up here. What do you think it is?" I asked after I swallowed hard.

"I don't know. I couldn't see it," he answered.

All this weird stuff was making me edgy. I looked down at him and with a scoff said, "Why am I up here first? Where in the rule book does it say that the older sibling leads the way into the haunted attic to be attacked? Where does it say that? Show me!"

"Page thirty one, paragraph four," he snapped back, starting to laugh. I didn't. He laughed for a few seconds, and then the music began to play again. It sounded like a tiny band with cymbals, drums, and a small piano.

"Jonny, do you hear that? We've got to find out what's making the music," I said.

"Go ahead," he said. He seemed really scared. I took a deep breath and entered the room.

The black thing blew by me again. I got a good look at it.

"Jonny, it's just a crow. I can't believe we acted so scared," I told him.

"We? What do you mean *we*? I wasn't scared." He was laughing again. But it was a laugh of relief. Jonny gave me a push and I stumbled over an old chest. When I hit it, a big box of toys slipped off the top and onto the floor. Then I heard it again. It sounded like a small band playing in the toys scattered across the floor.

"Did you find our musical ghost yet?" Jon asked as he entered the attic.

"I sure did. It's your old monkey band toy," I told him. I picked it up from the rubble of playthings. The monkey began to beat his little drum with one hand, clap cymbals together with his feet, and play the piano with the other hand. I flipped off the switch.

"I'm surprised the batteries still work," Jonny said. "But then again, Dad made them." He reached over and pulled the toy from my hands. "How did it get turned on? The switch doesn't come on by itself."

"It looks like the crow was pulling some of the monkey's hair off for a nest. It must have hit the switch and turned on the monkey," I told him. I pushed the toys out of the way and headed toward the steps.

"What about the crow?" he asked.

"We'll tell Dad about it when he gets home. Right now, I think we better get back to cleaning up the house. I don't want Mom and Dad to walk into this mess. And I pray that nothing else happens to make things worse."

I finished talking as I reached the bottom of the attic steps. Jonny was right behind me until he reached the last step. Then it hit him, and he hit me.

Whatever it was kept going down the hall and then down the front staircase.

"What was that?" Jonny asked, frightened.

"I don't know. You fell on top of me and I couldn't see a thing. I'm beginning to think that you are behind all this. You do all those crazy experiments down in the basement. One of them must have gone nuts."

"It wasn't me. Honest," Jonny responded.

Jonny looked toward the stairs with worried eyes. "We have to figure out what it was so we can go finish cleaning down there."

We tiptoed slowly toward the bottom of the steps. Whatever had attacked us could do it again if we weren't watching. At the bottom of the steps I saw the tail of a dark form twitching along the floor. It disappeared around the corner.

"Did you see that?" Jonny whispered.

"I did. What was it?"

"I don't know," I gulped. My throat felt dry again, and my hands broke out in a cold sweat. "I guess we should go find out."

"First let me get something." Jonny ran back up the stairs and into his bedroom, then he bounded back down with his baseball bat. "I got it. If this thing can smack a home run, it can certainly smack any monster creeping on our dining room floor."

Jonny approached the doorway with great care. He was scared. He moved around the corner like a cop in a TV show.

"Can you see what it is yet?" he mouthed.

"No. But it's there somewhere. We'll have to chase it down," I whispered.

We worked our way past the table and chairs. I noticed a movement near Mom's good dishes. "Over there. By the china closet," I yelled to Jon.

He pounced. His bat came down hard and cracked. The tip went flying in the air toward my head.

I ducked just in time.

Jonny smacked the monster again with the stub of his bat.

"What is it?" I asked him.

"I don't know. But I think I got it," he said.

He walked over and flipped on the light switch. "You won't believe this, but it's just an old sleeping bag." He rustled the material around. "I see a lump inside."

"What is it?"

He picked up the sleeping bag and shook it out. I watched as pieces from an old remote-controlled toy dropped out. "I guess we've found our monster," Jonny said.

"I wish this day were over," I told him.

But Jonny wasn't listening to me. "What's that sound?"

Jonny and I headed out of the room and raced through the kitchen. When we turned the corner toward the family room, the noises got louder. I should have stopped at the doorway, but my speed carried me through the opening. I had barely enough time to duck.

My nose ground into the carpet as something shot past my head. Several more whistled by me. I heard Jonny scream as he stood above me.

"Jonny, what is it?" I asked. I twisted my head and saw a silver disc stuck in the wall behind him. His eyes had grown to twice their size as he stood staring at one of Dad's CDs. It had barely missed him.

I heard Dad's CD player click again. It was loading up another plastic circle to spit our way. Jon still stood there like a statue. The next one could put a permanent crease in his forehead. Jonny was usually a pain in my neck, but I didn't want him to have a pain in his neck. And, at this point, I really wished Dad had upgraded to an MP3 player.

I grabbed Jonny by the pant leg and yanked. He came tumbling down beside me as another CD whistled past us.

"Anna, at first I thought all this stuff was funny. Then I laughed because I was nervous. Now I'm getting scared. I think the house is out to get us. Are you sure it isn't haunted?" he asked with a quiver in his voice.

"No, it isn't haunted, but there is something really weird going on. This place is starting to get to me too," I answered.

Another CD flew by us and bounced off the wall. It rolled to a stop by our feet. I picked it up. "Jonny, it's one of Dad's country music discs. I never liked this one. Did you?"

"Nope," he answered. Another CD hit the couch we were hiding behind. It flipped end over end and dropped in Jonny's lap. He picked it up and looked at the title. "*Great Organ Classics.* Another fine choice."

We both started to laugh. "So how do we stop this most recent attack of the killer house?" I asked.

"We could turn it off with the remote control," he answered.

"Where is the remote?" I asked.

"Dad keeps it on the shelf . . ."

We finished the rest of the statement together: ". . . next to the CD player."

"Idea number one down the drain. Do you have any others?" I quizzed.

"We could unplug it," he suggested. "I can see the plug from here."

"Okay, I'll give it a try," I told him. "How many CDs does that player hold?"

"Dad designed it to hold close to a hundred," he answered.

"I count about twenty-five flying CDs so far. I

better get to it before the wall is filled with them," I told him.

I sat up with my back against the back of the couch. I was preparing myself for the leap over it. Once I got over the couch, I would dive for the plug. I prayed I wouldn't get nailed by a CD.

"Here goes nothing," I told Jonny. I folded my legs under me and prepared them for the spring upward.

Jonny reached out and stopped me. "Hey, sis, I'm sorry for all the rotten things I've done to you."

"Why are you saying that?" I asked.

"It's just in case you don't come back," he told me and then broke into a big grin. I was glad that he was getting his sense of humor back. It helped me.

"Thanks for the confidence builder. I better do this before I chicken out," I said. I hopped over the couch and dived for the outlet. As I pulled the plug on the CD player, I heard a click and felt something stick to the back of my neck. At first, I thought Jonny was playing games again. But he was still sitting behind the couch. It wasn't him.

My hands flew to my neck. Jonny jumped over the couch and crouched next to me, staring at my face. I grasped at the leech-like thing and yanked it away from me. Jon began laughing hysterically. When I saw what was trying to separate me from the world of the living, I got really mad. Then the thought hit me. "This is scotch tape. How did tape get on me?" Then it hit me. Dad was going to ground us until we had grandchildren of our own when he saw what had happened to his patent-pending electronic tape dispenser.

Jon was crawling toward the source of the tape.

"The dispenser is spitting out tape and won't stop. It's everywhere. Forget about getting grounded. Dad will have us put on some island far, far away," he said with a very gloomy voice.

"Quick, pull the plug," I told him. "It's plugged in over there." I pointed. Jonny's feet stuck to the sticky tape. I felt tape wrap itself around my legs and arms.

I could barely move. I struggled to stand, but the tape was stuck to everything and was multiplying by the second.

Weaving, twisting tape nearly covered both legs. It held my arms tightly against me. I tried to tell Jonny to hurry up, but the tape was bunching around my mouth. I needed help now!

The sticky stuff was encircling my head, but I could hear the TV come to life again. I rolled my eyes just in time to see that horrible face from Dad's computer staring at me. His robotlike mouth moved.

Through a tiny opening, I watched Jonny pull the plug. He scrambled toward me.

"Anna, hold on. I'll help you," he yelled to me.

He pulled at the tape, and he struggled to keep from getting stuck to me. His hand reached out, and he started pulling it from my face. I winced in pain. His next handful ripped the tape from my hands. Soon we were both tearing at it.

Once I was free, Jonny picked up a handful of the tape, wadded it into a ball, and giggled. "I always hoped we'd stick together, but this is not what I meant."

I laughed with him as I began to gather the tangled tape into large balls to throw away. Then I heard it.

I knew the sounds. One was coming from the front of the house. A similar sound rang out from the back.

"Jonny, do you hear that?" I asked.

"Yes," he said with real fear in his eyes. "I'm beginning to believe that story you told me."

"You check out the back, and I'll go to the front door. Let's go," I barked.

We leaped to our feet. My legs felt rubbery and weak when I tried to run. I rounded the corner. I saw it, but I didn't believe my eyes. I stopped and yelled to Jonny, "What's happening back there?"

"I don't know. The back door is—"

"—opening and closing by itself!" I finished his sentence.

Jonny shot out of the kitchen and down the hall. When he got to my side, he grabbed me. "What's going on? Anna, I didn't see anything. My robot couldn't even have done it. It's got to be a ghost."

"You said yourself there's no such thing as

ghosts," I assured him. But I wished I was that sure of it myself. "We've got to close the doors and lock them."

"I thought we locked them before," he answered.

"We probably forgot. Things have been so crazy around here that it's hard to remember what we did. We need to get to the doors and shut them," I repeated.

"I'm ready."

Our day in the killer house was making us braver than we had thought possible.

Jonny walked right up to the door, turned to look at me, and smiled. With his left hand he gripped the door and pushed it closed. He reached up to lock it.

But the door popped open again. This time it caught my brother and flung him upward. The handle caught his belt, so when the door slammed shut, his body followed.

"Anna, help me. I don't think it's just the wind," he said. The word *wind* was pushed out of him when the door swung open again.

I looked around. I was hoping that an answer would catch my eye. Nothing did at first. Then I saw an antique iron my mom used for a doorstop. It was very heavy. If I could jam it against the door when it closed again, it would give me time to lock the door.

Jonny looked like a Ping-Pong ball that was being spiked from one side of the table to another.

I shoved the iron in front of the slamming door. The door stopped. My plan had worked! I jumped up and flipped the lock closed.

"Are you all right?" I said breathlessly. I pulled his bruised body down from the door handle. He was barely able to stand at first.

"I'm okay, but I need to rest a minute," he said.

"I'm going to check the back door. Come help as soon as you can." I walked to the back of the house. That door was doing the same as the front. We had to close it before any outside visitors made their entrance.

"Got any ideas?" Jonny said as he walked up behind me.

"Look around for something heavy," I told him.

"Too late," Jonny croaked out. "They're here!"

28

Standing near our back door was Jonny's robot and his little automotive buddies, the trucks. The robot's eyes were blinking. The robot seemed to be excited, as though it had missed terrorizing us. When it moved toward the door, I prayed, "Please stop these toys, Lord. They're starting to make me believe in things that I know don't exist."

"What do we do, Anna?"

"Shut the door!" I yelled.

He dived toward the back door and tried to push it shut. But the remote-controlled terrors beat him to it.

"Anna, they got in!"

"Get out of there fast. The trucks are going to make us their new racetrack." What were we going to do now?

The horns of the trucks beeped and the eyes of the robot twinkled as they moved across the threshold into our kitchen. The popcorn that covered the floor didn't slow them down for a second. They were

heading our way with only one goal surging through
their circuits—destroy.

Jonny was already on the staircase when he turned
to look back at me. His eyes popped open even wider.
When I saw his eyes, I knew something was going on
behind me. I was afraid, but I had to look.

I stopped. I shouldn't have. The robot's mechanical arm reached toward me. When it grabbed me, I
turned and screamed. While the robot held me still,
the trucks circled my feet. I was totally trapped.

Jonny whispered, "Anna, I'm going to try something."

"Jonny, I'm scared. What are you going to do?"

"Trust me," he said, gulping.

With that he disappeared. I looked at the trucks
circling my feet. The robot moved an inch closer.
Its Erector-set hand opened and closed around my
arm. Each time it pinched me, I fought back a yelp
by biting my lip.

"Jonny," I yelled at the top of my lungs. No sound
came back. Had something gotten him? My mouth
went dry. I tried to yell again, but my mouth and
lips couldn't form words.

I waited.

Still no Jonny.

The situation seemed hopeless. Jonny must have
been caught. I was about to give up when I heard
Jonny's footsteps.

"Jonny, quick, please."

"I'm almost there. Hang on," he hollered from the staircase.

"Its grip is getting harder every second," I called out.

He bounded down the stairs. I looked at his hand. He was carrying a spray can!

"Anna, this is spray glue. It should clog up their wheels. If they can't move, they can't chase us. If they can't chase us, then we can get away from them."

"Good thinking! Spray them! Quick!"

Jonny bent forward and stretched out his arm. His finger depressed the button at the top of the can. As it started to spray, one of the trucks leaped over me and hit Jon's hand. The can went flying. It hit the floor and bounced along the carpet and under the table.

My heart sank deep into my stomach. What kind of a chance did I have left? I had to break free, but the robot gripped tighter. The pain made me react. Without thinking, I reached down and grabbed the truck and hit the robot over the head with it. They both stopped moving and whirring.

Jonny retrieved his glue and faced the other truck. The first blast nailed its wheels. The little mechanical killer slowed as the glue gummed around it. The trucks were stopped.

"Anna, we did it! We stopped them."

I put my arm around his shoulders and said, "I'm so relieved. I'll be glad to get back to normal."

"I think I've forgotten what normal is."

"You said it," I agreed.

I sucked in a breath and pushed the back door shut. I turned toward Jonny and gave him a big smile. I could see the relief on his face, and I was sure my face showed it too. Our smiles soon turned to laughter. It was over.

Then we heard that familiar sound. Fear grabbed my stomach. Surely I was hearing things. But Jonny's face told me that I wasn't.

The doorbell rang again.

2 9

Fear struck us both. The house was giving me the creeps. There were too many spooky things going on. Sure, our house was always a little strange, thanks to Dad's inventions, but not like this.

I turned to Jonny. His face looked drained of blood. "Who do you think it is?" I asked him.

"I just don't want to think about it. What if it's the guy from the computer monitor?" he answered.

I shot back, "We've got to find out who's out there."

"You're right. So go ahead and open the front door," he told me.

"This time, Jonny, we are going to have a plan. I want you to grab your remote controls. Make sure you have them all. One of them might stop whoever or whatever is at the door. If that doesn't work, then we need to do something that will slow it down while we get away," I said. I searched the family room for things to help us.

"Anna, I've got it. I know what we can use. My Legos!" He was very excited.

"How in the world will that slow something down?" I scoffed at him.

"Remember what happened two days ago? You were so mad I saw sparks flying from your eyes," he said.

"Oh yeah, I nearly killed myself when I was running down the hall to get ready for ball practice. I slipped and fell on some stray Legos of yours. Oh, I get it now. They will do the trick. Go get them," I told him.

My brother raced up the stairs to get his remotes and the Legos. We needed to use everything in our arsenal to outsmart the killer house. Unfortunately we didn't have that many weapons.

Jonny landed on the first floor after his run to his room. "I've got them all," he told me.

We crept slowly toward the front door on our hands and knees. The bell was ringing constantly. Whatever was waiting for us was getting impatient. Isn't that just like motorized menaces? You keep them waiting outside, and they get impatient. Toys sure were inconsiderate these days.

When we got to the door, I stood to one side, and my brother moved to the other. He was closest to the small window by the door. The doorbell rang again.

I glanced up at the TV in the living room. The

face from the monitor was staring at me. I turned to Jonny and said, "The man on the TV screen is back."

"I guess that means he can't be at the door," he said.

I watched the man's lips move and heard him say: "So our hope is in the Lord. He is our help, our shield to protect us."

That was the verse Dad had used in his Sunday school class last week. Hey, all the messages were from Dad's lesson! "Jonny," I said, "I just realized that all the verses we've seen on the screens were from Dad's Sunday school lesson. This whole thing must have something to do with Dad's computers."

"Everything in this house has something to do with Dad's computers. Remember, he's been writing a program that controls all the electronic gadgets in the house," Jonny said.

Then he reached up for the doorknob. I jumped across, preventing him from grabbing the knob. Then Jonny started to laugh. "I got you that time."

"This is no time to kid around. Something on the other side of that door wants inside. We might be in real danger," I said, a little angry.

"You're right. I'm sorry," he said.

"Forget it. Just look out the window to see who's there," I instructed.

Jonny peeked through the window and yelled, "It's him!"

Jonny jumped up to open the door. I thought that he must have been taken over by whatever was causing the house to attack us.

"It's over! He's here!" Jonny yelled as he turned the doorknob and swung the door open. I screamed and turned my eyes away. I didn't want to see the horror waiting on the threshold of our house.

"Anna? What's wrong?" a voice said as it entered the house.

I knew that voice. I jumped from the floor. My shoes slid as I scrambled along the wood floor. A hand reached out and grabbed me.

"Anna, what's going on here?"

It was Dad. He had come home, and I was so glad to see him. He had used the doorbell because he had forgotten his key.

"Dad, you won't believe what happened. The house attacked us. It was horrible," I told him.

"This house is what's horrible. The place looks

like a storm hit it. What were you two doing?" he said with surprise on his face.

Jonny was the first to say, "We were attacked by the killer house."

"It was like everything in the house went out of control," I added. Then I told him all about the robot, the toys, the lawn mower, the microwave, and the face on the computer and TV.

Dad rubbed his chin and said, "I think I know what happened. Let me ask you a few questions, okay?"

Dad always seemed to know how things happened. "Sure, Dad, ask away," I answered.

"Did our electrical power go off in the storm?"

Jonny replied, "Yes, right after you left, lightning knocked out our lights. A little later they came back on. They were very bright, and then they went back to normal."

"All right, next question. Did everything that attacked you run by electrical power or by battery-powered remote control?"

My mouth was wide open. My guess had been right. The verses were the key; today's craziness did have something to do with the computers. "Yes, Dad, that's exactly right," I answered. "Were your computers behind all this weird stuff?"

He smiled and then spoke once more. "Kids, I'm glad to say that your killer house experience was nothing supernatural. I've been working on a new computer program that will run every appliance in our house. I entered different commands for things like the TV, the CD player, and the microwave. Then I set a timer to turn everything on at different times. It was all an experiment. The power surge must have damaged the hard drive on one of the computers.

"It sounds to me like the computer mixed up all the different bits and bytes of information. It was like the computer was trying to make a cake from a recipe for spaghetti sauce and chocolate pudding. The thing was sending the wrong commands to the wrong appliances and toys. I'm sorry, kids. I'm afraid that this whole frightening day was caused by one of my experiments malfunctioning."

I was still puzzled. "Dad, but what about my hair dryer? It flew around my room after me. A simple command to turn it on wouldn't have done that. And that face on the TV and computer spoke to us."

"That's simple. You complained about the dryer not blowing out enough air. I added a new engine to it. It came from one of Jonny's old model jets," he told me. He started to walk through the house and examine the damage.

"But why did it chase me?" I asked.

He smiled. I think Dad was really enjoying himself as he explained. "You know that each body has its own electrical charge. The appliances were simply attracted to your electrical charge. As for the face on the TV, it was a screen saver I use to protect my computer screen. It must have been sent to the TV in the command mix-up. Some of his words were from a letter I was working on this morning before I left. And the verses came from my Sunday school lesson."

We heard the door creak open and shut. Then another voice spoke. "So, how was your quiet little day at home, kids?" That question was followed by a sudden, "Aaaahhhh!"

We spun around just in time to see Mom's hands fly to her mouth. Mom looked at me, and then she looked at Jonny and said, "Both of you are grounded until you have your first grandchild."

I knew she wasn't kidding. I got up and headed for the living room to clean up.

But as I passed the TV, I couldn't help but look to see if the face was still there.

BIRTHDAY CAKE
AND I SCREAM

It's MacKenzie's twelfth birthday. He'd like a paintball party, but his mom books the party at Creepy the Clown's Pizza Palace. Unlimited play on the video games makes it pretty cool, until Creepy shows up with some games of his own. Soon, all the kids want to win is a chance to get out!

In a few days I was going to be twelve years old. You'd think that a guy's twelfth birthday should be special. I expected mine to be, but the best places to hold a party weren't cooperating.

I wanted to take a huge group of friends to play paintball. But when my mom called Pete's Paintball, it already had a party booked for Friday night.

Mom and I called all over town after that, looking for a fun place to celebrate my birthday. But we kept hearing over and over, "Sorry, but we're booked that night."

I had completely run out of ideas and hated the thought of having the party at home. My folks and I live in a small house with a little yard. It's not big enough for the number of friends I wanted to include. I'd have to uninvite a bunch of kids. I thought that would be the worst thing in the world. That is, until Mom gave me the "good news."

When I came home from school, I tossed my

backpack on the floor by the door and headed to the kitchen. After a long day at school and soccer practice, I needed to refuel with chocolate chip cookies and a big glass of milk.

As I poured myself a tall glass of cow juice, Mom came home from work. She didn't even put her briefcase down before she said excitedly, "Kiddo (she always calls me Kiddo, but you can call me Mac—MacKenzie Richard Griffin's the name), I have good news for the birthday boy."

"You decided to get me a four-wheeler?" I asked jokingly.

"Even better—I found a place for your party."

My face lit up, and my feet felt like dancing. "Where?"

"Creepy the Clown's Pizza Palace," she announced with a beaming smile.

My face went gray, and my dancing feet became lead. "Mom, we can't go there!" I said.

She knit her brows in puzzlement and asked, "Why?"

"It's for little kids," I protested. "I'll be the laughingstock of the century."

"Don't worry. You and your friends will have the entire Pizza Palace to yourselves." Mom smiled. "And Creepy the Clown told me they have a room filled with the latest video games. They even have your favorite, *Guardians*."

"*Guardians*? They've got *Guardians*? Hardly anyone has that one."

Mom made a good argument. If we had the place to ourselves, we wouldn't be bothered by little kids. And the games didn't hurt. But I wasn't convinced. "What about the important stuff like—"

"Like good food?" Mom interrupted. "You'll have all the pizza you can eat. Speaking of which, if we want to eat tonight, I better get moving." Mom headed to her bedroom to change out of her work clothes.

I sat at the kitchen table thinking while I polished off my glass of milk and three cookies. Mom had convinced *me* that Creepy's place could be fun. Could I convince my friends?

I felt uneasy, so I decided I'd wait until lunchtime the next day to tell anyone. Lots of people had planned to come to my party on Friday night. Would they change their minds when I told them to meet me at a place for little kids?

My morning classes went fast. As much as I liked lunchtime, I hadn't looked forward to this one. I was lost in thought as I entered the cafeteria. I heard Frankie call out, "Hey, over here."

I snapped my head up and noticed that I had almost walked right past our table. I gave her and my best friend, Barry, an embarrassed smile.

"Earth to Mac, earth to Mac," Barry said, imitating

the scratchy sound of an old science-fiction movie. "Please land at your earliest convenience."

I absently started to sit down and nearly plopped down on Lisa. She had slipped into the seat as I was snapping out of my what-do-I-tell-my-friends trance. "Sorry, Lisa. I didn't see you come up behind me."

Lisa smiled at me as I settled into the chair next to hers. I was with my three closest friends, and I dreaded what I had to say.

Barry Lennon had seen most of my twelve years with me. He lived right behind me. We'd played together, gone to the same schools, and attended the same Sunday school class at church for as long as I could remember.

Frankie and Lisa were cousins. They went to our church too. Lisa spent a lot of time at Frankie's house, which was only a few blocks from mine. Barry and I often walked down to join them. And, since they shared the last name Grey, the girls and I had sat next to each other in all of our elementary school classes. Our teachers had this thing about seating us alphabetically.

Frankie and Lisa were the most fun girls I knew. The four of us played on the same ball teams and attended the same youth group. I guess a person could say that we were inseparable. I hated to tell them my news about Creepy's.

"I have some bad news," I began as a warning.

That immediately got everyone's attention. I was ready to drop the news about Creepy's.

Then Davis Wong scooted into the seat at the end of the table and asked, "So, when do I get my paint-ball gun, and who wants to get hit first?"

Davis was a recent addition to our group. He had just started at the school this year; his dad was our new vice principal. We had met him during the summer at a youth group meeting. He was a pretty cool kid, and he had a crazy sense of humor.

I didn't know what to do. Without stopping to think, I blurted out, "The paintball place is booked."

"What?" Frankie cried out.

"No paintball?" Davis's mouth drooped into a gigantic frown.

"Are you kidding?" Barry asked.

"No, I'm not kidding. I guess this was a popular weekend for parties. We tried everywhere. Everybody had something going on this Friday night," I reported sorrowfully.

"So, what are you going to do?" Frankie asked with genuine concern.

"We booked Creepy the Clown's Pizza Palace," I answered.

Frankie asked, "Isn't that the new place in that old building on Tremble Avenue?"

"That's the one," I responded.

Lisa gasped and got a terribly serious look on her

face. Then she sat up straight and said firmly, "No, not Creepy's. Anyplace but Creepy the Clown's Pizza Palace."

"I figured some people wouldn't want to go because it's a place for little kids," I said. I slumped lower and lower in my chair.

Lisa shot back, "No, that's not it at all. It has nothing to do with little kids. Creepy the Clown's Pizza Palace is haunted!"

"Come on, Lisa, you don't really believe those silly stories, do you?" Frankie asked.

"I have heard that some pretty strange things have gone on in that old building," her cousin said defensively.

"What happens? Do ghosts jump out of pizzas to scare kids?" Davis quipped.

"Don't joke, Davis. There's something very unusual about that building. Nothing stays in business there very long," Barry said.

"Remember last year? Uncle Andy's House of Sandwiches only lasted about four months. When we were little kids, it was the Chunks of Cheese Pizza Parlor. I can't remember all the names that came in between."

Davis looked puzzled. He asked, "Why do you think so many places go out of business there?"

"It's simple," Lisa stated sharply. "The building is haunted, and the ghosts scare away customers."

In all my planning for my birthday party, I hadn't stopped to consider that Creepy's was located in the old Tremble Avenue building.

When my friends and I were a lot younger, the older kids used to tell us stories about that place. They scared us with their talk about ghosts. But that was years ago. We were the older kids now.

Surely Lisa and Barry didn't still believe those crazy stories. Besides, we'd given our lives to Christ. Believing in Jesus and ghosts at the same time just didn't fit.

"Do you think the ghosts are still there? Do you think they'll make a special appearance at Mac's party?" Barry asked us.

The bell rang, interrupting our conversation. We scattered to head to our next classes. As I walked down the hallway, I thought about the ghost stories the older kids used to tell us. There were nights when I had to keep a light on in my room because I was so scared. I felt a shiver run up my spine.

Get a grip on reality, Mac, I told myself. *You've given your life to the Lord, and you're too old to be spooked by silly ghost stories.*

The rest of the school day seemed pretty routine. Even soccer practice just sort of slipped by. We covered the same drills over and over. I guess the coach was looking for perfection, but today my heart just wasn't in the game. I was glad to get out of there.

After practice, I hurried to meet Frankie and Lisa at the town library, just across the street from our school. We had some research to do for a history report. I had chosen them as study partners because they were the two smartest students in the class.

When I got to the library, they had already started on the report.

"Sorry. Practice went long," I said after I greeted them. "How's the report coming?"

"Not too bad. We've found a lot of information on the Civil War. Our biggest problem is narrowing things down to a single topic," Lisa said.

"Maybe I can help," I offered.

"We were hoping you might contribute something to this team," Frankie said with a grin. "You could start by digging through these books."

Before I sat down, I said, "I saw another book last week that had some unusual Civil War stories in it. It's up on the third floor. It'll only take me a second to grab it."

I remembered that the book had lots of personal stories in it. Some quotes from people who had fought in the war could make our report outstanding.

Most people avoided the third floor with its stacks of musty-smelling books. But I liked to prowl and see what new worlds I could discover on the shelves upstairs. I remembered the book was somewhere in the back left corner of the building.

The third floor seemed unusually dim today. After all our talk at lunch about ghosts, the darkness spooked me a little. I walked very slowly between the shelves, listening carefully for sounds that didn't belong in a library.

Finding the book wasn't going to be as easy as I thought. It wasn't where I remembered. I kneeled, trying to focus on the book spines in the dim light.

Suddenly, a large shadow cut off my light. I immediately felt alarmed. What made it? I looked up, but the shadow, and whatever made it, was gone.

I told myself I was being silly. It was probably just someone looking for a book like I was. I went back to my search.

I spotted the book and reached for it with relief.

Then something blocked the light again. This time, when I looked up, I saw a dark form. It did not look like a person. It looked like it had wings.

Gripping my book, I stood up and backed against the wall. The thing moved between the rows of bookshelves—toward me. Its shadow shivered as it approached. Had it seen me?

I scanned the shelves. I wondered if I could climb them and get away. If I tossed books at the approaching menace, would it run?

The form took two more steps and stopped. I placed my foot on one of the shelves to start climbing. But the shelf bowed with my weight. It would never support me.

So I grabbed the heaviest books I could find and waited. If the ghoul came any closer, I was going to clobber it. I heard it taking slow, deep breaths. I wondered if it could hear that my heart had begun to beat like a wild conga drum.

The shadowy figure lunged toward me.

I tensed and aimed one of the heavy books at the shape. Before I could throw it, black cloth fluttered down toward me. In a panic, I fought my way free. In the next second, I realized what had happened.

"That was just a little birthday scare for you," Frankie said through her snorts of laughter.

The girls had threaded long rulers through the arms of Lisa's black raincoat. That's why it looked like it had wings. They had used the spooky shape to scare me.

"Hey, that wasn't cool at all. A guy can get really tense backed into a dark corner like that. If I had hit you with one of these big books, I could have knocked you out," I chastised them both.

Lisa reached out and took one of the books from my hands. She looked at the cover, and her eyes grew wide. "Very appropriate, Mac. Did you choose this book on purpose?"

"No, I just grabbed the fat ones. What is it?" I asked.

Frankie took the book from Lisa. She turned the spine my way. I read the title: *Middletown's Ghosts and Ghouls: And Their Favorite Haunts.*

Frankie handed it back to me. "Are you sure you didn't purposely choose that one?"

"No. I just grabbed it because it was thick. I couldn't even see the spines of the books. Remember, you cut off all my light," I replied.

"Then this whole thing is scaring me. Is there anything in there about the building on Tremble Avenue?" Lisa asked.

I opened the book to the contents page. I scanned the chapter titles and stopped when I reached chapter thirteen: "The Haunting on Tremble Avenue." I couldn't believe what I had just read. Maybe if I closed my eyes, the words would change. I squeezed them tight and opened them again.

I felt my mouth go dry. I managed to mumble, "You're not going to believe this." Lisa looked at me curiously as I handed her the book.

"Look at chapter thirteen." My voice was barely a squeak.

Lisa gasped.

"What?" Frankie asked, concern registering in her voice.

Lisa didn't answer. She flipped through the pages of the book. When she stopped, she began to read.

"The legend surrounding the building at 1313

Tremble Avenue can be traced back to the turn of the century. At that time Bertrand Bailey Cooley died mysteriously in the room he rented in the building's basement."

Lisa glanced up at me, then turned her eyes back to the book. She licked her lips and continued reading.

"Rumor has it that Cooley had stashed a fortune somewhere inside the building. The means by which Cooley gained such a fortune are uncertain, considering his employment."

Frankie and I stared at Lisa as she turned the page.

"Cooley worked in the building's first-floor restaurant during the winter season. The rest of the year he was employed as a clown in a traveling carnival."

Lisa abruptly stopped reading and looked wide-eyed at Frankie and me. "A clown!" Her voice sounded higher than normal, though she kept it quiet because we were in the library. "And now a clown is running the restaurant! Don't you think that's more than a coincidence?"

"You can't be serious," Frankie said. "The guy you're reading about died almost a hundred years ago. No. It's just a coincidence, Lisa. Keep reading."

I kept my mouth shut. I knew Frankie was right. A clown who had died almost a hundred years ago couldn't be linked to a clown who was alive and running a business today. But still, the thought was unsettling.

"Six months after Cooley's death, another man, Oscar R. Newcombe, also died mysteriously in the Tremble Avenue building," Lisa continued. "Newcombe, the manager of the carnival for which Cooley had worked, was allegedly in search of Cooley's hidden fortune. Newcombe claimed Cooley had stolen the money from the carnival.

"No facts were ever substantiated in the incidents, and no fortune has ever been found. Yet legend has it that the ghosts of Cooley and Newcombe roam the building, frightening anyone who threatens to find the hidden fortune."

I gulped. The fears I'd had as a little kid listening to the ghost stories about the Tremble Avenue building came rushing back. Fortunately, Frankie still had the voice of reason.

"Eerie legend," she said. "But that's all it is. A legend. There's no such thing as ghosts."

"Don't be so sure," Lisa answered. "The next section of the chapter is called 'Reports of Apparitions and Unexplainable Phenomena.'"

"Hey, we better get to work on our report," I said. I didn't want to hear any more about ghosts, but I didn't want to tell Frankie and Lisa that I was getting spooked.

"Why don't you take this home with you?" Lisa said, handing me the book. "You can read the rest of the chapter later."

I carried the haunting book and the one on the Civil War back to the main floor. We managed to get some work done, though I had trouble staying focused. I wanted to get home. The sun was already going down, and in my current state of mind, I didn't want to walk home in the dark.

The girls were heading to Frankie's, a few blocks from my home. We walked the several blocks from the library together talking about school, ghosts, the youth group, ghosts, other friends, and ghosts.

I was still concerned that some of my friends wouldn't come to my party. After all, Creepy's was for little kids. I wanted to make sure Frankie and Lisa would be there.

"Are you two still coming to my party Friday night?" I looked down at the sidewalk. "I mean, even though we can't have it at Pete's Paintball?"

"Of course we'll be there," Frankie said. "You're our friend, Mac."

I looked up at Frankie. She was smiling.

"It will be a private party," I said in an attempt to play up the positive side. "Mom rented the entire place for the night."

"Aren't you two scared of that building after what we read in that book?" Lisa asked.

"I don't see how a pizza place for little kids could be haunted. Isn't there some kind of law against that?" Frankie questioned.

I joked, "It's in the *Ghosts and Ghouls Rule Book.*"

We had come to Frankie's house. I watched until the girls were safely inside. Then I continued toward home.

We live on a very quiet dead-end street. Mom and Dad like that, but sometimes it gets a little eerie because of the giant trees that line both sides of the road. They block the streetlights and cast long shadows. Four of those trees are in our front yard. They make our front porch pretty dark.

I walked past the trees. I thought I saw something move around the side of the house. If we had a dog or a cat, I might have thought it was our pet. But all I have is a goldfish, and it doesn't usually go out at night for walks.

I kept walking toward the house. I was a little unnerved, but I figured my eyes were playing tricks on me.

When I was halfway to the door, I heard a crash behind the house. It could have been something simple and logical. Dad could have been dropping the trash into the garbage can.

I tried to convince myself, but I felt a shiver of fear. I started singing a worship song to bolster my courage.

I reached the porch on shaky legs. As I breathed a sigh of relief, something touched me from behind.

I felt long tentacles brushing against my head and neck. I also felt the panic rise up from my stomach and form a lump in my throat.

I twisted to my right and lunged, leaping toward the front door. But I misjudged the distance and hit the door with a loud crash. I caught my balance just in time to keep from landing in a crumpled heap.

As I steadied myself, I looked over my shoulder to see what kind of creature had attacked me. And I came face to face with the branch of a large tree. It was swaying peacefully in the gentle breeze.

I had been "attacked" by a tree! I guess it was after my carbon dioxide.

I leaned against the door and laughed at my carbon dioxide joke. Suddenly the door swung open. I tumbled through the opening.

"Your mom and I wondered when you'd get home," Dad said after he recovered from jumping out of my way.

I stared up from the foyer floor and greeted him. "Hi, Dad. Just thought I'd drop in."

He chuckled and said, "Mom thought she heard some sort of animal at the front door. I came to check it out—and it looks like there *was* some sort of animal at the front door."

Dad reached down and pulled me to my feet. I snatched up my backpack, which had dropped from my shoulder, and followed him into the living room. I dropped my pack into a chair near the stairs as Dad said, "Tell me about soccer practice. Did you work on passing skills?"

"Practice went okay," I answered. "Coach had us doing the same drills over and over today. He pretty much wore us out."

Dad always asked about my activities. I felt pretty lucky to have a dad who cared so much about my life.

Turning toward the kitchen, he called through the house to Mom, "Katherine, you'll never believe what I found on our front porch."

"Let me guess. Is his name MacKenzie?" she called back. When we got to the kitchen, she had popped my dinner in the microwave and poured a glass of milk for me.

"I called Creepy the Clown's Pizza Palace today," she said. "Everything is set for Friday night from 8:00 to 10:00 P.M. I also called Coach Reese and Pastor Daniels. They agreed to help get the word out. Between the three of us, everyone should know where to meet on Friday."

"Thanks, Mom," I said. Mom and Dad had already eaten, so I sat quietly thinking about ghosts while I ate. When I finished, I put my plate in the dishwasher and headed toward my room.

I wanted to get to bed early. Tomorrow I had a meeting in the school library before classes. Several of us wanted to start a new book club. We all like to read scary stories, so we decided to meet and talk about our favorites. We even planned to loan some of our own books to each other.

I got to the bottom of the stairs and picked my backpack up off the chair where I'd left it. The light in the upstairs hallway was off, and the stairs reached up into darkness. My thoughts instantly returned to ghosts, and I actually hesitated on the bottom step.

I'm going to be twelve. I shouldn't be afraid of the dark up there. Right, Lord? I thought. But what I thought and what I felt were two very different things.

I realized my fear was silly and started to climb the steps. My mouth felt dry, and I could barely swallow. My heart beat as if I had just run a mile. I don't like the dark to begin with, and tonight my mind was running wild with pictures of ghosts in pizza parlors.

At the top of the stairs, I gripped the banister.

Of course, nothing reached out of the dark hallway and grabbed me. Nothing ever did.

I stretched my hand over to turn on the lamp—just like I did every night. Then I hustled down the hall to my room and pushed the door open.

As I entered, I glanced up at the window in my room. I stifled a cry, jumped back into the hall, and dropped my backpack with a crash.

Two huge eyes had been staring at me.

"What happened, MacKenzie?" my dad asked with concern from the bottom of the stairs.

"I accidentally dropped my backpack," I answered. "Sorry." I told him only part of the story. I wasn't ready to tell him about the eyes until I checked them out myself.

I cautiously reached in and flipped on the light in my room. My eyes went immediately to the big window. Taped to it was a round yellow smiley face with huge eyes. Above it was a small banner that said HAPPY BIRTHDAY.

I laughed to myself. Mom had decorated my room with streamers and balloons that all said HAPPY BIRTHDAY. My mom was so sentimental sometimes. I'd have to give her a thank-you hug in the morning.

After another look around, I shook my head and snickered. I stashed my backpack. Then I got my pajamas out of a drawer. I felt tired and sore from the long soccer practice.

After washing up and brushing my teeth, I sank deep under the covers, wanting to sleep. But the smiley-face scare had jarred me awake. I needed something to relax me.

While digging through the books I had ready for tomorrow morning's meeting, I found one I had enjoyed years ago. I settled in to begin reading when I suddenly remembered the library book that I'd brought home. It was in my backpack.

I dug the heavy volume out of my pack and set it on my bed. It wasn't exactly what I would call light reading. The book must have weighed two to three pounds.

For a moment, I had second thoughts about cracking open the book. Did I really want to know right now about the ghosts at Creepy's pizza place? After all, I wanted to get a good night's sleep.

But I knew the ghosts weren't real. So, pretending to be Sherlock Holmes, I decided to see what I could discover. I crawled to the head of my bed and leaned back on my pillow. Then I pulled the big book up and rested it on my legs. It fell open to chapter thirteen.

I hadn't even started to read before I recognized the fear overcoming me. *Lord,* I prayed, *I know there's no truth in these stories. Please help me to overcome my fear.* As I took in a deep breath, I felt a little bit calmer. I began reading where Lisa had left off that afternoon:

In the last fifty years, the large red-brick building that sits in the middle of Tremble Avenue's business district has seen more than thirty tenants. Many of the tenants and customers witnessed strange, unexplainable disturbances.

In the 1940s, mysterious sightings of a gaunt gray figure occurred. At that time the building housed Dandy's Five and Dime Store.

In one instance, a customer had selected her items from one of the basement bargain areas and walked to the register. Without looking up, she placed her purchases on the checkout counter. While she rummaged in her purse for money, the items moved off the counter, and the register rang.

The customer looked up expecting to see a clerk. But the only thing she saw was the long kitchen knife she had selected. It was floating in midair. When she screamed, the knife dropped to the floor, and she heard a haunting, eerie laugh.

Big deal, I thought, still trying to dismiss my fears. *The woman probably needed to buy glasses instead of a kitchen knife. Besides, that happened before my dad was even born, and that was a long time ago.*

I debated with myself over whether I should read the rest of the chapter. I decided I was still curious, so I continued to read.

Over the years the building has changed hands many times. As of this writing, a new pizza restaurant for kids is planning to open after extensive remodeling. The previous owner ran a bakery that specialized in hand-decorated birthday cakes.

The bakery relocated because of recurring hauntings. In the final instance, one of the night shift bakers had gone to the basement for flour. The worker said that he was "attacked from behind. I didn't know what it was. I thought maybe a burglar had gotten in until these long, gray arms wrapped themselves around me. I struggled as hard as I could, and the two of us fell into the stacked bags of flour. Several of them broke, sending clouds of flour into the air. When it finally settled, I saw a thin, grayish-white form slipping into the next room."

The night shift baker said that he didn't follow the ghost but immediately ran upstairs and then outside, never to return to work on Tremble Avenue again.

I stopped reading for a moment and rubbed my eyes. It was getting hard to keep them open. I wanted a drink of water, but I didn't want to climb out of bed and get it. I was afraid of what I might discover in the dark hall. I decided to stay in bed and try to relax. I breathed deeply and closed my eyes.

After a few minutes I picked up the book and began reading again.

> The most recent encounter at the Tremble Avenue building occurred on September 23 . . .

This year? On my birthday? Surely I misread that, I thought. I read the sentence again.

> The most recent encounter at the Tremble Avenue building occurred on . . .

I hadn't misread it. It was this Friday's date. I felt my breath come in shorter gasps as I read on.

> MacKenzie Griffin, celebrating his twelfth birthday at Creepy the Clown's Pizza Palace, mysteriously disappeared . . .

I dropped the book. My name! My birthday party! My pulse quickened, and I concentrated hard to keep from shaking. *Calm down, Mac. Your imagination is in overdrive. You didn't really read what you thought you just read.*
I returned to where I had left off.

> Witnesses to the event reported strange occurrences. Barry Lennon, Griffin's best friend,

reported that a gray ghostlike being had cornered the young man in the basement.

Beads of perspiration broke out on my forehead.

"I closed my eyes out of fear," Lennon reported. "When I opened them again, MacKenzie was gone." MacKenzie Griffin is still missing . . .

Tears welled in my eyes. I could not explain what was happening.

Either I was going crazy, or this was some kind of phantom book that predicted the future.

A piercing wail shattered the silence. I jolted upright in my bed. The back of my pajama shirt was soaked with sweat and stuck to my skin.

Outside, the wail grew fainter.

My mind cleared, and I recognized the sound as an ambulance siren. I rubbed my eyes.

Unbelievable! I had fallen asleep and dreamed I was reading about my birthday disappearance.

Mom must have turned off my reading lamp before going to bed. I turned it on again and reached for *Middletown's Ghosts and Ghouls*, which lay on the floor.

I opened the book and scanned chapter thirteen with relief. No mention of my birthday party. In fact, the last sighting the book reported had happened a full year ago.

I placed the volume on my bedside table, turned out the light, and crawled under the covers. I prayed I wouldn't dream anymore.

On awaking the next morning, I hoped that lunch, school, homework, and bedtime would be more sane than my dream. I really needed to get my imagination under control.

After breakfast, I gathered up some of my scary book collection and headed for school. Several of us involved in forming the new book club walked into the library together. The lights were on, but no librarian was in sight. We sat down at the largest table.

I placed my collection in front of me. The others did the same. I looked over the stack next to mine. One kid brought a series for younger kids called *Boo! Books.*

While we waited for the librarian to come help us start our meeting, I said, "It looks like there are dozens of scary series. I'm not sure I've read many books in any of them. Maybe we should each give a short review on our favorites to start."

A girl from my math class said, "I thought they were all the same. Aren't they all about ghosts or monsters?"

The girl next to her responded, "No, my favorite books have historical backgrounds."

"One series I like is more about ghosts than monsters, and another is about a street called Scare Avenue," the boy across from me said.

"My favorites all have endings that will shock you. They've actually helped me deal with my fears," another boy added.

The boy across from me was just opening his mouth to say something else when the doors to the library flew open. Startled by the noise, I whipped my head around.

In the library's doorway stood a creature that looked like it had just climbed out of a grave.

We jumped from our seats and ran to the far corner of the library. The creature turned toward us, staring and moaning. Then it lurched in our direction.

I felt my heart beating in my throat. I had hoped today would be uneventful. Wrong.

We spread out along the back wall. The creature might be able to grab one or two of us, but some would be able to get away to get help. The refugee from the graveyard took a few more steps and twisted its head toward the table.

Our books diverted the thing's attention. It walked to a chair, pulled it out, and sat down. Slimy fingers reached out and grabbed one of my books and flipped it open.

We stood, shocked, watching the walking dead become the reading dead. The creature turned, stared at us, and spoke for the first time. "Good books."

Then the undead looked right at me and said,

"Mr. Griffin, if you can get your cohorts to sit down, I'd like to get started."

Suddenly, I recognized her voice—the librarian! Wow! Who would have expected the school librarian to do something so cool?

"I can't believe it's you," I said. "Why did you dress up to scare us?"

"That's simple. I dressed up like this because I wanted you to have a real experience that you can carry to your books. When you read, remember how you felt a few minutes ago. Such feelings help make stories come to life," she answered.

I didn't need her entrance to experience fright. I had pizza palace ghosts, floating raincoats, trees, and smiley faces to draw on for feelings of heart-pounding fear.

"That was really great," one of the other kids said.

"You should see what I do when classes study the ocean. Sea monsters are tough costumes to find, and seaweed isn't easy to clean up," she said as she smiled.

We gathered around her. She liked our idea about reviewing the different series. We decided which books to talk about at the next meeting. Then the bell rang, and we split up to start our classes.

The day passed quickly. Even soccer practice breezed by. When I walked out of the locker room into the late-afternoon sun, I saw Lisa waiting for me beneath the big elm tree.

"What's going on? Why are you still here?" I quizzed.

Usually, Lisa and Frankie hang out together after school. I felt uneasy when I saw Lisa alone. Her expression concerned me even more.

"It's Davis," Lisa answered in a troubled tone. She looked frightened by something.

"What's wrong with Davis? Did he get hurt or something?" My words flew out of my mouth as I walked closer to Lisa.

"He's all right now, but in a few minutes he may not be," Lisa said.

Lisa hadn't told me anything concrete, but she had managed to frighten me. My confusion and fear came out in my voice as I said, "Tell me what's going on. This suspense has to be worse than whatever is going to happen to Davis."

"When Frankie, Davis, and I were helping the biology teacher after school today, Davis started asking us lots of questions about Creepy's.

"We told him what we read in that library book yesterday, and he decided to have a look at that old building for himself. He left about ten minutes ago," Lisa stated.

"So, he'll walk by it, and it will look like a pizza place. Then he'll go home. What's the big deal?" I said to calm her fears for our friend, though my stomach was growing queasy with nervousness.

"That isn't exactly what he planned," Lisa continued. "He said he wants to disprove the legend before the party. He plans to get inside."

"I don't think there's anything to worry about," I said, trying to sound convincing to both Lisa and myself.

Lisa looked at me hard and said, "You're not listening to me, Mac. Davis plans to go around behind the building and find a way to get down to the basement. I told him it was a dumb idea, but Davis is trying so hard to be a part of our group. Sometimes, I think he tries too hard."

My thoughts were racing. Surely, Davis would be safe in broad daylight. The restaurant workers and the early dinner crowd would be there. And all the stories about ghosts were just fiction, weren't they?

But what about the people I had read about—the people who had witnessed the apparitions, the baker who had been attacked by a ghost? Or what if someone thought Davis was a burglar?

"We've got to get down there and stop him," I said. "Hurry." I bolted past Lisa, grabbing her hand to drag her along as I ran toward Creepy the Clown's Pizza Palace.

The restaurant was only a few blocks from the school. We could get there in five minutes. But Davis was probably already there. He could be in the hands of a ghost for all I knew.

We reached the building and stopped abruptly. I stared at the rough red-brick front. A large mural painted above the door showed an enormous clown's face. Out of his mouth came a dialogue balloon, like in comic books, saying, "Creepy the Clown's Pizza Palace is a killer-fun place."

I wished I hadn't read that. I turned to Lisa and said, "Davis may already be inside. We need to do something quick to save him."

Stepping back from the building, I thought about how Davis might have gone in. It didn't seem likely that he'd use the front door if he wanted to get into the basement. Someone would probably stop him. To the left of the building was a narrow walkway that led to the back of the building.

Lisa looked at me with wide, frightened eyes and said, "He said something about going in the back door. He must have gone down that way. We better follow him."

"No, we can't both go. I'll go alone. You stay here and be the lookout. If I don't come back soon, call my parents," I told her.

I didn't *want* to go by myself. I really wanted Lisa to come with me, but if I didn't return, I wanted Lisa to go for help. I had to do this by myself. I knew it, but I didn't like it.

As I moved slowly down the narrow walkway, I wanted to sing or whistle. But if Davis needed rescuing, I couldn't make any noise and give myself away. Instead I said a silent prayer for our safety.

At the end of the walkway I found myself in a narrow alley that ran behind the buildings in this block. The stores and restaurants kept their dumpsters back there, out of sight.

I forced myself to walk toward Creepy's back door. Each step brought me closer, but my legs were heavy and my feet fought me when I lifted them.

When I was about a foot from the door, I heard someone turn the knob. I quickly searched for a place to hide. I was close enough to get behind the garbage dumpster before the door opened. I took one big leap and ducked down.

Someone came out and headed toward the dumpster I had hidden behind. I heard the lid open and two huge bags drop in. Then the lid slammed shut. In another few seconds, the back door closed.

I sighed and stood up. I took one step forward and almost tripped on my shoelace. As I reached down to tie my shoe, I saw Davis's prized Pittsburgh Pirates baseball cap. I snatched it off the ground.

My heart began beating out of control. Davis must have gotten inside!

I raced down the walkway toward Lisa holding Davis's cap in front of me.

Lisa saw me coming and then looked at the hat in my hands. She covered her mouth with her hands and let out a groan of fear. She took a step back and leaned against a streetlight.

"I found this by the back door. Davis must have gone inside. We've got to help him," I told her.

"What can we do?" Lisa asked, holding tightly to the lightpole.

"Let's go home. I'll call Barry, and you call Frankie. We need every one of our crew to come back tonight. We've got to help Davis. Plan to meet me here after dinner," I said.

We ran to our houses. I crashed through the front door, dropped my backpack by the staircase, and rushed into the kitchen where Dad was cooking dinner. "Dad, can Barry sleep over tonight?" I asked.

"Hey, is that any way to greet your old dad, especially when he's sweating over a hot stove?" Dad grinned at me.

"Sorry. Hi, Dad," I said. "Now, can Barry sleep over?"

Dad looked at me and raised his eyebrows while he thought. "I guess so. Why don't you go make sure it's okay with your mother?"

After I checked with Mom, I called Barry.

"Hi, Barry," I said. "This is Mac. I don't have time to explain right now, but somebody's got Davis. Ask your parents if you can sleep over so we can get into Creepy's to help him."

Barry's folks said okay. He promised to come over after dinner.

As I ate with my parents, I tried to keep the conversation on school and soccer. I didn't want them to ask questions about Creepy's or my party. I was afraid I'd let something about Davis slip. I had gotten him into this mess, and I had to get him out—or so I thought.

As I was rinsing off the last dish from dinner, the doorbell rang. The next thing I knew, Barry was standing next to me with an intensely worried look on his face. "What's going on, Mac?" He asked quietly, so my parents wouldn't hear.

I quickly told him about the book, the legend of the clowns and the treasure, and what Davis had planned on doing. Then I pulled Davis's Pirates cap from my back pocket. I told him how I had found the cap behind the haunted pizza place.

Barry said very little. He was not often so quiet. When I finished, he asked, "So, what's the plan?"

"We've got to check out Creepy's basement tonight. We're going to meet Frankie and Lisa. Once we're inside we'll split into pairs and search for Davis," I answered.

After I finished putting the dishes in the dishwasher, Barry and I headed upstairs so I could grab a jacket. We were almost to the top step when the phone rang. Mom answered it.

I ignored the call until I heard Mom say, "Sure, let me call him to the phone. I'm sure he can help you out."

Barry and I exchanged a worried look. What had Mom promised I would do? We had to go meet the girls now.

"MacKenzie, the phone is for you," Mom called up to me.

"See if I can call back, Mom. Barry and I are really busy," I responded.

"Mac, it's Davis Wong. He says he really needs your help," she said.

Davis Wong? I suddenly had to sit down.

"Are you going to get it upstairs, Mac?" Mom asked.

"Yes, I'll get it in my room."

I stood up and raced Barry down the hall to my room. I snatched up the phone and said, "Thanks, Mom, I've got it."

I waited for her to hang up and whispered into the phone, "Davis, this is Mac. I know where you are, and we're planning to come over to get you out of there."

"What are you talking about?" Davis responded. "I'm at home watching TV. Why would I want you to come and get me out of my house?"

"Well, I thought that . . . oh, never mind." A big smile of relief spread across my face. So Barry would know what was going on, I asked, "How did you get out?"

"Out of what? Mac, what happened? Did you get hit on the head at soccer practice?" he quizzed.

"Didn't you go to Creepy's after school?"

Davis laughed and responded, "Sure, and that's why I'm calling. I went down the walkway next to the building and found the back door. I was going to sneak in, but someone came out, and I ran out of there. The only trouble is that I dropped my Pirates cap somewhere. I was wondering if you could go with me before school to look for it."

"Davis, I'll do even better than that. I went looking for you and found your cap. I'll bring it to school tomorrow," I answered.

Barry was almost jumping up and down as I got off the phone. He wanted to know what had happened. After I told him, I called Frankie and Lisa.

Later, Barry and I worked on our homework for a little while. Then I dug out one of my favorite video games and challenged Barry. I thought that since I had the home-court advantage, I could win. I should have known better. Video games are Barry's thing. He beats me every time.

"How do you do that? Do you practice every day?" I asked in frustration.

"You know that I play almost every day, but I also seem to have a gift for it," he answered.

"I don't think you can call being good at video games a gift," I challenged.

"No, that isn't the way I mean it. It takes a degree of concentration and hand-eye coordination. I just do these things well," he said. Then he sat back against the foot of the bed. I could tell he was deep in thought.

"What are you thinking about?" I asked. "Are you scared that I'll beat you so badly that you won't be able to show your face at school?" I asked, joking around.

He hesitated. "Do you think ghosts really exist?" he asked.

I sat back against the bed too. "Well, I do know that Ephesians 6:12 says, 'We are fighting against the rulers and authorities and the powers of this world's darkness.' And God's Spirit is greater than the darkness. So I guess that if there *are* ghosts there's really nothing to be afraid of."

We sat quietly until the wind moved a branch, and it brushed against my window. "Did you hear that?"

"It was just the wind, I think," he answered.

Funny how I could quote Scripture and still be spooked a minute later. My imagination had started to run away with even the smallest things. I was getting tired, and my mind always played tricks on me when I got tired. "I think we better hit the hay," I told him.

"Hit the what?" he asked in confusion.

"Hit the hay. It means 'go to bed,'" I told him. I thought everyone used that expression.

"Why does it mean 'go to bed'? Where do you suppose that expression comes from?" Barry pondered.

"Listen, I've already used up all my brain power on the plan to free Davis. Let's get some sleep and ask someone else in the morning."

We laughed and got ready for bed. I had two beds in my room, so I could have friends over. Barry used my spare bed more than anyone else I knew.

I had just started to drift off to sleep when I heard a crash from the backyard.

I slipped out of bed and shook Barry, but he was already awake.

"Hey, did you hear that?" I asked. "I heard the same thing yesterday when I was coming home from the library."

"Yes, I heard something like it around my house last night too," he answered. "My mom sent Dad out to see what caused it, but he didn't find anything. If we could figure out what's making the noise, my mom would sleep a whole lot better. Let's check it out . . . Or do you think it might be ghosts?"

I gave him my don't-be-ridiculous look, and we slipped out of our beds. I opened the door slowly. My parents were already in bed. It was quiet and dark downstairs.

I crept down the stairs as Barry stayed close behind me. We tiptoed past Mom and Dad's bedroom door and into the kitchen. I silently twisted the knob and pulled the back door open. We slipped silently outside into the dark night.

"Where do you think the noise came from?" my best friend whispered.

"I couldn't tell, but let's try near the garbage cans," I told him. As we crept toward the cans, we heard a noise. We spun ourselves around to face the garage.

Barry motioned to me to keep silent. Together we crept softly through the wet grass. I couldn't see anything by the small building.

As we got closer, something moved in the bushes in front of us. We looked at each other and I gulped. I thought, *Is it really a ghost? Is it one of the "powers of this world's darkness"?*

Another four steps put us next to the big bush. I searched near the ground. Barry let out a howl. I looked up as a dark form leaped at Barry's head from the bush.

Barry dove for the ground as the ghostly figure flew toward his head. It missed him by only two inches, but it didn't miss me.

"Help! Get it off me!" I cried out.

I twisted and turned in a wild attempt to free myself from the sharp claws of the phantom. I finally grabbed its head, and it hissed and growled.

A black cat decided I had scared it enough. It let go of my chest, dropped to the wet grass by my feet, and shot off into the night.

Barry had seen the terror in my eyes. Then he saw the cat and cracked up.

"Did that little kitty scare you?" he asked.

"At least I stayed on my feet," I fired back.

We both broke out in giggles as the tension eased out of us. Finally I got my breath back and said, "We better get back to bed before our little adventure wakes Mom and Dad."

We didn't say anything as we crossed the lawn and

climbed the back porch steps. As I pulled the screen door open, a sinking feeling hit my stomach. I had forgotten to turn the button to keep the door from locking behind us.

I grabbed the knob and tried twisting it. Nothing happened. We were locked out.

"I've got some bad news," I told my friend. "We locked ourselves out of the house."

"Then we'll just go around to the front door and ring the bell. Your dad will open the door, and we'll all go back to bed," he answered simply.

"Barry, I've had a tough enough time convincing them that I can be responsible. If they find out I did something stupid like locking myself out over a silly cat, they'll treat me like a little kid until I'm old enough for my beard to reach my navel."

"How about a window?" he suggested.

"That's a good idea. Dad usually leaves the one in his workroom open. He likes lots of fresh air. I'll bet he didn't lock it the last time he was in there," I said as I ran around to the side of the house.

The window was wide open. I bent over to inspect it. It would be tough to get through, but I thought we could. By then Barry was standing behind me.

"Maybe my first idea was better. Let's go around front and ring the bell," he suggested strongly.

I lay down flat on the ground. Technically, I guess I lay down right on top of Dad's prize flowers. I attempted to move them out of the way, but a good bed of flowers is hard to move. I'd have to tell my parents the whole story in the morning. But at least they'd get an uninterrupted night's sleep first.

I wiggled in through the window. Dad's workbench stood directly below the window. The drop was short, but Dad had left a glass jar of nuts and bolts near the edge. In the dark, I bumped it.

Nothing I did could stop its suicide leap to the floor. The crash of breaking glass and scattering metal sent shivers through me.

I tried to keep Barry from knocking anything else off the bench. But he kicked a mallet, and it toppled off. I could barely see it as my hand shot into the darkness to stop its fall. I snatched it out of the air.

We stood in the workroom. "If any ghouls got in here before us, I'll bet they're waiting for us in the family room," I said in a very low whisper.

"Do you think they came in so they could play foosball?" Barry joked.

I ignored him. Before I could open the door, I heard movement on the other side.

"What should we do?" Barry asked, his eyes wide.

"I don't know. Maybe we should grab a hammer and go after it," I answered.

"We don't have to go after it. It's coming to us!" Barry said in panic as he watched the knob turn slowly.

The door flew open.

"DAD!" I screamed as he began to swing a baseball bat in the air.

He stopped mid swing, reached over, and flipped on the light. Dad stared at us in surprise. Then he sucked in a deep breath and set the bat down.

"Could you please explain to me why you're sneaking into the house through my workroom window? And while you're at it, I'd like to know why you were outside in the first place. And don't you realize that it's dangerous to break into a house? I could have really hurt you. I thought you were thieves," he said, his anger rising as he realized what we'd done.

"It was really stupid, Mr. Griffin, but it was my idea." Barry attempted to take the blame.

"Thanks, Barry, but this is my house. I knew the rules, and I broke them. I'm sorry, Dad. We heard something crash, and we slipped outside to see what it was. But instead of finding some ghoul strolling around the garden, we locked ourselves out."

"You heard it too?" Dad said with interest. He seemed to forget he was mad at us. He totally refocused on the mysterious noise. "Did you see anything?"

"We heard something by the garage. When we went to investigate, a cat jumped on me."

"Hmm. Why don't we get some sleep and talk in the morning?" Dad suggested.

As we walked upstairs, he said, "You two can sleep in an extra fifteen minutes. I'll drive you to school."

When morning came, I expected crazy things to happen at school after all the excitement of the last few days, but it was rather dull until lunchtime.

Barry described to our friends how we'd confronted a horrible ghoul in my backyard. I liked his version. We sounded much braver than we'd been.

Frankie looked him right in the eyes and said, "I don't believe this story."

"It's true," Barry defended.

"Most of it is true," I added.

"Which part is true?" Davis asked.

"We did see a mysterious, dark shape that looked like a ghost in the backyard," I answered.

"I saw a ghost in my pajamas once," Davis said with a smile. "What he was doing in my pajamas, I'll never know."

Frankie and Lisa laughed so hard they nearly fell from their cafeteria seats. Barry and I were not amused.

I opened my lunch bag and pulled out my sandwich. When I unwrapped it, the bread had "Happy Birthday, Almost" written on it in mustard. *Thanks, Mom*, I thought.

"Cute—really cute," Frankie said. "I can't wait to see what the rest of your lunch looks like."

Lucky for me, Mom hadn't gotten too creative this morning. The rest of the school day seemed to slip by.

That evening, before I went into the house, I checked where we'd seen the cat by the garage. I wanted to make sure we hadn't missed something. I didn't find any clues. Maybe all the noise just came from the cat. Next, I made sure the window to Dad's workroom was closed. Assured that nothing could get in, I went inside.

I discovered that Mom and Dad were still at work. I looked around for anything unusual. I knew I was starting to get paranoid. It was crazy to think that ghosts would be lurking around the house waiting for me. I decided to think less about ghosts and more about the Protector *against* ghosts.

The rest of my last evening as an eleven-year-old was completely uneventful. I hoped my first day as a twelve-year-old would be as well.

I got up early on my birthday, showered, and dressed. I was pulling on my Dodgers cap as I stepped into the silent kitchen. Where were Mom and Dad? Then I noticed my spot at the table. A tower of pancakes just about glowed—twelve candles burned happily on top.

My parents leaped out from behind the kitchen counter yelling, "Happy Birthday!"

"Thanks, Mom and Dad. I can't believe that I'm twelve, almost a full-grown man." I threw that in as a hint to my mother.

"Hurry and blow out the candles," Dad said.

"Okay, please let my party tonight be the talk of the school on Monday," I wished. I puffed out the candles with a single blow.

The pancakes were great, and I was only halfway through when Barry showed up at the back door to walk to school with me.

"Wow!" he said as he peeked through the screen door. "That's the biggest pile of pancakes I've ever seen."

"You know how it is when you're the birthday boy," I said with a grin. I took a few more bites, grabbed my backpack, and we were on our way to school.

It was a quiet morning, but I knew lunch wouldn't be as quiet. Tonight was my party at Creepy's. I imagined we'd probably meet up with whatever was haunting that building. I was sure we'd talk about it while we ate.

At lunchtime, I walked into the cafeteria and sat at an empty table. Barry and Frankie arrived next from their class together. I saw Lisa in the lunch line beside Davis.

Since Davis's dad was the vice principal, they felt he should eat the sometimes mysterious cafeteria food. Vice Principal Wong wanted to emphasize how good the food could be. But it wasn't.

"How are the party plans for tonight, Mac?" Frankie asked.

"Just about everyone I invited is coming. To tell you the truth, after all the strange things that have happened this week, I have a feeling that tonight may be the weirdest night of my life," I told the others.

Lisa agreed, but Frankie didn't believe it would be scary. She told us, "A girl in my English class said her little brother had a party there last week and nothing unusual happened. No one saw any type of ghoul, ghost, or phantom. I think we're all getting a little carried away with the legend about the Tremble Avenue building."

But Davis insisted, "I heard just the opposite. A couple of guys from gym class said it was definitely haunted and that two kids went in and never came out last week. The police don't want to panic anyone, so nothing has been in the news about their disappearance."

"It doesn't matter what anyone's saying. Tonight, we'll all find out for ourselves," Barry told us.

I opened my lunch bag and pulled out my sandwich. Then I dumped out an apple and a bag of chips. A brightly wrapped gift fell onto the table from the bottom of my bag. The others looked at me.

"Open it," Frankie urged.

"Mom didn't say anything about a birthday gift in my lunch bag. How do I know it's from her? It could be from anybody, including the ghosts at Creepy's," I kidded, using my best scary voice.

I took the bow off the package. "Well, nothing happened—so far."

I undid a piece of tape on the bottom. "It still didn't blow up," I joked some more.

Then I ripped the Happy Birthday wrapping paper off the small box. "Nothing unusual," I said, stretching out the suspense.

"Well, are you going to open the box or not?" Frankie asked.

"Would you open a gift some ghost sneaked into your lunch bag?" Lisa said.

I wasn't sure if she was kidding or not. I looked at her face for a clue.

"Of course," she continued, "if some loving, caring ghost took the time to wrap a nice gift to make my birthday a little brighter, I'd open it a lot faster than Mac is." Then she started laughing.

I smiled and pulled the top off the box.

"Oh, no!" I gasped.

"HAPPY BIRTHDAY! HAPPY BIRTHDAY! HAPPY BIRTHDAY! HAPPY BIRTHDAY! HAPPY BIRTH-DAY! HAPPY BIRTHDAY! HAPPY BIRTHDAY!" a computer chip blared.

Everyone in the entire cafeteria stood up to see what was going on. Some kids even climbed on chairs to get a better look.

I didn't know what to do. My first instinct was to put the lid back on the box. But I couldn't find it. I must have dropped it on the floor. I stuck my head beneath the table to look for it. I sort of wanted to just stay under the table. Then the sound stopped as suddenly as it had begun.

I crawled out from under the table and found myself the focus of a roomful of stares. I smiled sheepishly. I was embarrassed, but I also felt the urge to giggle. I looked at everyone and asked, "Does anyone else have a birthday gift for me?" People started laughing and went back to their lunches.

We didn't have soccer practice today, so after school, I hurried home to tell Mom about the havoc she had caused, but she had gone out. She left me a note on the fridge that said she'd gone shopping for party favors. I could see her coming home with brightly colored little bags with plastic whistles, lollipops, and fake watches. I shook my head and decided to shoot a few hoops to burn off some of my pre–birthday-party excitement.

I got into a zone, hitting my shots one after another—nothing but net. I was so into shooting that I didn't realize Mom came home. Then I heard her call out my name. "MacKenzie, we need to get going, or you'll be late for your own birthday party."

I rolled the ball into the garage and headed for the minivan. Mom had already thrown things for the party into the back. For a long time, I'd told her that since I was an only child, she could get a sportier car. She sort of took my advice; she got a *red* minivan.

She picked up Barry, Davis, Frankie, and Lisa. Everyone else would meet us at Creepy's. I had invited kids from three different groups. There were the guys I played soccer with, my best friends in the van with me, and other kids from my church youth group. It should be a pretty big turnout.

We wanted to be the first to get there. Mom pulled to a stop in front of Creepy's as a bunch of little kids were leaving the Pizza Palace. Their party must have just ended. They all had bright helium balloons stringing from their wrists and traditional birthday bags of goodies in their hands.

I sighed. None of them looked scared; Creepy's really must be a place for little kids. I wouldn't be able to show my face at school, practice, or church. How much fun could this be for a bunch of middle schoolers if little kids looked unfazed? *This is going to be a drag,* I thought.

We all jumped out. I had taken only a few steps from the minivan when Barry stopped me. "Afraid to go in?" I asked. "Maybe you're afraid you'll lose at pin the tail on the donkey."

"Yeah, right. I just wanted to tell you I read something in the newspaper about this place," he said seriously.

"So?"

"This building really is haunted. It's like the Bermuda Triangle of town. Strange things happen here. The article talked about the last business to go under and the one before that. I asked my dad about it, and he said there are supposedly ghosts here looking for hidden treasure," he whispered.

"That's the legend," I told him.

"I'm not sure I want to go in . . . But I'm not staying out here by myself," he finished, and we walked in.

Mom checked in with Creepy while I greeted my guests as they came through the door. We were told to wait in the Pizza Palace foyer until everyone had arrived. The foyer's walls were covered with all kinds of crazy things. It looked a lot cooler than I thought it would.

On one wall was a stuffed clown head. Kind of like those moose heads people hang on their walls as trophies.

I nudged Davis and said, "Tough place. They even stuff the heads of dead clowns. Or do you think the ghosts did that to him? Maybe he got too close to the treasure and they put an end to him."

Frankie looked up and pointed at the stuffed head on the wall. She said, "My dad wants one of those with a purple dinosaur on it."

Davis and I cracked up. It helped me to forget what Barry had reminded me of.

We continued making jokes about the clown's head. Suddenly it opened its eyes and yelled, "Welcome to Creepy the Clown's Pizza Palace."

I jumped back and nearly knocked Lisa over. I heard my friends let out gasps and little shrieks. My heart leaped into my mouth, and I felt totally speechless.

Creepy pulled his head through a hole in the wall, and we heard him drop to the floor on the other side with a thump. When he opened a door, I saw several clown servers standing just beyond him. He said, "Hey, kids. Welcome to my Pizza Palace. Are you ready to have a fun and crazy evening with us? We've got some really wacky games and loony prizes. Ho, hey, ho! This is going to be one fun-n-n-n night!"

I rolled my eyes and shot a glance at the kids around me. "I knew it was really him all the time," I told them.

Frankie and Lisa giggled. I guess they didn't believe me.

Creepy came over, grabbed my arm, and ushered my friends and me to the door. I was surprised when

I looked into the next room. The place was enormous and filled with video games. One wall had several doors marked Hall of This and Hall of That. I stood there taking it all in as the games beeped, whirred, gasped, and dinged only a few feet away.

The game room looked like a blast. I just hoped that Creepy and his clown team wouldn't make us sing little kids' songs or play baby games later in the party. If they did, I might crawl under a table and not come out until I graduated from middle school.

Creepy spun around, clapped his hands together, and said, "Boys and girls, can I have your attention?"

Everyone groaned in unison.

"Oops, did I say something wrong? You know Creepy, just kidding around. Anyway, kids, please follow me and my fellow clowns into the party room."

We fell in behind the clown corps. The party room reminded me of a carnival midway. Games lined the sides of the room, and tables filled the center.

Creepy had gone all out for this place. Even the hologram characters near the midway games looked real. Of course, in the blinking, colored lights almost anything could have looked real. The lights cast an odd glow on everything.

We all wandered around as Creepy's clowns pushed chairs and tables into place. The holograms sang and danced.

In a dark corner, far from the entrance, a hologram

depicted a group of kids playing a game of ring-around-the-rosy. They pranced in a circle around an odd figure. From the distance, in the crazy light, the figure in the center looked like a dingy gray sheet draped over something.

I walked closer to get a better look. When I got about five feet away, I found myself looking into its eyes. It wore a baggy clown costume, but it wasn't brightly colored like the other clowns. Instead, everything, including its skin, was gray. A shiver ran up my spine. Could this be one of the ghosts that haunted the Tremble Avenue building?

I shook my head to knock that frightening thought loose, then took a step back. I bumped into someone. One of the clowns?

Before I could turn around to look, the person behind me asked, "Do you know about the legend behind that scene?"

I tried to face the owner of the voice, but two hands gripped my shoulders, holding me still. "Do you? Do you know where the rhyme ring-around-the-rosy came from?"

I answered, "No, sir. I came over to see what the kids were dancing around—"

The person behind me didn't let me finish. He said, "When England was struck with the plague hundreds of years ago, people thought the dirty air was killing them. So, they filled their pockets with flowers and walked around with handfuls of posies up to their noses. Don't you think it was silly of them to try to protect themselves with flowers?" He took his hands off my shoulders.

The eerie voice scared me so badly that my teeth started to chatter. I was too scared to turn around. When I tried to speak, my voice came out high and squeaky. "Uh, thank you for telling me about the rhyme. I guess you want me to join the others now?" I hoped I could escape this presence unharmed.

The voice didn't respond. Surprised, I spun around and discovered I was alone. Where did he go? I found myself beginning to buy into this ghost business. Had I just met one of them?

I didn't want to hang around and find out. I shot back toward my friends.

The others had already found places to sit around the tables. A large red velvet chair stood in the center of the room. I figured it was for me when Barry and Davis waved me over to it. They were sitting on either side of my birthday throne. Frankie and Lisa sat next to them, and the rest of my friends seemed to merge into a sea of faces.

Barry said something to me as I sat down, but the old-time organ music was so loud that I couldn't hear him. When I tried to yell into his ear that I had met a ghost, the music grew even louder.

The music didn't stop until Creepy joined us again

and clapped his hands. It was obvious that he was the clown in charge.

"Throughout the evening, we will escort you to different areas for different activities. I see that we can split you easily into groups of five. Sometimes one group will be one place while the others are someplace else. Don't worry. We'll all end up in the same room when the party ends," he explained.

"That is, if the ghosts of Tremble Avenue don't get us first," Barry whispered to me.

"That's what I was trying to tell you. I went over to check out that gray figure in the middle of the kids playing ring-around-the-rosy, and a ghost grabbed me," I whispered back excitedly.

Barry looked at me and then glanced at the hologram. He asked, "What did the ghost look like?"

"I don't know. He grabbed me from behind, and when I turned around, he was gone. But he told me some weird tale about ring-around-the-rosy. He really spooked me," I told him in a loud whisper.

He scrunched his eyebrows together and looked like he wanted to ask me another question. But before he could open his mouth, clowns swarmed all around us with plates and glasses.

These clowns sure didn't look happy. Most had their faces painted in demented, angry, or twisted expressions. As my waitress reached over my shoulder to set a glass down, she looked right at me and snarled.

For a second I thought that maybe Creepy's wasn't just for little kids. Maybe it was going to be too much for me, even if I was practically an adult.

I leaned over to Davis to ask if he'd gotten a good look at the waitress's face. "Hey, did you see that? I don't think she's—"

CRASH! The wall across from us blew apart in a puff of smoke, sending stone fragments into the air. As the air cleared, I heard a horn beep. I couldn't believe it.

A car had smashed through the wall and was heading, out of control, directly toward our table.

My friends and I dived for the floor as tires screeched. The almost cartoonish-looking car still slid toward us. The car's clown-faced driver's eyes were wide with what looked like terror.

I couldn't tell if she was terrified that she'd hit us or terrified that she'd miss us. It looked like she was steering deliberately at us.

"What's going on?" Davis yelled above the noise.

Lisa looked shocked as she screamed, "We've got to get out of here. That thing's still coming right at us."

We scrambled out of the way, just in time.

"It looks like my birthday party will be everybody's last party," I said to no one in particular. But I don't think anyone heard me above the screeching tires and screaming kids.

The car finally stopped. Thankfully no one got hit. The clown driver jumped out of her seat and yelled, "Howdy, am I late for the party?"

Creepy leaned on one of the tables, shaking with laughter. He could barely get the words out: "Look, kids! It's Penny the Party Crasher."

Penny had driven through a fake wall built out of plastic blocks. A smoke bomb made the explosion seem more realistic. I looked up and realized clown helpers had already begun to rebuild the wall.

After we all picked ourselves up and got back into our seats, Penny bounced from table to table doing silly magic tricks.

"Did I scare you kids?" she asked as we dug into our pizza.

"No, and we're not kids," I answered. I didn't want to give her the satisfaction of knowing that she'd just about terrified me.

She reached her white-gloved hand over and tousled my hair. Then Penny reached for my ear and produced some coins. She dropped them on the table, then reached for more. They just kept pouring out. Hundreds fell to the table as she giggled.

"Well, Birthday Boy, you really should clean your ears out more often," Penny said loudly. "You had all these tokens for Creepy's Hall of Games stuck inside your eardrum. But I beat them out of you. Get it? Beat them out? Eardrum? Beat drum?"

I understood her joke but didn't think it was very funny. Did she really think I'd believe she had pulled those coins out of my ear? I must have looked dubious because Penny snapped her fingers in front of my face.

"Hey, Birthday Boy, are you still with me?" she asked.

I smiled. "That was a great trick. Do you think if you looked harder you might find a new video game in there?" I joked. She smiled and moved on to another group of kids.

When all the pizza had been devoured, Creepy whistled to get everyone's attention. Then he said, "Okay, gang, it's time to head for the Hall of Games for a good time. That is, if Mac will share the tokens Penny found in his ear."

I smiled as Creepy continued. "Try to stay in your groups of five. We're going to have a big surprise for some of you."

Creepy directed everyone to take a handful of tokens off the table in front of me. Then we all ran toward the game room. I went right to my favorite game, *Guardians*. Superhero angels fight with the bad guys who look like ghouls and ghosts. It's really cool. It's based on the characters from my favorite comic book series, also called *Guardians*.

Barry and I had all the editions. We both wanted to play the game, but he let me go first because it was my birthday and my favorite game.

I dropped in the tokens and reached for the start button—but the game began by itself. I didn't want to waste a second of playing time. I grabbed the joystick and started moving it while I pushed the weapons buttons.

I was racking up lots of points. I laughed at how good I was getting. I was in the video game zone.

Others started crowding around me. Someone accidentally pushed Davis, and he knocked my elbow. I momentarily lost my grip on the controls, but the game continued to play. It was as if something invisible had taken over the joystick.

The game was approaching the final level. I had gotten there only once before. There were so few of the *Guardians* video games around that I hadn't had much practice. I was almost afraid to tighten my grip on the controls again, but I didn't want to frighten the other kids.

I closed my fingers around the joystick. Even though it looked like I was playing great, I knew I wasn't controlling the game. Was it haunted? Several of the kids from school cheered as my score continued to climb.

I was about to make the highest score in my video game career, but something else had control over the game. I watched my score mount up. As I stared at the screen, I saw a shadow of a face slowly form over the graphics. It had a grayish tinge.

In fear, I recognized the face of the gray clown from the ring-around-the-rosy hologram. As the picture sharpened, I watched a hand with long, sharp nails move up near the face.

The horrible clown came into crystal-clear view and motioned for me to come closer. Then I heard a weird whisper: "Come and play with me. Come closer and play my game, but don't touch my treasure." I watched as flower petals dropped from the sharp-nailed hand and floated away.

I backed away from the game. Hadn't anyone else seen the face?

Barry slipped into my place and said, "Don't quit now. You're almost—ahhhhh!" Barry yelped off the end of his sentence as the face became visible to him. I guess you had to stand directly in front of the game to see it. He jumped back in surprise and landed on one of my feet.

"Ouch!" I yelled out in pain.

Everyone in the room looked at us. I saw Creepy lean close to Penny's ear and say something then snicker. I did not like the looks of that.

I turned back to the *Guardians* game, but the face had disappeared. All that was left was a frowning yellow circle of a face with the words "Better luck next time" beneath it. I tried to shake off what I had seen as I pulled my group away from the video game.

I put my head close to Barry's so no one else would hear us.

"Did you see what I saw?" I asked.

"The face? That's not what I expected when you got to that level of the game," Barry answered.

I shook my head. "I don't think it had anything to do with the game. It was too real looking. Besides, I wasn't controlling the score at all. I even let go of the joystick, and the game continued on its own. I'm not sure I like this place anymore."

"Neither do I, especially after what you said was in that book you read," Barry added. Frankie and Davis interrupted us when they grabbed our arms and yanked us toward a booth called The Game of Life.

Lisa was standing in front of it reading something. She started instructing us, "According to these directions, we need to get inside the booth and sit down. Then we drop our tokens in the slot and grip the controls in front of us. Sounds easy enough."

I was about to tell them what had happened when Barry said, "After the last game, I could use something a little more sane."

Lisa pushed me into the seat. Lisa, Davis, Barry, and Frankie slid in beside me. We were firmly in place when Frankie dropped in the tokens.

The doors shut quickly, and a bar dropped over our laps. As we all instinctively put our hands on the bar, it locked tight across our knees. We were caught in The Game of Life as it began to flash and groan.

In front of us a large curved screen flicked on as loud music poured into the booth. The Game of Life flashed across the screen. We looked at one another.

I said, "This doesn't seem like some kind of kids' game to me. Creepy's place is starting to get to me. Barry, maybe we should tell them about *Guardians.*"

Frankie said, "Relax, Mac, this is probably one of those virtual reality rides. It will look and feel like we're in a roller coaster or a spaceship or something."

A face appeared on the screen. As it came into focus, Frankie remarked, "Why is that clown face in black and white?"

I stared at the grayish clown face. "Barry, it's him! It's the face from ring-around-the-rosy and *Guardians.*"

Before anyone could say another word, the ghostly clown spoke in an eerie, hollow voice: "Welcome to The Game of Life. I'm your host, George Ghouless.

Now, let's begin the game. The rules are simple. If you score enough points, we'll open the doors and let you out. And if you don't, we won't."

We tried to jump out, but the lap bar held us tight. We twisted and pulled up on the bar, but it was useless.

"What do we do?" Davis asked.

Lisa fairly hissed, "I guess we'd better answer the questions right. I don't want to end up as an eternal guest of Creepy's game room."

The spooky gray clown spoke again. "Here are your category choices: the History of European Wars, the Mammals of New Zealand, and Horror Movie Trivia. Which do you prefer?"

Barry answered for us all. "I don't think we have much choice. We haven't covered European history at school yet. I don't know much about New Zealand's mammals. Do you?" he asked as he looked at the rest of us.

When we shook our heads, he continued. "Right now, I wish Dracula were here to help us."

"I guess Horror Movie Trivia is my choice. What about you guys?" I asked.

Everyone agreed.

Our computer host said, "Horror Movie Trivia it will be then. Here is your first question: Who was the Bride of Frankenstein supposed to marry?"

I smiled. This might not be so hard. "That's easy," I said. "She was made for Frankie himself."

"Correct. Let's move to question two. What did Dracula sleep in, and what did it sit on?"

We all knew he slept in his coffin, but no one knew what it sat on. When we made several wild guesses, a horn buzzed so loud that our teeth rattled.

Our game host chimed in, "Dracula's coffin had to sit on dirt from his home in Transylvania. Are you ready for the third question?"

We all shook our heads, but the question came anyway: "What famous cartoon dog chased ghosts?"

"That one's easy," said Frankie. She broke out in the song, "Scooby-Dooby-Doo, where are you?"

"Correct," George Ghouless said. "One more correct answer, and I'll set you free. Two more incorrect answers, and you'll be locked inside forever. Question number four is: When does a werewolf come out?"

"At night," Barry yelled.

The horn buzzed again, so loud that it made us all jump.

"I think the questions are getting harder," I said to the others. "We better come up with the answer to the next question. By the way, werewolves come out only during a full moon."

Then George said, "Time for our last question. Answer it right, and you'll go free. Answer it wrong, and prepare to stay for a long time."

"Thanks for the encouragement, George," Frankie commented.

Lisa said, "We absolutely have to answer this one right."

I could hear panic in her voice. I realized that she felt the same way I did.

"Attention!" George commanded. "Question number five . . ." He paused dramatically. "What did Dr. Jekyll turn into?"

Barry almost blurted out an answer, but I shot him a glance. "What are our choices?" I whispered to the others. I didn't want to say anything too loudly until we were sure. We couldn't afford to give another wrong answer.

"A monster," Davis let out quietly, as if one were breathing down his neck.

"An evil relative of the werewolf?" Lisa's high-pitched voice sounded unnatural.

"We don't have time to guess. The clock is ticking. Doesn't anyone know the real answer?" I pleaded.

Frankie thought for a moment, then he nearly shouted, "Mr. Hyde!"

George gave a ghoulish bark of laughter.

Had we won?

Had we lost?

The rest of us stared at Frankie. She had sealed our fate. Had she given the wrong answer?

Our host gave us a sinister smile as he reached for a switch. Instantly the door to our booth slid open, the bar across our knees lifted, and the seat tipped up, dumping us on the floor.

"Yes, Frankie! You saved us," I cried. "I'll live to see another birthday."

"Nothing to it," she said, but her eyes looked distracted.

A few feet away, five other guests were entering a booth similar to the one we had just escaped from. It was called The Game of Chance.

Frankie ran their way, but the group was already inside and the door was sliding shut.

"What should I do?" she asked, turning back to us.

"Try forcing the door open," Davis suggested.

By then Barry and I had joined Frankie next to The Game of Chance. Together we pressed hard on the door, and it slowly slid open. I expected to see five surprised faces. Instead, we found an empty booth.

"Where did they go?" Barry asked me.

I stuck my head inside the booth but found no sign of my friends. I looked carefully for a trapdoor, but the walls of the booth looked seamless. On the seat I noticed a few flower petals. I thought about the posies in the ring-around-the-rosy game. Had George Ghouless taken five of my friends?

I turned back to the others. "I don't see how they could have gotten out, but I found these."

Frankie looked confused and said, "Five people disappear and you're worried about flower petals?"

I started to tell them about the hologram, but Davis cut me off by saying, "We better tell Creepy."

Frankie gave him a hard, long look. "Don't you realize he's probably behind all this weird stuff? We can't tell Creepy."

The moment she mentioned his name, Creepy's voice blasted from the speaker above my head. "The Hall of Games time is over. Please follow my assistants to the Hall of Food."

Doors opened and several clowns escorted us into a room that looked like something out of the 1950s. The center of the room was empty and had an interesting black-and-white square-patterned floor. Along one wall stood an old-fashioned counter with high red stools. Two sides of the room held red cushioned booths. Above the booths the walls were covered with mirrors. The fourth wall was draped in red velvet.

A tall, thin man wearing a white paper hat greeted us with, "Welcome to Big Rick's Cafe. Have a seat. In a few minutes we'll be having—"

Creepy interrupted by yelling over the noise we were making, "Before we have cake and ice cream, we're going to play some party games."

I said to the others, "He sure is rude. He didn't let Big Rick finish."

"Who?" Frankie turned to me and asked.

"He's right over there." I pointed to where Big Rick had been. No one was there. "I'm sure he was standing right there. I wonder where he went."

Barry gave me a puzzled look and said, "To leave the room, he'd have had to walk right through us to get to the door. That's the only exit."

He was right. I must have been seeing things, or . . . "Do you think it could have been a ghost?" I asked.

"I think you're getting delirious from too much pizza and too many flashing lights. Besides, we saw a bunch of little tykes leave this place. If they weren't scared, we shouldn't be either," Frankie said.

I was beginning to wonder if anything rattled my friend.

Frankie could have been right, but I was sure that I'd seen something.

As we gathered where Creepy had indicated, I looked around for the group that had gone into The Game of Chance. None of them were here.

Before I could comment to anyone, Creepy yelled again, "Quiet down, everyone. It's time for some traditional party games."

"Pin the tail on the donkey?" Davis asked. "Oooo! That one really scares me."

"We're going to start with Hot Potato. I need you all to get into a circle," Creepy instructed. This handy little plastic potato winds up and explodes when the timer expires. And I do mean *explodes*. Whoever's left holding it when it goes off is out of the game—really out of the game. Does everyone understand?" Something about the tone of his voice made me wonder about how safe this game would be.

The hot potato flew from one set of hands to another. The loud ticking it made was a little unnerving.

KABOOM! The potato shook, rattled, and blinked, but no pain followed the excruciatingly loud noise.

Our expressions changed from fear to relief. Hot Potato was only a game.

Within a few minutes most of the players had been eliminated. Only Frankie, Barry, Davis, Lisa, and I remained. Creepy looked us over, then said, "Let's make this game a little more interesting. I'm going to replace the plastic game potato with something that will give you a *real* bang."

Creepy reached into a deep pocket in his baggy clown pants. He pulled out a small black ball that looked like a cartoon-style bomb. "This is set for just a few seconds. Don't get stuck holding the bomb," the clown said with a sinister snicker.

I looked at Frankie and quietly asked, "Is Creepy trying to get rid of us because he thinks we're after the treasure? Maybe he heard us talking when we first came in. Remember? We thought he was just a stuffed head on the wall. I wonder if we said something to tip him off."

"Maybe. It must be worth a lot for him to go through all this trouble. Personally, I'd rather leave safely than find the treasure," she answered.

I responded, "I don't see how we can leave."

Then I had to focus on the bomb. Creepy had wound it and tossed it toward Lisa.

She gasped and pitched it into the air toward Davis.

Davis didn't even grab it. He batted it to Barry, who bobbled it. He yelled at me, "Find a window. Find someplace to get rid of this thing."

The little timer read thirteen seconds when Barry pitched it to Frankie. With her superb athletic ability, she had the bomb into the air and flying at me within seconds.

As I caught the sinister sphere, I yelled at Barry, "This can't be happening. A clown can't blow up a group of kids and expect to keep his business alive."

Creepy called out to me, "You better concentrate on keeping yourself alive."

I started to panic. I tried to pitch the bomb into a far corner where no kids were standing. But I took too long.

Time had run out. It was all over. I'd never see thirteen.

The red timer flashed zero. I turned my face away as I closed my eyes and waited for the explosion. Instead of a bang, I heard Creepy laugh. I opened my eyes in confusion.

When I looked at the bomb, the word *BANG!* flashed over and over again on the red light panel.

"Really funny," I said to Creepy.

"Oh, come on, Birthday Boy. Lighten up. We've only just begun. You're getting the best party package we offer, and there's a lot more frightening fun to come.

"Okay everyone, find a seat where you can see the velvet curtain. The magic show is about to begin," Creepy directed.

As we found places to sit, several clowns pulled the red velvet cloth aside to reveal a stage full of magic show props. I couldn't believe all that stood in front of us. Creepy the Clown had quite a setup.

In his first trick he put Penny the Party Crasher into a box and sawed her in half. The special effects were great. I couldn't figure out how he did it until the trick was over and Penny broke out of the upper half of the box. Another clown jumped out of the lower half. Everybody cracked up.

"How embarrassing. It's so hard to find good help these days. Maybe if I used one of you for my next trick, it would turn out better." Creepy barely spoke the words before every kid in the room but me had a hand up in the air. Creepy laughed and pointed at a boy on the left side of the room. He couldn't have chosen a more perfect candidate. The kid was always joking around, so being on stage would probably come naturally to him.

I watched as Creepy put the boy into a box and closed the door.

"I will say the magic words," Creepy said to his audience, "and right before your very eyes, one of your buddies will disappear."

Davis leaned over Frankie and whispered close to my ear. "I'm starting to get a bad feeling about this."

Creepy then said the magic words: "Treasure divine, treasure I'll find, treasure is mine."

What?! I could see the words had the same effect on the others who knew about the treasure.

"Creepy must be working with the ghosts to find the treasure," I whispered. "That's probably why he calls himself Creepy. We should have figured that out a long time ago."

I looked up at the stage. Creepy opened the box, but instead of our friend, a tall, sinister-looking clown with long, sharp fangs stepped out. Creepy tried to stop him, but the spooky clown pushed him away and started moving toward me and my friends.

Kids scattered everywhere. Frankie, Barry, and I made the mistake of running toward a corner of the room. The figure glided slowly in our direction.

"I think I believe the legend completely now," Frankie cried out.

"Lord, what should we do?" I prayed. I didn't realize I'd said it out loud until Frankie responded with a plan.

"Everybody run a different way," she said. "It might confuse him. Maybe we can all escape."

It wasn't a perfect plan, but then again this wasn't the perfect birthday party. I decided I'd be glad if I got home alive.

Barry shot to the right. Frankie shot to the left. I ran straight toward the tall clown's legs.

At the last possible second, I tried to dive between his large feet. I figured if I could get through his legs, I could be long gone before he could turn around. But he was quicker than I expected. He snatched me off the floor and held me high in the air. I found myself face-to-face with what I was now sure was one of the building's ghosts.

He growled loudly, "Now I've got you, and I guarantee that you won't get what you came for."

I closed my eyes and sent up a silent prayer for help.

I was afraid I would soon join my friend who had disappeared.

I couldn't help myself; I peeked at the clown as he pulled me closer with one hand and raised his other hand in the air. I felt sure he was going to shove me into his mouth. Instead, the free hand reached for the top of his head and pulled off a mask.

"Happy birthday, MacKenzie," the clown said. Without his mask, he didn't look the least bit scary. He lowered me to the floor, and I dusted off my clothes.

"Thanks for the fright," I returned.

"Wow!" Creepy said as everyone started to calm down. "That was terrifying, wasn't it? If you'll all take your seats once again, we can continue with the magic show." Then he pulled the boy who had disappeared out of a hidden panel in the wall. The kid kept asking, "What happened? What happened?"

I went back to my seat, rather embarrassed that I had let the clown get the best of me. Frankie and Barry came up next to me.

"That was really brave when you tried to dive between his feet. It really drew his attention away from us. I was sure that we were all goners. This ghost thing has me on edge," Barry said.

"Me too," I agreed.

Davis joined us and said, "I was so worried that clown would eat you." He paused and added, "And then not floss."

I groaned and rolled my eyes.

Lisa said, "That was pretty scary, but I know it wasn't for real. If the ghost was just someone in a mask, maybe all the other stuff isn't real either . . ."

She sounded like she was trying to convince herself. I gave a small smile, and I hoped she was right.

After Creepy performed a few more magic tricks, he announced, "Now it's time to play hide-and-seek.

"In a moment, the doors behind the stage will open up, and you will have three minutes to run through. Find a place to hide before it comes after you," he instructed.

"Does he mean 'it' as in 'you're it' in a game? Or does he mean 'it' as in 'it lives in the basement and wants to protect its treasure'?" I asked.

Before anyone could answer me, the doors popped open, and everyone swarmed toward the stage.

When we ran through the door, we found ourselves in a big, dimly lit room. Huge Styrofoam shapes—squares, triangles, and columns—littered the floor. Kids ran to hide behind them. We also found tubes to crawl into and other shapes with holes cut in them. This game was going to be a blast!

Barry and I rolled out to our right and shot along the wall until we reached something that looked like a cave with an opening at each end.

"This will be perfect," Barry said. "If he sees us at one end, we can escape out the other."

I agreed and we crawled inside. Leading the way, I crept as far into the shadows as I could. Then something grabbed me. I let out a small eek before I heard, "Hey, this is our spot." I recognized Frankie's voice immediately.

"What do you mean, 'our spot'?" I asked.

"Lisa, Davis, and I got here first," she said. "But I guess there's enough room for everyone."

We fell silent when we heard a ghoulish cackle. "It" had just entered the room. We heard it grab one kid after another. Their screams echoed throughout the room. It was dragging away our friends one by one.

Soon everyone was caught but us. We could hear it move restlessly around the room as it searched for us. I held my breath and waited. I shifted silently, trying to find a more comfortable position.

I backed into someone and whispered, "I'm sorry." In the dark it was hard to tell who I'd bumped into.

I nearly yelled out when I received a hard shove to my ribs. I slammed forward into someone else.

"What are you doing?" Davis growled in a stern whisper.

"It wasn't my fault. Somebody pushed me from behind," I answered.

"That's impossible. We're all in front of you," Lisa said with a hint of panic in her voice.

"Then who pushed me?" I asked as fear seeped into my bones.

"I did," croaked a cold, dead voice behind us.

"Run! It's the ghost of Tremble Avenue!" I yelled to the others.

We flew out of the cave with Frankie leading the way. Screaming and sucking in air, we tried our best to not knock each other over in the confusion.

We stumbled around the room, hiding behind the various geometric shapes scattered around. I thought we were safe. Then I heard it shuffling across the floor behind me and to the right.

"Run!" I yelled to Lisa, who had hidden with me. I decided right then that if I lived to see thirteen, I wouldn't have any more birthday parties, especially at Creepy the Clown's Pizza Palace.

"Hey, ho, hey, kids! It's just me, Creepy the Clown. Come out, come out wherever you are. You five won the game! Everyone else has been caught and is waiting in the next room. Even *it* gave up and left," he told us.

"Then who was chasing us?" Davis asked.

"I don't know. There's only the six of us here," the clown answered.

I didn't believe him. I was sure Creepy's presence was keeping it from attacking us.

I started toward the door when I heard someone whisper, "Birthday Boy, I'll be back with my gift later. Maybe I'll even stop by for some birthday cake and I scream."

"Let's get out of here, and I mean now," I commanded the others.

"That's right. It's time to go play musical chairs," Creepy reported cheerfully.

"No, I mean out of this Pizza Palace," I snapped at him.

"I'm sorry, but I can't let you do that. There is still so much more planned for this party, and we wouldn't want to disappoint any of our guests. So, let's all go back to the Hall of Games," Creepy said.

Since none of us knew the way out, we had to follow him.

When we entered the Hall of Games, I hoped to see the other guests waiting for us, but the room was empty. "Where is everyone?" I asked.

"It got them," the bizarre clown said without concern. I tried to press the question again, but Creepy put his hand over my mouth as he said, "Our last game will be musical chairs. Tonight we'll play a very special version. My helpers have set up five chairs.

You'll each have a place to sit when the music stops. But beware, one of the chairs . . . well, let's just say that you'll feel the earth move beneath your feet. Or rather beneath your seat."

"A trapdoor?" Frankie questioned in my direction. I shrugged my shoulders.

"We sometimes call this Musical Chairs That Dance," Creepy reported. "Now, take your places. The music is about to begin."

Reluctantly, we walked around the circle of chairs when the music played. With each note our tension grew. We knew that one of us was headed for trouble, but which one?

When the music stopped, we tentatively chose chairs and sat. I looked around. My friends were all still there. Maybe the trapdoor system had broken . . . In the next instant, four chairs dropped through the floor, sending everyone but me to who knew where.

I gripped the sides of the seat. The chair rocked a little. I gasped and prepared to jump to safety when I looked up and saw that Creepy and his clown team had surrounded me.

Suddenly, the trapdoor seemed like the better of the two options. The clowns got to within a few feet of me before my chair went out from under me. I slipped down a cold, slick slide.

I zoomed past flashing lights that lined the slide.

I tried to focus on where I was heading. I shouldn't have.

Below my feet I saw a ball of flames licking toward the slide. I was heading straight toward it with no way to stop. I tried digging my heels into the slide, but it was too slick and I was going too fast.

Then I grabbed for the edges, but I couldn't feel anything to hold on to. I was only a yard or so away from the flames. I'd had a good twelve years. Too bad it would all come to an end in a few moments.

I closed my eyes and waited to feel the scorching heat of the flames. I slid for another few seconds, then I lost contact with the slide. I felt myself float through the air. I was too afraid to open my eyes.

I bounced to a landing on something soft. Then a bunch of hands grabbed and pulled at me.

"No, leave me alone. I don't want to die!" I screamed, squirming desperately to escape the tightening grips.

"Get a grip, Mac. What's your problem?" Frankie asked.

I opened my eyes and saw my four friends standing around me, trying to help me off the soft pillow I had landed on.

"What happened? Where are we? The last thing I saw was a ball of fire. Then I flew through the air without getting burned. Where are we?" I asked in bewilderment.

"We don't know. We just got here too," Lisa said.

She pointed at several orange strips of fabric fluttering around the pillow I had landed on. "These look a lot like flames when the air circulating system blows them around."

Frankie added, "That ball of fire thing looked pretty scary."

"Who was scared?" I asked, pretending that I hadn't been.

"You were," Barry blurted out.

I grimaced. "You're right. I was petrified," I said as Barry and Davis pulled me to my feet. "Creepy the Clown's Pizza Palace is not at all what I expected. This place scares me to death. How did those kids from the party before us make it out of here without their hair standing on end?"

"They're braver than we are?" Lisa tossed out as a possibility.

Davis had been looking around the room and called back to us, "Hey, I don't know where we are, but I do know where we are heading. There is one door out of here, but it leads to the Hall of Fear. That sounds like a nice place to visit. I wonder if it's anywhere near the Tombs of Torture?"

"The Hall of Fear?" Lisa asked. "Do we really have to go there?"

"Remember what we studied in Sunday school last week, Lisa? Deuteronomy 31:8 says: 'The Lord himself will be with you. He will not leave you or forget you. Don't be afraid . . .' I think it's good to remember that God's always with us. Come on, let's try to find some other way out of here," Barry said.

To get the others moving, I told them, "I want to get out of here before Creepy and his clowns come for us."

Barry added, "Or worse, the ghosts."

Davis led the way, followed by Barry and Lisa. Frankie and I hurried along behind them. I said to her, "You're not as afraid as I am. Is there anything that really scares you?"

Frankie looked around as if she didn't want anyone else to hear her. "I do have this silly fear . . . You'll laugh if I tell," she said.

I shook my head to let her know I wouldn't laugh.

After a moment, she continued. "I'm afraid of the dark. I've always imagined that there is someone waiting for me at the top of our steps. Sometimes I'm afraid to go upstairs alone at night."

My mouth fell open. "I've always had that same fear," I blurted out. Then I quietly told Frankie how nice it was to be able to share my fears with her.

"Listen, if you two are finished whispering back there, could we get the show on the road?" Barry said to bring us back to our predicament. "Someone needs to enter the Hall of Fear and tell the others what it's like. I nominate the birthday boy since it's his party that got us into all this," Barry insisted.

Barry pulled the door open. All I could see was a pretty dark room. For some reason, I felt like we needed to be really quiet.

Frankie was standing right behind me. I could tell she felt the same way because she whispered, "I'll go in with you."

We started into the Hall of Fear. When nothing happened to us, the others followed cautiously behind us.

Lisa pointed at something and said in a stage whisper, "Over there. I see a tiny light blinking."

We went to investigate the light and found a booth that looked like The Game of Life in the Hall of Games.

"This is the only way out of here," Davis said.

Barry laughed and asked, "How do you know that?"

Davis pointed to a small sign on the door that said: This Is the Only Way Out.

Barry laughed again. "I guess you're right. Do we have any other choice?" Barry asked as he climbed into the booth.

Lisa stopped the rest of us from joining him. "I don't think we should all go in together. Let's split up so that at least some of us survive to tell the world what really goes on here."

Barry butted in. "Great idea, but it won't work. Look at this control panel. The fuel gauge on this baby says empty, and by the looks of the controls, it must be preprogrammed. It may not come back to this room. We don't have any choice. We have to risk all of us going at once."

I inhaled deeply and let the air out slowly to try to relax. I wished again that Mom had never booked my party here. And I wished that I had never read chapter thirteen in *Middletown's Ghosts and Ghouls*. Finally I prayed that we would all make it safely out of this place.

We crowded into the booth, and the door slid shut behind us. Even though we expected it to shut on us, the sound of it closing made us jump.

We watched the red numbers on the control panel count down from ten to nine to eight . . . all the way to zero. Then we felt the booth start to shake and rumble.

On the viewing screen before us we could see that we were climbing slowly. We passed through an opening in the roof and continued to climb into the air. The buildings, cars, and people below us looked smaller and smaller. Without warning, the booth stopped high in the air.

"What happened?" I asked. I was so frightened by the height that I felt dizzy.

"I think we're stuck at the top of a long pole," a high, shrill voice said. It took me a few seconds to figure out that Davis had spoken. *He must be really scared*, I thought.

"Why do you think that?" I asked.

Davis pointed across the skyline. When he answered me, he talked way too fast. "Look over there. There's another booth on a pole. That pole doesn't look strong enough to hold a bird up."

"Now what?" Barry cried.

"I don't think we have many options. I guess we have to wait and see what happens," I told the others.

"Why is this booth just sitting up here?" Lisa asked as she choked back tears.

"Heights scare some people pretty badly," Frankie told her. She tried to keep her voice as calm as possible to soothe Lisa.

"But we're just sitting here and not doing anything. I want down before this thing starts to rock back and forth. Ahhh! I should never have opened my mouth. We're starting to rock!" Lisa yelled.

"Calm down. A little wobble would be normal at this height," Barry said, trying to reassure her. But the whole booth tipped so far to one side that we all screamed while we slid around on the seat.

I just knew the booth was going to break off the pole. We were goners for sure.

We held each other tight, but it didn't stop the fear from getting a good hold on us too. I wanted out. Now!

"We've got to get out of here!" I yelled. Beads of perspiration formed on my forehead.

"How?" Davis screamed back. Terror poured out along with his question.

Barry scrambled toward a red flashing button on the control panel.

"Barry, what are you trying to do?" I yelled.

"This might be the way down. We've got to try it." He almost reached the button, but then the booth dipped backward. We all slid toward the back wall. When the contraption tipped forward again, Barry practically fell on top of the button.

As soon as he touched the flashing red spot, we felt the booth straighten up. Then we started to descend. We cheered, but our joy didn't last long. We had started to fall so quickly that our landing could flatten us permanently.

"This can't get any worse," Frankie moaned.

"Oh yes, it can," Lisa responded as her eyes widened in panic.

She started shaking uncontrollably and then she shrieked, "We're breaking up. Look! Cracks!"

I looked down where Lisa pointed and saw a bunch of small cracks. Then I looked at the walls. Like lightning bolts flashing through the sky, jagged cracks split the wall panels.

I knew we'd never make it to the ground before the booth split into a zillion pieces.

"Hang on to something!" Davis bellowed.

As the booth around us broke apart, we braced ourselves for the long fall to earth.

22

I hit the ground much sooner than I expected.
Nothing hurt. How could that be? Was I dead? I
quickly ran my hands along my arms and legs to
see if I were intact. Then I reached for my head.
Still there. I finally felt brave enough to open my
eyes.

I couldn't believe it. I sat up and in the dim light I
saw that my friends were right beside me, all in perfect shape. The whole time the booth had only been
a few feet off the ground. The terrifying experience
had all just been special effects.

"What was that all about?" Barry asked, shaking
his head.

"Fear," answered Frankie simply. "We were in the
Hall of Fear. We faced the fear of heights, the fear
of falling, and the fear of death. What's left?"

Davis spotted a door that we'd missed earlier. As
he walked toward it, he said, "I don't care what happens next, as long as it gets us out of here."

We pulled ourselves together and scrambled to follow him. The door led to another dark room. We could hear the wind whistling and bat wings flapping all around us.

"Where are we?" I asked.

No one answered. We had all heard the sound of heavy footsteps and deep breathing. It had to be one of the ghosts. The sound got closer and closer.

An excruciating screech cut through the darkness.

"Run!" somebody yelled. But it wasn't necessary. Our shoe soles were already slapping the hard floor.

We ran through another door and ended up in a long hallway. None of us knew where it led, but we could see another door at its end.

Frankie was right in front of me. I could hear her say over and over to herself: "Run, Frankie, run."

My birthday party seemed more like a nightmare every minute. I wished Creepy's had turned out to be safe and boring. Maybe a little pizza, a little birthday cake, and pin the tail on the donkey would have been fun.

I watched as Davis, Barry, and Lisa shot through the door at the end of the hall. Then I realized the sounds behind us had stopped.

"Frankie, wait up. I don't hear anything behind us anymore."

She stopped at the doorway and looked into the room.

"Mac, I don't want to go in there. It's so dark. I hate the dark," she said. I could tell she was really afraid.

I wanted to tell her I was afraid too when a blood-curdling scream crackled through the darkness.

"What do we do?" Frankie asked.

"We've got to go help whoever that was. Maybe we can find a light switch," I answered.

We slipped through the door and slid along the wall using our hands as our eyes. I was also praying that we would discover the way out.

Something tapped me on my shoulder. I turned my head to see what Frankie wanted.

But it wasn't her voice I heard.

"Birthday Boy, do you still have the treasure?"

I gulped as hands gripped my shoulders and squeezed them tight. *What treasure does he think I have?*

It had to be one of the ghosts! I shook off the hands and spun around to face him. In the dim light from the doorway, I watched as he grabbed Frankie.

My blood ran cold. I panicked.

"Let her go!" I demanded as I lunged forward. The only thing in my mind was that I had to save my friend. But I misjudged the distance and missed.

The ghost dragged her, kicking and screaming, deeper into the room.

"Wait," I yelled. "I'm the birthday boy. Take me, not her."

His sinister laugh cut into me.

"Come and take her away from me," he taunted.

In the next second the darkness engulfed them. I ran to where they had been standing.

"I don't think this is part of the birthday party games." The voice startled me, and I nearly had a cardiac arrest.

"Barry, is that you?" I blurted out. Then I asked,

"Where are the others?"

"Right here. We saw that ghoul drag Frankie over here," Davis answered.

"We've got to find her," Lisa pleaded.

"We will. Frankie's screams ended too abruptly. There has to be a door on this wall. Help me find it," I urged.

I ran my hands along the wall. When they hit a button, I pushed it. The wall spun around, taking me with it.

Suddenly, a door across the room opened, admitting a little light. I still couldn't see the ghost, but I heard him calling to me: "Birthday Boy."

My eyes started to adjust to the dim light. I walked toward the open door and read the sign over it: Hall of Amazing Mazes. I couldn't believe it. How would I find my way through a maze in near darkness? I stepped into the room. I could go either to the right or to the left.

"The Lord himself will be with you. He will not leave you or forget you. Don't be afraid . . ." I heard myself repeating the Bible verse out loud.

I began to feel calmer, secure that I wasn't alone.

"Help, Ralph!" I heard Frankie yell. *Ralph? Who was Ralph?* Then I got it. She must be able to see me, even though I couldn't see her. Ralph was an expression we used to call out directions. If you wanted someone to turn right, you said, "Hang a Ralph." Frankie was directing me through the maze.

I turned to my right. When I came to another choice, I needed help again.

I yelled, "Louie, are you out there?" Louie was the code word for left. I heard a muffled noise in response, so I turned left.

I didn't get very far before I had to make another choice. "Louie?" I yelled. No answer.

Then I called out, "It's Ralph." Still no answer. The ghost must have figured out our code. I went to the right and came to a dead end. I turned and ran back the other way.

When I had to make another decision, I heard Frankie yell, "Ralph, help me!"

I was getting closer. Her voice sounded near.

As I stumbled into another hallway, I saw a dark staircase. Behind me a door slammed shut with a resounding bang. I turned around and discovered that the door had locked.

My only option was the stairs. At the top, I saw the ghastly grayish figure. Frankie stood right next to him.

"Birthday Boy," the ghost called in his raspy, gasping voice. "I've been waiting for you. I'm willing to exchange your friend for the treasure. Come on, Birthday Boy."

"But I don't have any treasure. Please let her go," I pleaded.

He only cackled and held Frankie in front of him so I could see her. "Here she is. Are you willing to trade?"

"Let her go!" I screamed, trying to make myself sound menacing.

The ghost taunted me with his laughter. I felt terrible. I was too afraid to go up the steps to save my friend. All my life, I'd had that terrible fear that something was waiting for me at the top of a dark stairway. I never thought I'd have to face it.

Although the fear was almost overwhelming, I had to help Frankie.

I took the first step. My legs went weak. My knees

seemed to turn into jelly, but I forced myself to keep climbing.

"Birthday Boy, it's time for you to give me back my treasure. Have you brought it?" the ghost asked again.

I closed my eyes, lowered my head, and charged up the remaining steps. I planned to ram myself into the ghost. Then again, if it was a ghost, maybe I would pass right through it. The thought startled me, and I opened my eyes.

The ghost had disappeared. I saw Frankie standing there alone.

"Frankie, where did the ghost go?" I asked frantically.

"He went through that door," Frankie told me. "I'm so glad he's gone. I was afraid I'd never get free. Let's go back through the maze and get out of here."

I thought for a moment. "We can't," I told her slowly. "A door locked behind me. I guess the only way out of here is to follow the ghost of Tremble Avenue."

Frankie looked pretty unhappy about that idea. "Where are the others?" she asked, stalling for time.

"I don't know. They didn't come with me through the maze. I hope we can find them when we get out of here," I responded.

Frankie seemed to have made up her mind to be brave. "Let's go. The longer I wait, the harder it's going to be to walk through this door."

I gave her a smile. "Here goes nothing," I said. I pushed on the door, and it popped open.

"Careful. The ghost may be waiting for you on the other side," she reminded me.

I eased the door open and looked cautiously through the opening.

"Ho, hey, ho!" Creepy boomed at us. "We thought we'd lost you. It's time to open your present."

"Where is everyone?" I demanded.

"Right this way. They're waiting to watch you open your gift. It's from everyone here at Creepy the Clown's Pizza Palace. We want you to know how much we've appreciated being able to give you this very special party. It isn't every day that a group of your fame celebrates a birthday here," he said.

What he said confused me. What kind of special group were we?

He led us back to the Hall of Food, where some of my friends had gathered. I still didn't see Barry, Lisa, and Davis, or the kids who disappeared in The Game of Chance. One of Creepy's clowns shoved a large box into my hands.

"What's this?" I asked.

"That's the gift I was telling you about. Come on in here and sit down," Creepy said.

I sat down in the seat with the big box on my lap.

"Go ahead and open it," Creepy encouraged.

I was afraid to. It could have been a box of snakes, exploding bombs, insects, or anything. I just stared at it.

"Hey, are you going to open it?" Frankie asked.

"Would you?" I responded.

"No, but then again, I'm not the birthday boy, am I?" she said.

Creepy looked at me kind of funny, as if he couldn't believe a twelve-year-old wouldn't want to tear into a present. Then he shrugged his shoulders and said, "Okay, if you aren't going to open the gift, we'll have some cake and ice cream. Bring in the food," he yelled.

Several clowns rolled two big carts into the room. One had a cake on it in the shape of Creepy's head. The other cart held a gigantic tub of vanilla ice cream.

Creepy led the kids in the room through a loud and off-key rendition of "Happy Birthday to You."

Then he said, "Okay, Birthday Boy, you cut the cake, then you get to dish out the ice cream. That's a tradition here at Creepy's."

"You've only been open a week. How could you have traditions already?" Frankie asked.

"We are very old in our hearts. Now the cake," he insisted.

I half expected something to jump out when I sank the knife into the thick white icing and chocolate cake. I sliced a number of pieces then handed Frankie the knife to cut more.

"Now for the ice cream," Creepy said as he slapped the ice-cream scoop into my hand. "Dig in, but I want to warn you that the ice cream is very hard, so use a little muscle."

I thought to myself that Creepy was a very strange clown. I've scooped ice cream before. I didn't need that much instruction.

I stepped over to the cart holding the ice cream. The container was huge. It certainly looked like more than enough to go around.

I looked at Creepy and said, "You and your clowns are welcome to share in my birthday cake and ice cream. Of course, around here, maybe we should call it birthday cake and I scream."

"No thanks," he said through his clown makeup smile. "Just go ahead and serve the kids."

I leaned over the ice cream and asked Frankie, "How much do you want?"

"Mmmm. I really like ice cream. Can I have two or three scoops?" she requested.

"Sure," I said as I began to dip the scoop into the frozen dessert. I remembered what Creepy had said and pressed down hard. To my surprise, the scoop sank into the ice cream as if it were a melting milkshake. Before I could stop my motion, I was dipped up to my elbow in the white foam.

Another one of Creepy's stupid jokes, I thought as I pulled my hand out of the ooze. Something tugged on my arm from deep inside the ice cream. I pulled back. Then I saw the hand with long, sharp nails reaching out of the ice cream. The ghost!

I pulled hard in an attempt to free my arm, but the ghoul dragged me deeper into the vat. I felt the gooey ooze at my ear.

The next thing I knew, two hands had grabbed my shoulders and saved me from the fake ice cream. The ghost's hand slipped off my arm, and I popped out of the ooze. I stumbled backward, staring at the ice-cream tub.

Creepy made a huge show of wiping me off and apologizing as his helpers wheeled the cart of ice cream out of the room. "I'm sorry," he said. "Our ice cream always comes frozen solid. Someone must have left it out to make it easier to scoop. Apparently it got left out too long. I'm so sorry about the mess."

"Didn't you see the hand that grabbed me and tried to pull me in?" I asked frantically.

"Maybe you encountered a wild vanilla bean, but I don't think they're strong or vicious enough to pull you in. Your strong scooping motion must have made you lose your balance. You fell in," he explained. "Besides, those tubs of ice cream aren't deep enough for something to have hidden inside it."

"But I know something pulled on my arm. It was probably the same thing that took Frankie through the Amazing Maze."

"Amazing Maze? . . . If it will make you feel better, I'll have BooBoo the Clown bring the ice cream back so you can see there's nothing in it."

BooBoo answered, "Sorry, Creepy, but we already poured that stuff into the garbage can out back. Here's another tub so the kids can have their party treat."

"I guess I can't prove anything to you, but we can get this wild and crazy party going again. BooBoo, you dish up the rest of the cake and ice cream. While he does that, Mac, why don't you go ahead and open your gift?" Creepy was all smiles.

"So many weird things have happened here, I'm not sure that I want to open this gift," I answered.

"Go ahead. Open it. I picked it out especially for you. Here, I'll help." Creepy grabbed the gift from my lap and started ripping the paper off.

I grabbed it back.

"Okay, I'll open it. After all, it is my gift," I said. I pulled the bow off and tossed it to the floor.

I ripped the remaining paper off the box. Then I pulled the top off, revealing a Creepy the Clown plastic snow globe.

A roar of noise surrounded me.

I jumped, almost dropping the snow globe. In the same motion, I turned around to see where all the noise had come from. The rest of my party guests had entered from another room. I saw all the kids I thought were missing.

"Mac, this is the greatest party I've ever been to," several of them said in unison.

Barry and Davis ran up to me.

"Mac, watch out. It all looks like everyone's having fun, but don't forget the ghost," Davis whispered.

The other kids lined up to get cake and ice cream from BooBoo. I could tell from all the noise that they were having a great time. Barry plopped down next to me.

"What happened to you guys? I thought we planned to stay together. I had to make my way through a maze alone in the dark." I felt annoyed with my friends, even though I was relieved to see they were safe.

Barry smiled at me and said, "We tried to follow you, but we couldn't figure out how you got that wall to flip around. Then Creepy showed up out of nowhere and led us back to the Hall of Games. He said that you'd meet us there. We didn't see you, but other groups kept joining us. Then Creepy's clowns brought us in here. Thanks for starting the cake and ice cream without us," he teased.

Lisa came over and joined us. "It sure looks like everyone's having a blast," she said. "Most of the kids keep saying they want to throw their next party here. I think you've started a real fad."

Davis said, "But none of them saw the ghost, and none of them went through the Hall of Fear. To them it's just the most fantastic birthday celebration they've ever been to."

Barry added, "You're going to be a legend. The whole school is going to know about the kind of parties that you throw."

"Personally, I just want out of here. Before you came in, the ghost tried to pull me into a tub of melted ice cream," I whispered.

Creepy called for our attention. When everyone had quieted down, he announced, "I hate to say this, but our party is almost over. If you enjoyed yourself, tell everyone. If you didn't like the place, don't tell anyone." Then he broke into his goofy laugh. "Ho, hey, ho!"

"I don't hate to say this party is over," Frankie whispered to the rest of us. "Creepy acts as if he doesn't even know what's going on. He seems oblivious to the ghost roaming around in his Pizza Palace."

Creepy said, "But before you all head home, I want to do one last magic trick. I need a volunteer. Well, not actually a volunteer—someone has made a special request for MacKenzie Griffin to be a part of this trick."

"What do I do?" I asked the other four.

"Maybe Creepy doesn't know about the ghost. If not, he can't be in on it. All his other tricks seemed pretty safe. Go ahead and finish out the party with one last blast," Barry advised quickly and quietly.

"If the ghost gets me, you won't be my best friend anymore," I warned Barry.

With a smile, he responded, "If the ghost gets you, can I have your new bike?"

I didn't have a chance to answer. Creepy's clowns surrounded me and lifted my chair high into the air. They carried me across the room and set me on the stage next to Creepy.

He waved his hand in my direction and said, "This is a very simple trick. I will lay this piece of cloth over MacKenzie."

He dropped a thick, black piece of material over me. As it hit my head, I felt a platform start to lower, and Creepy's voice trailed off. I looked up, and a wire shaped like the back of the chair gave the illusion that I was still sitting on stage.

The platform lowered into a dingy little room below the floor. I could see a tall, dark shape in the poorly lit corner.

I had a bad feeling. I knew I had seen this silhouette before.

He took a large step closer and asked in a menacing growl, "Have you come to return my treasure?"

27

"I don't have your treasure. We never found any treasure," I stammered at the ghost. "I don't know why you think we have it. Please just let me go home."

"I can't let that happen," he answered me.

"Any second now, Creepy is going to bring this platform back to the floor, and I better be in the chair or . . . or . . . or . . ."

"Or what?" the ghost asked in an icy voice. "I control the platform with this button." The ghost pointed a long, sharp nail at the button. "Where is my treasure?"

"What treasure? I don't have any treasure," I pleaded.

I felt my eyes fill with tears. But I couldn't cry. I couldn't let him know how frightened I was.

The ghoul stared deep into my eyes. He opened his mouth and sneered out, "Give me back my treasure. Penny the Party Crasher stole it from me and gave it to you."

I sagged in relief. The tokens! All he wanted were the tokens Penny had "pulled" out of my ear. The other kids had taken lots of them, but I had some somewhere. I dug into my left pocket. None there. I must have put them in my right pocket. Hmm, not there either. I thrust my hands deeply into every pocket in my clothing. Nothing.

The ghost took another step closer.

I frantically braced myself in the chair. My hand brushed the plastic snow globe Creepy had given me. Maybe the ghost would take that and leave me alone.

He didn't want the cheap globe. I eyed the button that would take me back up to Creepy.

"Don't think that you're going to get away until I have what I want," my captor said in his raspy voice.

Think, Mac! You've got to get out of here, I thought to myself. If only I could find a way to push the button.

I stretched my arm out, but I couldn't reach far enough.

"Naughty birthday boy, are you trying to leave so soon? And just when I was enjoying myself," the gray, grim form teased.

As much as I hated soccer drills, even that sounded better than being at the mercy of this ghoul.

Soccer! That was it! That was my answer.

My aim was pretty good. I bet I could kick Creepy's snow globe across the little room and strike the button with it.

The ghost moved around to my left side, and I pretended to make a move to my right. I faked him out, and I had a clear shot at the button.

I kicked. Thwump!

The globe sailed through the air. The ghost realized what I had done and dived through the air to stop the flying globe.

I held my breath and closed my eyes. I didn't want to see what would happen. It was my only chance to escape. If the ghost stopped the globe, I was doomed.

Then I heard the plastic ball crash. Did it hit the button? Did it hit the wall? Did the ghost knock it to the ground?

All I could do was pray.

I felt the platform and chair jerk. I started to rise!

I looked over and saw the ghost lying on the floor. He tried to get up, but the plastic orb had smashed, splashing its liquid all over the floor. He slipped on it and fell back to the ground.

Ascending into the black cloth, I could hear Creepy say, "I think our birthday boy has finally returned from the great beyond. I've never had anyone take so long to come back before. I do hope—"

I startled Creepy the Clown by ripping off the black cloth and running for the exit.

"Where are you going, Mac?" Creepy called after me.

"My mother should be here by now. She hates it when I'm late. In fact, she grounds me. I've got to go," I yelled over my shoulder as I ran out.

When I got to the door, I stopped and motioned for everyone to follow. The entire group of party guests raced out behind me.

I heard a familiar voice say, "So, how was the party, kiddo?"

Only one person ever called me kiddo. It was my mom. The only thing I wanted to do was to get out of Creepy's.

I didn't have to tell my mother anything about the party. All the other kids were telling their parents about the fantastic time they'd had. Most of them asked to have their next party at Creepy's.

I smiled and nodded my head. My party was a hit. I might have been scared to death by the ghosts haunting the building, but everyone else had a great time.

"Give me a moment to pay and thank Creepy for the great time you all had, then we can get going," my mom said.

Frankie and Lisa walked up behind me. Lisa asked, "Did you have another run-in with the ghost while you were under that cloth?"

"Yes, I thought I was a goner for sure."

"So did we," Barry said as Davis put his hand on my shoulder.

"I can't believe we're getting out of here safe. I'm going to hurry Mom up so we all can go home," I told them as I walked to the counter where Mom was paying for the party.

Creepy had handed her a business card, and she slid it to me to carry home. As my mom wrote a check, I leaned over and read the desk calendar by the phone. I wondered what other groups would have to face the ghosts of Creepy's Pizza Palace.

Suddenly, my mouth dropped open and my head became light. I couldn't believe what I read. Written over today's date was "National Horror Movie Fan Club Birthday Party." Underneath was a memo that said, "Rent ghost costumes and really scare the kids." Across Saturday's date I saw my name.

Creepy had written the wrong party groups on the wrong days. I had gotten the party for the Horror Movie Fan Club.

The greatest birthday party of my life was all a mistake. Cool!

I smiled at Mom and said, "We're ready to go."

"Good, wait for me in the minivan. I'll only be a few seconds," she responded in her usual joyful way.

As I walked up to the others, I looked down at Creepy's business card. Below the words *Creepy the Clown's Pizza Palace* was imprinted *Alexander C. Reepy, Owner and Chief Executive Clown.* I chuckled to myself. The name Creepy had nothing to do with ghosts. It was actually the clown's name, C. Reepy.

I told the others, "Mom said for us to wait for her in the van."

We all started to head outside. Before I left, I wanted to look around at the greatest party place in the world. Just then something floated down on my head.

Looking up at the stuffed heads on the walls, I gasped.

For a second I had seen one of the gray clown ghosts. It looked right at me and winked. I blinked and it disappeared.

I shook my head and noticed another flower petal float to the ground.

I knew it was only someone in a costume. I whistled and strolled out the door to the sidewalk. As the door swung shut behind me, I was sure I heard someone say in a raspy voice, "Good-bye, Birthday Boy."

I ran to the van.